John Galsworthy

John Galsworthy was born in 1867. An early encounter with Joseph Conrad helped inspire him to write, and he went on to emerge as one of the most widely read novelists of his day, a reputation standing the test of time. He was elected the first president of International PEN, the association of writers, in 1912. He is best remembered for his trilogy *The Forsyte Saga*, which clinched his award of the Nobel Prize for Literature in 1932. He died in 1933, aged 65.

Anthony Gardner is a freelance writer who contributes features, travel articles and book reviews to, among others, the *Daily Telegraph, Sunday Times Magazine* and the *Mail on Sunday*. He is a Fellow of the Royal Society of Literature and edits the Society's annual journal, the *RSL*.

The Dark Flower

The Dark Flower

John Galsworthy

FOREWORD BY ANTHONY GARDNER

CAPUCHIN CLASSICS

CAPUCHIN CLASSICS
LONDON

The Dark Flower
First published in 1913
This edition published by Capuchin Classics 2008
Reprinted 2008

© Capuchin Classics 2008
4 6 8 0 9 7 5 3

Capuchin Classics
128 Kensington Church Street, London W8 4BH
Telephone: +44 (0)20 7221 7166
Fax: +44 (0)20 7792 9288
E-mail: info@capuchin-classics.co.uk
www.capuchin-classics.co.uk

Châtelaine of Capuchin Classics: Emma Howard

ISBN: 978-0-9555196-7-3

FOREWORD

In 1893, on a ship returning to England from Australia, a young British law student struck up a friendship with a Polish seaman. Both had ambitions to become authors, and with each other's encouragement went on to pursue enormously successful literary careers. The law student was John Galsworthy; the seaman, Joseph Conrad.

During his lifetime, Galsworthy was the more celebrated of the pair. In 1932 he won the Nobel Prize for Literature, and he remains the only British novelist apart from Rudyard Kipling and William Golding to have done so. But posterity has not been kind to him. While Conrad's *Heart of Darkness* remains an essential text for students, most would struggle to name a single one of Galsworthy's novels. If he is remembered by the public at large, it is mainly for the epic television series based on six of his books, *The Forsyte Saga* – such addictive viewing in pre-video days that a *Punch* cartoon showed a middle-aged couple climbing the Berlin Wall *into* East Germany to catch a re-run of it.

Why has he fallen from fashion? Perhaps because his characters' speech – however representative of the age – strikes the modern reader as clichéd and absurd ('Look here old girl!'); perhaps because the exclamation marks which fill his paragraphs are no longer considered a desirable form of punctuation. In addition, he has received a mauling from critics who identify him damningly with the upper-middle-class view of life embodied by the Forsytes: one described the saga as 'a type-piece of that social fossilisation of literature in this century, which now deserves the museum'.

This is harsh on a man whose novels and plays often challenged convention and drew attention to social injustice; and on opening *The Dark Flower*, it soon becomes irrelevant. Within a dozen pages, Galsworthy establishes his mastery of compelling narrative, and sketches an irresistible plot. It is the kind of book one can devour in a single day, though Galsworthy was thoughtful enough to divide it into three courses – Spring, Summer and Autumn.

The novel covers almost 30 years in the life and loves of a man roughly contemporaneous with the author. (Born in 1867 and dying in 1933, Galsworthy symmetrically spanned the last third of the nineteenth century and the first third of the twentieth.) It opens in 1880, with its hero Mark Lennan an 18-year-old undergraduate studying art at Oxford – unaware that his tutor's Austrian wife Anna, twice his age, has fallen in love with him. When her husband casually suggests that Mark joins them for a holiday in the Alps, the scene is set for the first of the passionate involvements which will characterise the young man's life.

'Summer' jumps forward seven years, and finds Mark – now establishing himself as a sculptor – in love with another married woman, this time of his own age. Mark tells himself that because Olive Cramier is unhappy with her domineering husband, social conventions should be thrown aside: an argument which Galsworthy must have conducted in his own heart, since he himself had pursued an affair with his cousin's wife for ten years, until she finally obtained a divorce and married him instead. But in *The Dark Flower* the lovers' mutual infatuation allows for no such waiting game, and matters swiftly come to a head in the most dramatic fashion.

In 'Autumn', a further twenty years have elapsed. Mark is now 46, long married and ostensibly happy with his wife; but he finds himself filled with an inescapable restlessness. Today we would call his condition a mid-life crisis; in the more mature and shorter-lived world of the 1900s, he feels himself on the threshold of old age and death. When a beautiful teenage girl throws herself at him, it seems a miraculous opportunity to grasp youth and life once more; but he knows that the consequences would be devastating to the wife for whom he still feels affection. For Mark it is the last and most disturbing manifestation of the 'dark flower' of passion, and again Galsworthy writes from the heart, having himself experienced the infatuation of a 19-year-old dancer at a similar stage in his life.

The book might have been subtitled 'An Englishman in Love', for its male characters all typify to a greater or lesser extent the repression of emotion for which this country is notorious. Mark, when we first meet him, has had virtually no acquaintance with women apart from his sister; complimenting Anna on her appearance, the best he can manage is 'You do look jolly'. And while the book traces his journey from inarticulate public-school Romantic to almost Bohemian man of the world, it is made clear that his fellows – without the benefit of an artistic temperament and six years spent in Paris and Rome – remain prisoners of their inhibitions. His old school friend Dromore, revealing in an unguarded moment that he had a mistress who died in childbirth, sums up his devastation in the words 'Women have no luck!'; Olive's politician husband, faced with losing her, is reduced to 'a low moaning'.

Much of Galsworthy's achievement lies in the mixture of pathos and humour which he derives from characters so little able to express their feelings. His attitude towards Mark is at once tender and ironic, as the youth discovers 'this miracle, that no one had ever felt before, the miracle of love'; despite such mocking asides, it is hard to think of another male British novelist apart from DH Lawrence (a fierce critic of Galsworthy) who explores a lover's heart so painstakingly. Galsworthy's women, by contrast, are far better attuned to emotional matters, and often able to manipulate their men accordingly. The unexpected vein of high comedy which emerges in 'Summer' derives mainly from the relationship between Olive's uncle and aunt, Colonel and Mrs Ercott – she schooled in the works of 'that dangerous authoress George Eliot', he baffled by the idea that love might exist outside marriage.

There is much else to admire in *The Dark Flower*, from

Galsworthy's impressionistic descriptions and eye for detail to the subtle symmetry he creates between his characters, emphasising the cyclical nature of the story. (Mark at the end of the novel is the same age that his desiccated tutor is at the beginning, and drawn to his teenage admirer by the same instincts that drew Anna to his younger self.) Published in 1913, it also holds the fascination of a world about to be transformed by war: one in which *billets doux* could still be delivered by the hand of a discreet manservant, and the residents of Piccadilly kept their horses stabled close by so that they could gallop down to Richmond for fresh air. But *The Dark Flower* is never just a period piece: its wisdom is timeless.

Anthony Gardner
London, March 2008

PART I — SPRING

I

He walked along Holywell that afternoon of early June with his short gown drooping down his arms, and no cap on his thick dark hair. A youth of middle height, and built as if he had come of two very different strains, one sturdy, the other wiry and light. His face, too, was a curious blend, for, though it was strongly formed, its expression was rather soft and moody. His eyes — dark grey, with a good deal of light in them, and very black lashes — had a way of looking beyond what they saw, so that he did not seem always to be quite present; but his smile was exceedingly swift, uncovering teeth as white as a negro's, and giving his face a peculiar eagerness. People stared at him a little as he passed — since in eighteen hundred and eighty he was before his time in not wearing a cap. Women especially were interested; they perceived that he took no notice of them, seeming rather to be looking into distance, and making combinations in his soul.

Did he know of what he was thinking — did he ever know quite definitely at that time of his life, when things, especially those beyond the immediate horizon, were so curious and interesting? — the things he was going to see and do when he had got through Oxford, where everybody was 'awfully decent' to him and 'all right' of course, but not so very interesting.

He was on his way to his tutor's to read an essay on Oliver Cromwell; and under the old wall, which had once hedged in the town, he took out of his pocket a beast. It was a small tortoise, and, with an extreme absorption, he watched it move its little inquiring head, feeling it all the time with his short, broad fingers, as though to discover exactly how it was made. It was mighty hard in the back! No wonder poor old Aeschylus felt a bit sick when it fell on his head! The ancients used it to stand the world on — a pagoda world, perhaps, of men and beasts and trees, like that carving on his guardian's Chinese cabinet. The Chinese made jolly beasts and trees, as if they believed in everything having a soul, and not only being just fit for people to eat or drive or make houses of. If only the Art School would let him model things 'on his own,' instead of copying and copying — it was just as if they imagined it would be dangerous to let you think out anything for yourself!

He held the tortoise to his waistcoat, and let it crawl, till, noticing that it was gnawing the corner of his essay, he put it back into his pocket. What would his tutor do if he were to know it was there? — cock his head a little to one side, and say: "Ah! there are things, Lennan, not dreamed of in my philosophy!" Yes, there were a good many not dreamed of by 'old Stormer', who seemed so awfully afraid of anything that wasn't usual; who seemed always laughing at you, for fear that you should laugh at him. There were lots of people in Oxford like that. It was stupid. You couldn't do anything decent if you were afraid of being laughed at! Mrs. Stormer wasn't like that; she did things because — they came into her head. But then, of course, she was Austrian, not English, and ever so much younger than old Stormer.

And having reached the door of his tutor's house, he rang the bell . . . .

II

When Anna Stormer came into the study she found her husband standing at the window with his head a little on one side — a tall, long-legged figure in clothes of a pleasant tweed, and wearing a low turn-over collar (not common in those days) and a blue silk tie, which she had knitted, strung through a ring. He was humming and gently tapping the window-pane with his well-kept finger-nails. Though celebrated for the amount of work he got through, she never caught him doing any in this house of theirs, chosen because it was more than half a mile away from the College which held the 'dear young clowns,' as he called them, of whom he was tutor.

He did not turn — it was not, of course, his habit to notice what was not absolutely necessary — but she felt that he was aware of her. She came to the window seat and sat down. He looked round at that, and said: "Ah!"

It was a murmur almost of admiration, not usual from him, since, with the exception of certain portions of the classics, it was hardly his custom to admire. But she knew that she was looking her best sitting there, her really beautiful figure poised, the sun shining on her brown hair, and brightening her deep-set, ice-green eyes under their black lashes. It was sometimes a great comfort to her that she remained so good-looking. It would have been an added vexation indeed to have felt that she ruffled her husband's fastidiousness. Even so, her cheekbones were too high for his taste, symbols of that something in her character which did not go with his — the dash of desperation, of vividness, that lack of a certain English smoothness, which always annoyed him.

"Harold!" — she would never quite flatten her r's — "I want to go to the mountains this year."

The mountains! She had not seen them since that season at San Martino di Castrozza twelve years ago, which had ended in her marrying him.

"Nostalgia!"

"I don't know what that means — I am homesick. Can we go?"

"If you like — why not? But no leading up the Cimone della Pala for ME!"

She knew what he meant by that. No romance. How splendidly he had led that day! She had almost worshipped him. What blindness! What distortion! Was it really the same man standing there with those bright, doubting eyes, with grey already in his hair? Yes, romance was over! And she sat silent, looking out into the street — that little old street into which she looked day and night. A figure passed out there, came to the door, and rang.

She said softly: "Here is Mark Lennan!"

She felt her husband's eyes rest on her just for a moment, knew that he had turned, heard him murmur: "Ah, the angel clown!" And, quite still, she waited for the door to open. There was the boy, with his blessed dark head, and his shy, gentle gravity, and his essay in his hand.

"Well, Lennan, and how's old Noll? Hypocrite of genius, eh? Draw up; let's get him over!"

Motionless, from her seat at the window, she watched those two figures at the table — the boy reading in his queer, velvety bass voice; her husband leaning back with the tips of his fingers pressed together, his head a little on one side, and that faint, satiric smile which never reached his eyes. Yes, he was dozing, falling asleep; and the boy, not seeing, was going on. Then he came to the end and glanced up. What eyes he had! Other boys would have laughed; but he looked almost sorry. She heard him murmur: "I'm awfully sorry, sir."

"Ah, Lennan, you caught me! Fact is, term's fagged me out.

We're going to the mountains. Ever been to the mountains? What — never! You should come with us, eh? What do you say, Anna? Don't you think this young man ought to come with us? "

She got up, and stood staring at them both. Had she heard aright?

Then she answered — very gravely:

"Yes; I think he ought. "

"Good; we'll get HIM to lead up the Cimone della Pala!"

III

W hen the boy had said goodbye, and she had watched him out into the street, Anna stood for a moment in the streak of sunlight that came in through the open door, her hands pressed to cheeks which were flaming. Then she shut the door and leaned her forehead against the window-pane, seeing nothing. Her heart beat very fast; she was going over and over again the scene just passed through. This meant so much more than it had seemed to mean. . . .

Though she always had Heimweh, and especially at the end of the summer term, this year it had been a different feeling altogether that made her say to her husband: "I want to go to the mountains!"

For twelve years she had longed for the mountains every summer, but had not pleaded for them; this year she had pleaded, but she did not long for them. It was because she had suddenly realized the strange fact that she did not want to leave England, and the reason for it, that she had come and begged to go. Yet why, when it was just to get away from thought of this boy, had she said: "Yes, I think he ought to come!" Ah! but life for her was always a strange pull between the conscientious and the desperate; a queer, vivid, aching business! How long was it now since that day when he first came to lunch, silent and shy, and suddenly smiling as if he were all lighted up within — the day when she had said to her husband afterwards: "Ah, he's an angel!" Not yet a year — the beginning of last October term, in fact. He was different from all the other boys; not that he was a prodigy with untidy hair, ill-fitting clothes, and a clever tongue;

but because of something — something — Ah! Well — different; because he was — he; because she longed to take his head between her hands and kiss it. She remembered so well the day that longing first came to her. She was giving him tea, it was quite early in the Easter term; he was stroking her cat, who always went to him, and telling her that he meant to be a sculptor, but that his guardian objected, so that, of course, he could not start till he was of age. The lamp on the table had a rose-coloured shade; he had been rowing — a very cold day — and his face was glowing; generally it was rather pale. And suddenly he smiled, and said: "It's rotten waiting for things, isn't it?" It was then she had almost stretched out her hands to draw his forehead to her lips. She had thought then that she wanted to kiss him, because it would have been so nice to be his mother — she might just have been his mother, if she had married at sixteen. But she had long known now that she wanted to kiss, not his forehead, but his lips. He was there in her life — a fire in a cold and unaired house; it had even become hard to understand that she could have gone on all these years without him. She had missed him so those six weeks of the Easter vacation, she had revelled so in his three queer little letters, half-shy, half-confidential; kissed them, and worn them in her dress! And in return had written him long, perfectly correct epistles in her still rather quaint English. She had never let him guess her feelings; the idea that he might shocked her inexpressibly. When the summer term began, life seemed to be all made up of thoughts of him. If, ten years ago, her baby had lived, if its cruel death — after her agony — had not killed for good her wish to have another; if for years now she had not been living with the knowledge that she had no warmth to expect, and that love was all over for her; if life in the most beautiful of all old cities had been able to grip her — there would have been forces to check this feeling. But there was nothing in the world to divert the current. And she was so brimful of life, so conscious of vitality running to sheer waste. Sometimes it had been terrific, that feeling within her, of wanting to live — to find outlet for her energy. So many hundreds of lonely walks she had taken during all these years, trying to lose herself in Nature — hurrying alone, running in the woods, over the fields, where people did not come, trying to get rid of that sense of waste, trying once more to feel as she had felt when a girl, with the whole world before her. It was not for nothing that her figure was superb, her hair so bright a brown, her eyes so full of light. She had tried many distractions. Work in the back streets, music, acting, hunting; given them up one after the other; taken to them passionately again. They had served in the past. But this year they had not served. . . . One Sunday, coming from confession unconfessed, she had faced herself. It was wicked. She would have to kill this feeling — must fly from this boy who moved her so! If she did not act quickly, she would be swept away. And then the thought had come: Why not? Life was to be lived — not torpidly dozed through in this queer cultured place, where age was in the blood! Life was for love — to be enjoyed! And she would be thirty-six next month! It seemed to her already an enormous age. Thirty-six! Soon she would be old, actually old — and never have known passion! The worship, which had made a hero of the distinguished-looking Englishman, twelve years older than herself, who could lead up the Cimone della Pala, had not been passion. It might, perhaps, have become passion if he had so willed. But he was all form, ice, books. Had he a heart at all, had he blood in his veins? Was there any joy of life in this too beautiful city and these people who lived in it — this place where even enthusiasms seemed to be formal and have no wings, where everything was settled and sophisticated as the very chapels and cloisters? And yet, to have this feeling for a boy — for one almost young enough to be her son! It was so — shameless! That thought haunted her, made her flush in the dark, lying awake at night. And desperately she would pray

— for she was devout — pray to be made pure, to be given the holy feelings of a mother, to be filled simply with the sweet sense that she could do everything, suffer anything for him, for his good. After these long prayers she would feel calmed, drowsy, as though she had taken a drug. For hours, perhaps, she would stay like that. And then it would all come over her again. She never thought of his loving her; that would be — unnatural. Why should he love her? She was very humble about it. Ever since that Sunday, when she avoided the confessional, she had brooded over how to make an end — how to get away from a longing that was too strong for her. And she had hit on this plan — to beg for the mountains, to go back to where her husband had come into her life, and try if this feeling would not die. If it did not, she would ask to be left out there with her own people, away from this danger. And now the fool — the blind fool — the superior fool — with his satiric smile, his everlasting patronage, had driven her to overturn her own plan. Well, let him take the consequences; she had done her best! She would have this one fling of joy, even if it meant that she must stay out there, and never see the boy again!

Standing in her dusky hall, where a faint scent of woodrot crept out into the air, whenever windows and doors were closed, she was all tremulous with secret happiness. To be with him among her mountains, to show him all those wonderful, glittering or tawny crags, to go with him to the top of them and see the kingdoms of the world spread out below; to wander with him in the pine woods, on the Alps in all the scent of the trees and the flowers, where the sun was hot! The first of July; and it was only the tenth of June! Would she ever live so long? They would not go to San Martino this time, rather to Cortina — some new place that had no memories!

She moved from the window, and busied herself with a bowl of flowers. She had heard that humming sound which often heralded her husband's approach, as though warning the world to recover its good form before he reached it. In her happiness she felt kind and friendly to him. If he had not meant to give her joy, he had nevertheless given it! He came downstairs two at a time, with that air of not being a pedagogue, which she knew so well; and, taking his hat off the stand, half turned round to her.

"Pleasant youth, young Lennan; hope he won't bore us out there!"

His voice seemed to have an accent of compunction, to ask pardon for having issued that impulsive invitation. And there came to her an overwhelming wish to laugh. To hide it, to find excuse for it, she ran up to him, and, pulling his coat lapels till his face was within reach, she kissed the tip of his nose. And then she laughed. And he stood looking at her, with his head just a little on one side, and his eyebrows just a little raised.

IV

When young Mark heard a soft tapping at his door, though out of bed, he was getting on but dreamily — it was so jolly to watch the mountains lying out in this early light like huge beasts. That one they were going up, with his head just raised above his paws, looked very far away out there! Opening the door an inch, he whispered:

"Is it late?"

"Five o'clock; aren't you ready?"

It was awfully rude of him to keep her waiting! And he was soon down in the empty dining-room, where a sleepy maid was already bringing in their coffee. Anna was there alone. She had on a flax-blue shirt, open at the neck, a short green skirt, and a grey-green velvety hat, small, with one black-cock's feather. Why could not people always wear such nice things, and be as splendid-looking! And he said:

"You do look jolly, Mrs. Stormer!"

She did not answer for so long that he wondered if it had been rude to say that. But she DID look so strong, and swift, and happy-looking.

Down the hill, through a wood of larch-trees, to the river, and across the bridge, to mount at once by a path through hay-fields. How could old Stormer stay in bed on such a morning! The peasant girls in their blue linen skirts were already gathering into bundles what the men had scythed. One, raking at the edge of a field, paused and shyly nodded to them. She had the face of a Madonna, very calm and grave and sweet, with delicate arched brows — a face it was pure pleasure to see. The boy looked back at her. Everything to him, who had never been out of England before, seemed strange and glamorous. The chalets, with their long wide burnt-brown wooden balconies and low-hanging eaves jutting far beyond the walls; these bright dresses of the peasant women; the friendly little cream-coloured cows, with blunt, smoke-grey muzzles. Even the feel in the air was new, that delicious crisp burning warmth that lay so lightly as it were on the surface of frozen stillness; and the special sweetness of all places at the foot of mountains — scent of pine-gum, burning larch-wood, and all the meadow flowers and grasses. But newest of all was the feeling within him — a sort of pride, a sense of importance, a queer exhilaration at being alone with her, chosen companion of one so beautiful.

They passed all the other pilgrims bound the same way — stout square Germans with their coats slung through straps, who trailed behind them heavy alpenstocks, carried greenish bags, and marched stolidly at a pace that never varied, growling, as Anna and the boy went by: "Aber eilen ist nichts!"

But those two could not go fast enough to keep pace with their spirits. This was no real climb — just a training walk to the top of the Nuvolau; and they were up before noon, and soon again descending, very hungry. When they entered the little dining-room of the Cinque Torre Hutte, they found it occupied by a party of English people, eating omelettes, who looked at Anna with faint signs of recognition, but did not cease talking in voices that all had a certain half-languid precision, a slight but brisk pinching of sounds, as if determined not to tolerate a drawl, and yet to have one. Most of them had field-glasses slung round them, and cameras were dotted here and there about the room. Their faces were not really much alike, but they all had a peculiar drooping smile, and a particular lift of the eyebrows, that made them seem reproductions of a single type. Their teeth, too, for the most part were a little prominent, as though the drooping of their mouths had forced them forward. They were eating as people eat who distrust the lower senses, preferring not to be compelled to taste or smell.

"From our hotel," whispered Anna; and, ordering red wine and schnitzels, she and the boy sat down. The lady who seemed in command of the English party inquired now how Mr. Stormer was — he was not laid up, she hoped. No? Only lazy? Indeed! He was a great climber, she believed. It seemed to the boy that this lady somehow did not quite approve of them. The talk was all maintained between her, a gentleman with a crumpled collar and puggaree, and a short thick-set grey-bearded man in a dark Norfolk jacket. If any of the younger members of the party spoke, the remark was received with an arch lifting of the brows, and drooping of the lids, as who should say: "Ah! Very promising!"

"Nothing in my life has given me greater pain than to observe the aptitude of human nature for becoming crystallized." It was the lady in command who spoke, and all the young people swayed their faces up and down, as if assenting. How like they were, the boy thought, to guinea-fowl, with their small heads and sloping shoulders and speckly grey coats!

"Ah! my dear lady" — it was the gentleman with the crumpled collar — "you novelists are always girding at the precious quality of conformity. The sadness of our times lies in this questioning spirit. Never was there more revolt, especially among the young. To find the individual judging for himself is a grave symptom of national degeneration. But this is not a subject — "

"Surely, the subject is of the most poignant interest to all young people." Again all the young ones raised their faces and moved them slightly from side to side.

"My dear lady, we are too prone to let the interest that things arouse blind our judgment in regard to the advisability of discussing them. We let these speculations creep and creep until they twine themselves round our faith and paralyze it."

One of the young men interjected suddenly: "Madre" — and was silent.

"I shall not, I think" — it was the lady speaking — "be accused of licence when I say that I have always felt that speculation is only dangerous when indulged in by the crude intelligence. If culture has nothing to give us, then let us have no culture; but if culture be, as I think it, indispensable, then we must accept the dangers that culture brings."

Again the young people moved their faces, and again the younger of the two young men said: "Madre —"

"Dangers? Have cultured people dangers?"

Who had spoken thus? Every eyebrow was going up, every mouth was drooping, and there was silence. The boy stared at his companion. In what a strange voice she had made that little interjection! There seemed a sort of flame, too, lighted in her eyes. Then the little grey-bearded man said, and his rather whispering voice sounded hard and acid:

"We are all human, my dear madam."

The boy felt his heart go thump at Anna's laugh. It was just as if she had said: "Ah! but not you — surely!" And he got up to follow her towards the door.

The English party had begun already talking — of the weather.

The two walked some way from the 'hut' in silence, before Anna said:

"You didn't like me when I laughed?"

"You hurt their feelings, I think."

"I wanted to — the English Grundys! Ah! don't be cross with me! They WERE English Grundys, weren't they — every one?"

She looked into his face so hard, that he felt the blood rush to his cheeks, and a dizzy sensation of being drawn forward.

"They have no blood, those people! Their voices, their supercilious eyes that look you up and down! Oh! I've had so much of them! That woman with her Liberalism, just as bad as any. I hate them all!"

He would have liked to hate them, too, since she did; but they had only seemed to him amusing.

"They aren't human. They don't FEEL! Some day you'll know them. They won't amuse you then!"

She went on, in a quiet, almost dreamy voice:

"Why do they come here? It's still young and warm and good out here. Why don't they keep to their Culture, where no one knows what it is to ache and feel hunger, and hearts don't beat. Feel!"

Disturbed beyond measure, the boy could not tell whether it was in her heart or in his hand that the blood was pulsing so. Was he glad or sorry when she let his hand go?

"Ah, well! They can't spoil this day. Let's rest."

At the edge of the larch-wood where they sat, were growing numbers of little mountain pinks, with fringed edges and the sweetest scent imaginable; and she got up presently to gather them. But he stayed where he was, and odd sensations stirred in him. The blue of the sky, the feathery green of the larch-trees, the mountains, were no longer to him what they had been early that morning.

She came back with her hands full of the little pinks, spread her fingers and let them drop. They showered all over his face and neck. Never was so wonderful a scent; never such a strange feeling as they gave him. They clung to his hair, his forehead, his eyes, one even got caught on the curve of his lips; and he stared up at her through their fringed petals. There must have been something wild in his eyes then, something of the feeling that was stinging his heart, for her smile died; she walked away, and stood with her face turned from him. Confused, and unhappy, he gathered the strewn flowers; and not till he had collected every one did he get up and shyly take them to her, where she still stood, gazing into the depths of the larch-wood.

V

What did he know of women, that should make him understand? At his public school he had seen none to speak to; at Oxford, only this one. At home in the holidays, not any, save his sister Cicely. The two hobbies of their guardian, fishing, and the antiquities of his native county, rendered him averse to society; so that his little Devonshire manor-house, with its black oak panels and its wild stone-walled park along the river-side was, from year's end to year's end, innocent of all petticoats, save those of Cicely and old Miss Tring, the governess. Then, too, the boy was shy. No, there was nothing in his past, of not yet quite nineteen years, to go by. He was not of those youths who are always thinking of conquests. The very idea of conquest seemed to him vulgar, mean, horrid. There must be many signs indeed before it would come into his head that a woman was in love with him, especially the one to whom he looked up, and thought so beautiful. For before all beauty he was humble, inclined to think himself a clod. It was the part of life which was always unconsciously sacred, and to be approached trembling. The more he admired, the more tremulous and diffident he became. And so, after his one wild moment, when she plucked those sweet-scented blossoms and dropped them over him, he felt abashed; and walking home beside her he was quieter than ever, awkward to the depths of his soul.

If there were confusion in his heart which had been innocent of trouble, what must there have been in hers, that for so long had secretly desired the dawning of that confusion? And she, too, was very silent.

Passing a church with open door in the outskirts of the village, she said:

"Don't wait for me — I want to go in here a little."

In the empty twilight within, one figure, a countrywoman in her black shawl, was kneeling — marvellously still. He would have liked to stay. That kneeling figure, the smile of the sunlight filtering through into the half darkness! He lingered long enough to see Anna, too, go down on her knees in the stillness. Was she praying? Again he had the turbulent feeling with which he had watched her pluck those flowers. She looked so splendid kneeling there! It was caddish to feel like that, when she was praying, and he turned quickly away into the road. But that sharp, sweet stinging sensation did not leave him. He shut his eyes to get rid of her image — and instantly she became ten times more visible, his feeling ten times stronger. He mounted to the hotel; there on the terrace was his tutor. And oddly enough, the sight of him at that moment was no more embarrassing than if it had been the hotel concierge. Stormer did not somehow seem to count; did not seem to want you to count him. Besides, he was so old — nearly fifty!

The man who was so old was posed in a characteristic attitude — hands in the pockets of his Norfolk jacket, one shoulder slightly raised, head just a little on one side, as if preparing to quiz something. He spoke as Lennan came up, smiling — but not with his eyes.

"Well, young man, and what have you done with my wife?"

"Left her in a church, sir."

"Ah! She will do that! Has she run you off your legs? No? Then let's walk and talk a little."

To be thus pacing up and down and talking with her husband seemed quite natural, did not even interfere with those new sensations, did not in the least increase his shame for having them. He only wondered a little how she could have married him — but so little! Quite far and academic was his wonder — like his wonder in old days how his sister could care to play with dolls. If he had any other feeling, it was just a longing to get away and go down the hill again to the church. It seemed cold and lonely after all that long day with her — as if he had left himself up there, walking along hour after hour, or lying out in the sun beside her. What was old Stormer talking about? The difference between the Greek and Roman views of honour. Always in the past — seemed to think the present was bad form. And he said:

"We met some English Grundys, sir, on the mountain."

"Ah, yes! Any particular brand?"

"Some advanced, and some not; but all the same, I think, really."

"I see. Grundys, I think you said?"

"Yes, sir, from this hotel. It was Mrs. Stormer's name for them. They were so very superior."

"Quite."

There was something unusual in the tone of that little word. And the boy stared — for the first time there seemed a real man standing there. Then the blood rushed up into his cheeks, for there she was! Would she come up to them? How splendid she was looking, burnt by the sun, and walking as if just starting! But she passed into the hotel without turning her head their way. Had he offended, hurt her? He made an excuse, and got away to his room.

In the window from which that same morning he had watched the mountains lying out like lions in the dim light, he stood again, and gazed at the sun dropping over the high horizon. What had happened to him? He felt so different, so utterly different. It was another world. And the most strange feeling came on him, as of the flowers falling again all over his face and neck and hands, the tickling of their soft-fringed edges, the stinging sweetness of their scent. And he seemed to hear her voice saying: "Feel!" and to feel her heart once more beating under his hand.

VI

Alone with that black-shawled figure in the silent church, Anna did not pray. Resting there on her knees, she experienced only the sore sensation of revolt. Why had Fate flung this feeling into her heart, lighted up her life suddenly, if God refused her its enjoyment? Some of the mountain pinks remained clinging to her belt, and the scent of them, crushed against her, warred with the faint odour of age and incense. While they were there, with their enticement and their memories, prayer would never come. But did she want to pray? Did she desire the mood of that poor soul in her black shawl, who had not moved by one hair's breadth since she had been watching her, who seemed resting her humble self so utterly, letting life lift from her, feeling the relief of nothingness? Ah, yes! what would it be to have a life so toilsome, so little exciting from day to day and hour to hour, that just to kneel there in wistful stupor was the greatest pleasure one could know? It was beautiful to see her, but it was sad. And there came over Anna a longing to go up to her neighbour and say: "Tell me your troubles; we are both women." She had lost a son, perhaps, some love — or perhaps not really love, only some illusion. Ah! Love. . . . Why should any spirit yearn, why should any body, full of strength and joy, wither slowly away for want of love? Was there not enough in this great world for her, Anna, to have a little? She would not harm him, for she would know when he had had enough of her; she would surely have the pride and grace then to let him go. For, of course, he would get tired of her. At her age she could never hope to hold a boy more than a few years —

months, perhaps. But would she ever hold him at all? Youth was so hard — it had no heart! And then the memory of his eyes came back — gazing up, troubled, almost wild — when she had dropped on him those flowers. That memory filled her with a sort of delirium. One look from her then, one touch, and he would have clasped her to him. She was sure of it, yet scarcely dared to believe what meant so much. And suddenly the torment that she must go through, whatever happened, seemed to her too brutal and undeserved! She rose. Just one gleam of sunlight was still slanting through the doorway; it failed by a yard or so to reach the kneeling countrywoman, and Anna watched. Would it steal on and touch her, or would the sun pass down behind the mountains, and it fade away? Unconscious of that issue, the black-shawled figure knelt, never moving. And the beam crept on. "If it touches her, then he will love me, if only for an hour; if it fades out too soon —" And the beam crept on. That shadowy path of light, with its dancing dust-motes, was it indeed charged with Fate — indeed the augury of Love or Darkness? And, slowly moving, it mounted, the sun sinking; it rose above that bent head, hovered in a golden mist, passed — and suddenly was gone.

Unsteadily, seeing nothing plain, Anna walked out of the church. Why she passed her husband and the boy on the terrace without a look she could not quite have said — perhaps because the tortured does not salute her torturers. When she reached her room she felt deadly tired, and lying down on her bed, almost at once fell asleep.

She was wakened by a sound, and, recognizing the delicate 'rat-tat' of her husband's knock, did not answer, indifferent whether he came in or no. He entered noiselessly. If she did not let him know she was awake, he would not wake her. She lay still and watched him sit down astride of a chair, cross his arms on its back, rest his chin on them, and fix his eyes on her. Through her veil of eyelashes she had unconsciously contrived that his face should be the one object plainly seen — the more intensely visualized, because of this queer isolation. She did not feel at all ashamed of this mutual fixed scrutiny, in which she had such advantage. He had never shown her what was in him, never revealed what lay behind those bright satiric eyes. Now, perhaps, she would see! And she lay, regarding him with the intense excited absorption with which one looks at a tiny wildflower through a magnifying-lens, and watches its insignificance expanded to the size and importance of a hothouse bloom. In her mind was this thought: He is looking at me with his real self, since he has no reason for armour against me now. At first his eyes seemed masked with their customary brightness, his whole face with its usual decorous formality; then gradually he became so changed that she hardly knew him. That decorousness, that brightness, melted off what lay behind, as frosty dew melts off grass. And her very soul contracted within her, as if she had become identified with what he was seeing — a something to be passed over, a very nothing. Yes, his was the face of one looking at what was unintelligible, and therefore negligible; at that which had no soul; at something of a different and inferior species and of no great interest to a man. His face was like a soundless avowal of some conclusion, so fixed and intimate that it must surely emanate from the very core of him — be instinctive, unchangeable. This was the real he! A man despising women! Her first thought was: And he's married — what a fate! Her second: If he feels that, perhaps thousands of men do! Am I and all women really what they think us? The conviction in his stare — its through-and-through conviction — had infected her; and she gave in to it for the moment, crushed. Then her spirit revolted with such turbulence, and the blood so throbbed in her, that she could hardly lie still. How dare he think her like that — a nothing, a bundle of soulless inexplicable whims and moods and sensuality? A thousand times, No! It was HE who was the soulless one, the dry, the godless one; who, in his sickening superiority, could thus deny her, and with her all women! That stare was as if he saw her — a doll tricked out in garments labelled soul, spirit, rights, responsibilities, dignity, freedom — all so many words. It was vile, it was horrible, that he should see her thus! And a really terrific struggle began in her between the desire to get up and cry this out, and the knowledge that it would be stupid, undignified, even mad, to show her comprehension of what he would never admit or even understand that he had revealed to her. And then a sort of cynicism came to her rescue. What a funny thing was married life — to have lived all these years with him, and never known what was at the bottom of his heart! She had the feeling now that, if she went up to him and said: "I am in love with that boy!" it would only make him droop the corners of his mouth and say in his most satiric voice: "Really! That is very interesting!" — would not change in one iota his real thoughts of her; only confirm him in the conviction that she was negligible, inexplicable, an inferior strange form of animal, of no real interest to him.

And then, just when she felt that she could not hold herself in any longer, he got up, passed on tiptoe to the door, opened it noiselessly, and went out.

The moment he had gone, she jumped up. So, then, she was linked to one for whom she, for whom women, did not, as it were, exist! It seemed to her that she had stumbled on knowledge of almost sacred importance, on the key of everything that had been puzzling and hopeless in their married life. If he really, secretly, whole-heartedly despised her, the only feeling she need have for one so dry, so narrow, so basically stupid, was just contempt. But she knew well enough that contempt would not shake what she had seen in his face; he was impregnably walled within his clever, dull conviction of superiority. He was for ever intrenched, and she would always be only the assailant. Though — what did it matter, now?

Usually swift, almost careless, she was a long time that evening over her toilette. Her neck was very sunburnt, and she lingered, doubtful whether to hide it with powder, or accept her gipsy colouring. She did accept it, for she saw that it gave her eyes, so like glacier ice, under their black lashes, and her hair, with its surprising glints of flame colour, a peculiar value.

When the dinner-bell rang she passed her husband's door without, as usual, knocking, and went down alone.

In the hall she noticed some of the English party of the mountain hut. They did not greet her, conceiving an immediate interest in the barometer; but she could feel them staring at her very hard. She sat down to wait, and at once became conscious of the boy coming over from the other side of the room, rather like a person walking in his sleep. He said not a word. But how he looked! And her heart began to beat. Was this the moment she had longed for? If it, indeed, had come, dared she take it? Then she saw her husband descending the stairs, saw him greet the English party, heard the intoning of their drawl. She looked up at the boy, and said quickly: "Was it a happy day?" It gave her such delight to keep that look on his face, that look as if he had forgotten everything except just the sight of her. His eyes seemed to have in them something holy at that moment, something of the wonder-yearning of Nature and of innocence. It was dreadful to know that in a moment that look must be gone; perhaps never to come back on his face — that look so precious! Her husband was approaching now! Let him see, if he would! Let him see that someone could adore — that she was not to everyone a kind of lower animal. Yes, he must have seen the boy's face; and yet his expression never changed. He noticed nothing! Or was it that he disdained to notice?

VII

Then followed for young Lennan a strange time, when he never knew from minute to minute whether he was happy — always trying to be with her, restless if he could not be, sore if she talked with and smiled at others; yet, when he was with her, restless too, unsatisfied, suffering from his own timidity.

One wet morning, when she was playing the hotel piano, and he listening, thinking to have her to himself, there came a young German violinist — pale, and with a brown, thin-waisted coat, longish hair, and little whiskers — rather a beast, in fact. Soon, of course, this young beast was asking her to accompany him — as if anyone wanted to hear him play his disgusting violin! Every word and smile that she gave him hurt so, seeing how much more interesting than himself this foreigner was! And his heart grew heavier and heavier, and he thought: If she likes him I ought not to mind — only, I DO mind! How can I help minding? It was hateful to see her smiling, and the young beast bending down to her. And they were talking German, so that he could not tell what they were saying, which made it more unbearable. He had not known there could be such torture.

And then he began to want to hurt her, too. But that was mean — besides, how could he hurt her? She did not care for him. He was nothing to her — only a boy. If she really thought him only a boy, who felt so old — it would be horrible. It flashed across him that she might be playing that young violinist against him! No, she never would do that! But the young beast looked just the sort that might take advantage of her smiles. If only he WOULD do something that was not respectful, how splendid it would be to ask him to come for a walk in the woods, and, having told him why, give him a thrashing. Afterwards, he would not tell her, he would not try to gain credit by it. He would keep away till she wanted him back. But suddenly the thought of what he would feel if she really meant to take this young man as her friend in place of him became so actual, so poignant, so horribly painful, that he got up abruptly and went towards the door. Would she not say a word to him before he got out of the room, would she not try and keep him? If she did not, surely it would be all over; it would mean that anybody was more to her than he. That little journey to the door, indeed, seemed like a march to execution. Would she not call after him? He looked back. She was smiling. But HE could not smile; she had hurt him too much! Turning his head away, he went out, and dashed into the rain bareheaded. The feeling of it on his face gave him a sort of dismal satisfaction. Soon he would be wet through. Perhaps he would get ill. Out here, far away from his people, she would have to offer to nurse him; and perhaps — perhaps in his illness he would seem to her again more interesting than that young beast, and then — Ah! if only he could be ill!

He mounted rapidly through the dripping leaves towards the foot of the low mountain that rose behind the hotel. A trail went up there to the top, and he struck into it, going at a great pace. His sense of injury began dying away; he no longer wanted to be ill. The rain had stopped, the sun came out; he went on, up and up. He would get to the top quicker than anyone ever had! It was something he could do better than that young beast. The pine-trees gave way to stunted larches, and these to pine scrub and bare scree, up which he scrambled, clutching at the tough bushes, terribly out of breath, his heart pumping, the sweat streaming into his eyes. He had no feeling now but wonder whether he would get to the top before he dropped, exhausted. He thought he would die of the beating of his heart; but it was better to die than to stop and be beaten by a few yards. He stumbled up at last on to the little plateau at the top. For full ten minutes he lay there on his face without moving, then rolled over. His heart had given up that terrific thumping; he breathed luxuriously, stretched out his arms along the steaming grass — felt happy. It was wonderful up here, with the sun burning hot in a sky clear-blue already. How tiny everything looked below — hotel, trees, village, chalets — little toy things! He had never before felt the sheer joy of being high up. The rain-clouds, torn and driven in huge white shapes along the mountains to the South, were like an army of giants with chariots and white horses hurrying away. He thought suddenly: "Suppose I had died when my heart pumped so! Would it have mattered the least bit? Everything would be going on just the same, the sun shining, the blue up there the same; and those toy things down in the valley." That jealousy of his an hour ago, why — it was nothing — he himself nothing! What did it matter if she were nice to that fellow in the brown coat? What did anything matter when the whole thing was so big — and he such a tiny scrap of it?

On the edge of the plateau, to mark the highest point, someone had erected a rude cross, which jutted out stark against the blue sky. It looked cruel somehow, sagged all crooked, and out of place up here; a piece of bad manners, as if people with only one idea had dragged it in, without caring whether or no it suited what was around it. One might just as well introduce one of these rocks into that jolly dark church where he had left her the other day, as put a cross up here.

A sound of bells, and of sniffing and scuffling, roused him; a large grey goat had come up and was smelling at his hair — the leader of a flock, that were soon all round him, solemnly curious, with their queer yellow oblong-pupilled eyes, and their quaint little beards and tails. Awfully decent beasts — and friendly! What jolly things to model! He lay still (having learnt from the fisherman, his guardian, that necessary habit in the presence of all beasts), while the leader sampled the flavour of his neck. The passage of that long rough tongue athwart his skin gave him an agreeable sensation, awakened a strange deep sense of comradeship. He restrained his desire to stroke the creature's nose. It appeared that they now all wished to taste his neck; but some were timid, and the touch of their tongues simply a tickle, so that he was compelled to laugh, and at that peculiar sound they withdrew and gazed at him. There seemed to be no one with them; then, at a little distance, quite motionless in the shade of a rock, he spied the goatherd, a boy about his own age. How lonely he must be up here all day! Perhaps he talked to his goats. He looked as if he might. One would get to have queer thoughts up here, get to know the rocks, and clouds, and beasts, and what they all meant. The goatherd uttered a peculiar whistle, and something, Lennan could not tell exactly what, happened among the goats — a sort of "Here, Sir!" seemed to come from them. And then the goatherd moved out from the shade and went over to the edge of the plateau, and two of the goats that were feeding there thrust their noses into his hand, and rubbed themselves against his legs. The three looked beautiful standing there together on the edge against the sky. . . .

That night, after dinner, the dining-room was cleared for dancing, so that the guests might feel freedom and gaiety in the air. And, indeed, presently, a couple began sawing up and down over the polished boards, in the apologetic manner peculiar to hotel guests. Then three pairs of Italians suddenly launched themselves into space — twirling and twirling, and glaring into each other's eyes; and some Americans, stimulated by their precept, began airily backing and filling. Two of the 'English Grundys' with carefully amused faces next moved out. To Lennan it seemed that they all danced very well, better than he could. Did he dare ask HER? Then he saw the young violinist go up, saw her rise and take his arm and vanish into the dancing-room; and leaning his forehead against a window-pane, with a sick, beaten feeling, he stayed, looking out into the moonlight, seeing nothing. He heard his name spoken; his tutor was standing beside him.

"You and I, Lennan, must console each other. Dancing's for the young, eh?"

Fortunately it was the boy's instinct and his training not to show his feelings; to be pleasant, though suffering.

"Yes, sir. Jolly moonlight, isn't it, out there?"

"Ah! very jolly; yes. When I was your age I twirled the light fantastic with the best. But gradually, Lennan, one came to see it could not be done without a partner — there was the rub! Tell me — do you regard women as responsible beings? I should like to have your opinion on that."

It was, of course, ironical — yet there was something in those words — something!

"I think it's you, sir, who ought to give me yours."

"My dear Lennan — my experience is a mere nothing!"

That was meant for unkindness to her! He would not answer. If only Stormer would go away! The music had stopped. They would be sitting out somewhere, talking! He made an effort, and said:

"I was up the hill at the back this morning, where the cross is. There were some jolly goats."

And suddenly he saw her coming. She was alone — flushed, smiling; it struck him that her frock was the same colour as the moonlight.

"Harold, will you dance?"

He would say 'Yes,' and she would be gone again! But his tutor only made her a little bow, and said with that smile of his:

"Lennan and I have agreed that dancing is for the young."

"Sometimes the old must sacrifice themselves. Mark, will you dance?"

Behind him he heard his tutor murmur:

"Ah! Lennan — you betray me!"

That little silent journey with her to the dancing-room was the happiest moment perhaps that he had ever known. And he need not have been so much afraid about his dancing. Truly, it was not polished, but it could not spoil hers, so light, firm, buoyant! It was wonderful to dance with her. Only when the music stopped and they sat down did he know how his head was going round. He felt strange, very strange indeed. He heard her say:

"What is it, dear boy? You look so white!"

Without quite knowing what he did, he bent his face towards the hand that she had laid on his sleeve, then knew no more, having fainted.

VIII

Growing boy — over-exertion in the morning! That was all! He was himself very quickly, and walked up to bed without assistance. Rotten of him! Never was anyone more ashamed of his little weakness than this boy. Now that he was really a trifle indisposed, he simply could not bear the idea of being nursed at all or tended. Almost rudely he had got away. Only when he was in bed did he remember the look on her face as he left her. How wistful and unhappy, seeming to implore him to forgive her! As if there were anything to forgive! As if she had not made him perfectly happy when she danced with him! He longed to say to her: "If I might be close to you like that one minute every day, then I don't mind all the rest!" Perhaps he would dare say that tomorrow. Lying there he still felt a little funny. He had forgotten to close the ribs of the blinds, and moonlight was filtering in; but he was too idle, too drowsy to get up now and do it. They had given him brandy, rather a lot — that perhaps was the reason he felt so queer; not ill, but mazy, as if dreaming, as if he had lost the desire ever to move again. Just to lie there, and watch the powdery moonlight, and hear faraway music throbbing down below, and still feel the touch of her, as in the dance she swayed against him, and all the time to have the scent about him of flowers! His thoughts were dreams, his dreams thoughts — all precious unreality. And then it seemed to him that the moonlight was gathered into a single slip of pallor — there was a thrumming, a throbbing, and that shape of moonlight moved towards him. It came so close that he felt its warmth against his brow; it sighed, hovered, drew back soundless, and was gone. He must have fallen then into dreamless sleep. . . .

What time was it when he was awakened by that delicate 'rat-tat' to see his tutor standing in the door-way with a cup of tea?

Was young Lennan all right? Yes, he was perfectly all right — would be down directly! It was most frightfully good of Mr. Stormer to come! He really didn't want anything.

Yes, yes; but the maimed and the halt must be attended to!

His face seemed to the boy very kind just then — only to laugh at him a very little — just enough. And it was awfully decent of him to have come, and to stand there while he drank the tea. He was really all right, but for a little headache. Many times while he was dressing he stood still, trying to remember. That white slip of moonlight? Was it moonlight? Was it part of a dream; or was it, could it have been she, in her moonlight-coloured frock? Why had he not stayed awake? He would not dare to ask her, and now would never know whether the vague memory of warmth on his brow had been a kiss.

He breakfasted alone in the room where they had danced. There were two letters for him. One from his guardian enclosing money, and complaining of the shyness of the trout; the other from his sister. The man she was engaged to — he was a budding diplomat, attached to the Embassy at Rome — was afraid that his leave was going to be curtailed. They would have to be married at once. They might even have to get a special licence. It was lucky Mark was coming back so soon. They simply MUST have him for best man. The only bridesmaid now would be Sylvia. . . . Sylvia Doone? Why, she was only a kid! And the memory of a little girl in a very short holland frock, with flaxen hair, pretty blue eyes, and a face so fair that you could almost see through it, came up before him. But that, of course, was six years ago; she would not still be in a frock that showed her knees, or wear beads, or be afraid of bulls that were never there. It was stupid being best man — they might have got some decent chap! And then he forgot all — for there was SHE, out on the terrace. In his rush to join her he passed several of the 'English Grundys, '

who stared at him askance. Indeed, his conduct of the night
before might well have upset them. An Oxford man, fainting in
an hotel! Something wrong there!. . .

And then, when he reached her, he did find courage.

"Was it really moonlight?"

"All moonlight."

"But it was warm!"

And, when she did not answer that, he had within him just the
same light, intoxicated feeling as after he had won a race at
school.

But now came a dreadful blow. His tutor's old guide had suddenly
turned up, after a climb with a party of Germans. The war-horse had
been aroused in Stormer. He wished to start that afternoon for a
certain hut, and go up a certain peak at dawn next day. But Lennan
was not to go. Why not? Because of last night's faint; and because,
forsooth, he was not some stupid thing they called 'an expert'. As if
—! Where she could go he could! This was to treat him like a child.
Of course he could go up this rotten mountain. It was because she
did not care enough to take him! She did not think him man enough!
Did she think that he could not climb what — her husband —
could? And if it were dangerous SHE ought not to be going, leaving
him behind — that was simply cruel! But she only smiled, and he
flung away from her, not having seen that all this grief of his only
made her happy.

And that afternoon they went off without him. What deep,
dark thoughts he had then! What passionate hatred of his own
youth! What schemes he wove, by which she might come back,
and find him gone up some mountain far more dangerous and
fatiguing! If people did not think him fit to climb with, he would
climb by himself. That, anyway, everyone admitted, was
dangerous. And it would be her fault. She would be sorry then.
He would get up, and be off before dawn; he put his things out
ready, and filled his flask. The moonlight that evening was more
wonderful than ever, the mountains like great ghosts of

themselves. And she was up there at the hut, among them! It was very long before he went to sleep, brooding over his injuries — intending not to sleep at all, so as to be ready to be off at three o'clock. At NINE o'clock he woke. His wrath was gone; he only felt restless and ashamed. If, instead of flying out, he had made the best of it, he could have gone with them as far as the hut, could have stayed the night there. And now he cursed himself for being such a fool and idiot. Some little of that idiocy he could, perhaps, retrieve. If he started for the hut at once, he might still be in time to meet them coming down, and accompany them home. He swallowed his coffee, and set off. He knew the way at first, then in woods lost it, recovered the right track again at last, but did not reach the hut till nearly two o'clock. Yes, the party had made the ascent that morning — they had been seen, been heard jodelling on the top. Gewiss! Gewiss! But they would not come down the same way. Oh, no! They would be going home down to the West and over the other pass. They would be back in house before the young Herr himself.

He heard this, oddly, almost with relief. Was it the long walk alone, or being up there so high? Or simply that he was very hungry? Or just these nice friendly folk in the hut, and their young daughter with her fresh face, queer little black cloth sailor hat with long ribbons, velvet bodice, and perfect simple manners; or the sight of the little silvery-dun cows, thrusting their broad black noses against her hand? What was it that had taken away from him all his restless feeling, made him happy and content? . . . He did not know that the newest thing always fascinates the puppy in its gambols! . . . He sat a long while after lunch, trying to draw the little cows, watching the sun on the cheek of that pretty maiden, trying to talk to her in German. And when at last he said: "Adieu!" and she murmured "Kuss die Hand. Adieu!" there was quite a little pang in his heart. . . . Wonderful and queer is the heart of a man! . . . For all that, as he neared home he hastened, till he was actually running. Why had he stayed so long up there? She would be back — she would expect to see him; and that young beast of a violinist would be with her, perhaps, instead! He reached the hotel just in time to rush up and dress, and rush down to dinner. Ah! They were tired, no doubt — were resting in their rooms. He sat through dinner as best he could; got away before dessert, and flew upstairs. For a minute he stood there doubtful; on which door should he knock? Then timidly he tapped on hers. No answer! He knocked loud on his tutor's door. No answer! They were not back, then. Not back? What could that mean? Or could it be that they were both asleep? Once more he knocked on her door; then desperately ruined the handle, and took a flying glance. Empty, tidy, untouched! Not back! He turned and ran downstairs again. All the guests were streaming out from dinner, and he became entangled with a group of 'English Grundys' discussing a climbing accident which had occurred in Switzerland. He listened, feeling suddenly quite sick. One of them, the short grey-bearded Grundy with the rather whispering voice, said to him: "All alone again tonight? The Stormers not back?" Lennan did his best to answer, but something had closed his throat; he could only shake his head.

"They had a guide, I think?" said the 'English Grundy.'

This time Lennan managed to get out: "Yes, sir."

"Stormer, I fancy, is quite an expert!" and turning to the lady whom the young 'Grundys' addressed as 'Madre' he added:

"To me the great charm of mountain-climbing was always the freedom from people — the remoteness."

The mother of the young 'Grundys,' looking at Lennan with her half-closed eyes, answered:

"That, to me, would be the disadvantage; I always like to be mixing with my own kind."

The grey-bearded 'Grundy' murmured in a muffled voice:

"Dangerous thing, that, to say — in an hotel!"

And they went on talking, but of what Lennan no longer

knew, lost in this sudden feeling of sick fear. In the presence of these 'English Grundys,' so superior to all vulgar sensations, he could not give vent to his alarm; already they viewed him as unsound for having fainted. Then he grasped that there had begun all round him a sort of luxurious speculation on what might have happened to the Stormers. The descent was very nasty; there was a particularly bad traverse. The 'Grundy,' whose collar was not now crumpled, said he did not believe in women climbing. It was one of the signs of the times that he most deplored. The mother of the young 'Grundys' countered him at once: In practice she agreed that they were out of place, but theoretically she could not see why they should not climb. An American standing near threw all into confusion by saying he guessed that it might be liable to develop their understandings. Lennan made for the front door. The moon had just come up over in the South, and exactly under it he could see their mountain. What visions he had then! He saw her lying dead, saw himself climbing down in the moonlight and raising her still-living, but half-frozen, form from some perilous ledge. Even that was almost better than this actuality of not knowing where she was, or what had happened. People passed out into the moonlight, looking curiously at his set face staring so fixedly. One or two asked him if he were anxious, and he answered: "Oh no, thanks!" Soon there would have to be a search party. How soon? He would, he must be, of it! They should not stop him this time. And suddenly he thought: Ah, it is all because I stayed up there this afternoon talking to that girl, all because I forgot HER!

And then he heard a stir behind him. There they were, coming down the passage from a side door — she in front with her alpenstock and rucksack — smiling. Instinctively he recoiled behind some plants. They passed. Her sunburned face, with its high cheek-bones and its deep-set eyes, looked so happy; smiling, tired, triumphant. Somehow he could not bear it, and when they were gone by he stole out into the wood and threw himself down in shadow, burying his face, and choking back a horrible dry sobbing that would keep rising in his throat.

IX

Next day he was happy; for all the afternoon he lay out in the shade of that same wood at her feet, gazing up through larch-boughs. It was so wonderful, with nobody but Nature near. Nature so alive, and busy, and so big!

Coming down from the hut the day before, he had seen a peak that looked exactly like the figure of a woman with a garment over her head, the biggest statue in the world; from further down it had become the figure of a bearded man, with his arm bent over his eyes. Had she seen it? Had she noticed how all the mountains in moonlight or very early morning took the shape of beasts? What he wanted most in life was to be able to make images of beasts and creatures of all sorts, that were like — that had — that gave out the spirit of — Nature; so that by just looking at them one could have all those jolly feelings one had when one was watching trees, and beasts, and rocks, and even some sorts of men — but not 'English Grundys.'

So he was quite determined to study Art?

Oh yes, of course!

He would want to leave — Oxford, then!

No, oh no! Only some day he would have to.

She answered: "Some never get away!"

And he said quickly: "Of course, I shall never want to leave Oxford while you are there."

He heard her draw her breath in sharply.

"Oh yes, you will! Now help me up!" And she led the way back to the hotel.

He stayed out on the terrace when she had gone in, restless

and unhappy the moment he was away from her. A voice close by said:

"Well, friend Lennan — brown study, or blue devils, which?"

There, in one of those high wicker chairs that insulate their occupants from the world, he saw his tutor leaning back, head a little to one side, and tips of fingers pressed together. He looked like an idol sitting there inert, and yet — yesterday he had gone up that mountain!

"Cheer up! You will break your neck yet! When I was your age, I remember feeling it deeply that I was not allowed to risk the lives of others."

Lennan stammered out:

"I didn't think of that; but I thought where Mrs. Stormer could go, I could."

"Ah! For all our admiration we cannot quite admit — can we, when it comes to the point?"

The boy's loyalty broke into flame:

"It's not that. I think Mrs. Stormer as good as any man — only — only —"

"Not quite so good as you, eh?"

"A hundred times better, sir."

Stormer smiled. Ironic beast!

"Lennan," he said, "distrust hyperbole."

"Of course, I know I'm no good at climbing," the boy broke out again; "but — but — I thought where she was allowed to risk her life, I ought to be!"

"Good! I like that." It was said so entirely without irony for once, that the boy was disconcerted.

"You are young, Brother Lennan," his tutor went on. "Now, at what age do you consider men develop discretion? Because, there is just one thing always worth remembering — women have none of that better part of valour."

"I think women are the best things in the world," the boy blurted out.

"May you long have that opinion!" His tutor had risen, and was ironically surveying his knees. "A bit stiff!" he said. "Let me know when you change your views!"

"I never shall, sir."

"Ah, ah! Never is a long word, Lennan. I am going to have some tea;" and gingerly he walked away, quizzing, as it were, with a smile, his own stiffness.

Lennan remained where he was, with burning cheeks. His tutor's words again had seemed directed against her. How could a man say such things about women! If they were true, he did not want to know; if they were not true, it was wicked to say them. It must be awful never to have generous feelings; always to have to be satirical. Dreadful to be like the 'English Grundys'; only different, of course, because, after all, old Stormer was much more interesting and intelligent — ever so much more; only, just as 'superior.' "Some never get away!" Had she meant — from that superiority? Just down below were a family of peasants scything and gathering in the grass. One could imagine her doing that, and looking beautiful, with a coloured handkerchief over her head; one could imagine her doing anything simple — one could not imagine old Stormer doing anything but what he did do. And suddenly the boy felt miserable, oppressed by these dim glimmerings of lives misplaced. And he resolved that he would not be like Stormer when he was old! No, he would rather be a regular beast than be like that! ...

When he went to his room to change for dinner he saw in a glass of water a large clove carnation. Who had put it there? Who could have put it there — but she? It had the same scent as the mountain pinks she had dropped over him, but deeper, richer — a scent moving, dark, and sweet. He put his lips to it before he pinned it into his coat.

There was dancing again that night — more couples this time, and a violin beside the piano; and she had on a black frock. He had never seen her in black. Her face and neck were powdered over their sunburn. The first sight of that powder gave him a faint shock. He had not somehow thought that ladies ever put on powder. But if SHE did — then it must be right! And his eyes never left her. He saw the young German violinist hovering round her, even dancing with her twice; watched her dancing with others, but all without jealousy, without troubling; all in a sort of dream. What was it? Had he been bewitched into that queer state, bewitched by the gift of that flower in his coat? What was it, when he danced with her, that kept him happy in her silence and his own? There was no expectation in him of anything that she would say, or do — no expectation, no desire. Even when he wandered out with her on to the terrace, even when they went down the bank and sat on a bench above the fields where the peasants had been scything, he had still no feeling but that quiet, dreamy adoration. The night was black and dreamy too, for the moon was still well down behind the mountains. The little band was playing the next waltz; but he sat, not moving, not thinking, as if all power of action and thought had been stolen out of him. And the scent of the flower in his coat rose, for there was no wind. Suddenly his heart stopped beating. She had leaned against him, he felt her shoulder press his arm, her hair touch his cheek. He closed his eyes then, and turned his face to her. He felt her lips press his mouth with a swift, burning kiss. He sighed, stretched out his arms. There was nothing there but air. The rustle of her dress against the grass was all! The flower — it, too, was gone.

X

Not one minute all that night did Anna sleep. Was it remorse that kept her awake, or the intoxication of memory? If she felt that her kiss had been a crime, it was not against her husband or herself, but against the boy — the murder of illusion, of something sacred. But she could not help feeling a delirious happiness too, and the thought of trying to annul what she had done did not even occur to her.

He was ready, then, to give her a little love! Ever so little, compared to hers, but still a little! There could be no other meaning to that movement of his face with the closed eyes, as if he would nestle it down on her breast.

Was she ashamed of her little manoeuvres of these last few days — ashamed of having smiled at the young violinist, of that late return from the mountain climb, of the flower she had given him, of all the conscious siege she had laid since the evening her husband came in and sat watching her, without knowing that she saw him? No; not really ashamed! Her remorse rose only from the kiss. It hurt to think of that, because it was death, the final extinction of the mother-feeling in her; the awakening of — who knew what — in the boy! For if she was mysterious to him, what was he not to her, with his eagerness, and his dreaminess, his youthful warmth, his innocence! What if it had killed in him trust, brushed off the dew, tumbled a star down? Could she forgive herself for that? Could she bear it if she were to make him like so many other boys, like that young violinist; just a cynical youth, looking on women as what they called 'fair game'? But COULD she make him into such — would he ever grow like that? Oh! surely not; or she would not have loved him from the moment she first set eyes on him and spoke of him as 'an angel.'

After that kiss — that crime, if it were one — in the dark she had not known what he had done, where gone — perhaps wandering, perhaps straight up to his room. Why had she refrained, left him there, vanished out of his arms? This she herself hardly understood. Not shame; not fear; reverence perhaps — for what? For love — for the illusion, the mystery, all that made love beautiful; for youth, and the poetry of it; just for the sake of the black still night itself, and the scent of that flower — dark flower of passion that had won him to her, and that she had stolen back, and now wore all night long close to her neck, and in the morning placed withered within her dress. She had been starved so long, and so long waited for that moment — it was little wonder if she did not clearly know why she had done just this, and not that!

And now how should she meet him, how first look into his eyes? Would they have changed? Would they no longer have the straight look she so loved? It would be for her to lead, to make the future. And she kept saying to herself: I am not going to be afraid. It is done. I will take what life offers! Of her husband she did not think at all.

But the first moment she saw the boy, she knew that something from outside, and untoward, had happened since that kiss. He came up to her, indeed, but he said nothing, stood trembling all over and handed her a telegram that contained these words: "Come back at once Wedding immediate Expect you day after tomorrow. Cicely." The words grew indistinct even as she read them, and the boy's face all blurred. Then, making an effort, she said quietly:

"Of course, you must go. You cannot miss your only sister's wedding."

Without protest he looked at her; and she could hardly bear that look — it seemed to know so little, and ask so much. She said: "It is nothing — only a few days. You will come back, or we will come to you."

His face brightened at once.

"Will you really come to us soon, at once — if they ask you? Then I don't mind — I — I —" And then he stopped, choking.

She said again:

"Ask us. We will come."

He seized her hand; pressed and pressed it in both his own, then stroked it gently, and said:

"Oh! I'm hurting it!"

She laughed, not wishing to cry.

In a few minutes he would have to start to catch the only train that would get him home in time.

She went and helped him to pack. Her heart felt like lead, but, not able to bear that look on his face again, she kept cheerfully talking of their return, asking about his home, how to get to it, speaking of Oxford and next term. When his things were ready she put her arms round his neck, and for a moment pressed him to her. Then she escaped. Looking back from his door, she saw him standing exactly as when she had withdrawn her arms. Her cheeks were wet; she dried them as she went downstairs. When she felt herself safe, she went out on the terrace. Her husband was there, and she said to him:

"Will you come with me into the town? I want to buy some things."

He raised his eyebrows, smiled dimly, and followed her. They walked slowly down the hill into the long street of the little town. All the time she talked of she knew not what, and all the time she thought: His carriage will pass — his carriage will pass!

Several carriages went jingling by. At last he came. Sitting there, and staring straight before him, he did not see them. She heard her husband say:

"Hullo! Where is our young friend Lennan off to, with his luggage — looking like a lion cub in trouble?"

She answered in a voice that she tried to make clear and steady:

"There must be something wrong; or else it is his sister's wedding."

She felt that her husband was gazing at her, and wondered what her face was like; but at that moment the word "Madre!" sounded close in her ear and they were surrounded by a small drove of 'English Grundys.'

XI

That twenty mile drive was perhaps the worst part of the journey for the boy. It is always hard to sit still and suffer.

When Anna left him the night before, he had wandered about in the dark, not knowing quite where he went. Then the moon came up, and he found himself sitting under the eave of a barn close to a chalet where all was dark and quiet; and down below him the moon-whitened valley village — its roofs and spires and little glamorous unreal lights.

In his evening suit, his dark ruffled hair uncovered, he would have made a quaint spectacle for the owners of that chalet, if they had chanced to see him seated on the hay-strewn boards against their barn, staring before him with such wistful rapture. But they were folk to whom sleep was precious. . . .

And now it was all snatched away from him, relegated to some immensely far-off future. Would it indeed be possible to get his guardian to ask them down to Hayle? And would they really come? His tutor would surely never care to visit a place right away in the country — far from books and everything! He frowned, thinking of his tutor, but it was with perplexity — no other feeling. And yet, if he could not have them down there, how could he wait the two whole months till next term began! So went his thoughts, round and round, while the horses jogged, dragging him further and further from her.

It was better in the train; the distraction of all the strange crowd of foreigners, the interest of new faces and new country; and then sleep — a long night of it, snoozed up in his corner, thoroughly fagged out. And next day more new country, more new faces; and slowly, his mood changing from ache and bewilderment to a sense of something promised, delightful to look forward to. Then Calais at last, and a night-crossing in a wet little steamer, a summer gale blowing spray in his face, waves leaping white in a black sea, and the wild sound of the wind. On again to London, the early drive across the town, still sleepy in August haze; an English breakfast — porridge, chops, marmalade. And, at last, the train for home. At all events he could write to her, and tearing a page out of his little sketch-book, he began:

"I am writing in the train, so please forgive this joggly writing —"

Then he did not know how to go on, for all that he wanted to say was such as he had never even dreamed of writing — things about his feelings which would look horrible in words; besides, he must not put anything that might not be read, by anyone, so what was there to say?

"It has been such a long journey," he wrote at last, "away from the Tyrol;" (he did not dare even to put "from you,") "I thought it would never end. But at last it has — very nearly. I have thought a great deal about the Tyrol. It was a lovely time — the loveliest time I have ever had. And now it's over, I try to console myself by thinking of the future, but not the immediate future — THAT is not very enjoyable. I wonder how the mountains are looking today. Please give my love to them, especially the lion ones that come and lie out in the moonlight — you will not recognize them from this" — then followed a sketch. "And this is the church we went to, with someone kneeling. And this is meant for the 'English Grundys,' looking at someone who is coming in very late with an alpenstock — only, I am better at the 'English Grundys' than at the person with the alpenstock. I wish I were the 'English Grundys' now, still in the Tyrol. I hope I shall get a letter from you soon; and that it will say you are getting ready to come back. My guardian will be awfully keen for you to come and stay with us. He is not half bad when you know him, and there will be his sister, Mrs. Doone, and her daughter left there after the wedding. It will be simply disgusting if you and Mr. Stormer don't come. I wish I could write all I feel about my lovely time in the Tyrol, but you must please imagine it."

And just as he had not known how to address her, so he could not tell how to subscribe himself, and only put "Mark Lennan."

He posted the letter at Exeter, where he had some time to wait; and his mind moved still more from past to future. Now that he was nearing home he began to think of his sister. In two days she would be gone to Italy; he would not see her again for a long time, and a whole crowd of memories began to stretch out hands to him. How she and he used to walk together in the walled garden, and on the sunk croquet ground; she telling him stories, her arm round his neck, because she was two years older, and taller than he in those days. Their first talk each holidays, when he came back to her; the first tea — with unlimited jam — in the old mullion-windowed, flower-chintzed schoolroom, just himself and her and old Tingle (Miss Tring, the ancient governess, whose chaperonage would now be gone), and sometimes that kid Sylvia, when she chanced to be staying there with her mother. Cicely had always understood him when he explained to her how inferior school was, because nobody took any interest in beasts or birds except to kill them; or in drawing, or making things, or anything decent. They would go off together, rambling along the river, or up the park, where everything looked so jolly and wild — the ragged oak-trees, and huge boulders, of whose presence old Godden, the coachman, had said: "I can't think but what these ha' been washed here by the Flood, Mast' Mark!" These and a thousand other memories beset his conscience now. And as the train drew closer to their station, he eagerly made ready to jump out and greet her. There was the honeysuckle full out along the paling of the platform over the waiting-room; wonderful, this year — and there was she, standing alone on the platform. No, it was not Cicely! He got out with a blank sensation, as if those memories had played him false. It was a girl, indeed, but she only looked about sixteen, and wore a sunbonnet that hid her hair and half her face. She had on a blue frock, and some honeysuckle in her waist-belt. She seemed to be smiling at him, and expecting him to smile at her; and so he did smile. She came up to him then, and said:

"I'm Sylvia."

He answered: "Oh! thanks awfully — it was awfully good of you to come and meet me."

"Cicely's so busy. It's only the T-cart. Have you got much luggage?"

She took up his hold-all, and he took it from her; she took his bag, and he took it from her; then they went out to the T-cart. A small groom stood there, holding a silver-roan cob with a black mane and black swish tail.

She said: "D'you mind if I drive, because I'm learning."

And he answered: "Oh, no! rather not."

She got up; he noticed that her eyes looked quite excited. Then his portmanteau came out and was deposited with the other things behind; and he got up beside her.

She said: "Let go, Billy."

The roan rushed past the little groom, whose top boots seemed to twinkle as he jumped up behind. They whizzed round the corner from the station yard, and observing that her mouth was just a little open as though this had disconcerted her, he said:

"He pulls a bit."

"Yes — but isn't he perfectly sweet?"

"He IS rather decent."

Ah! when SHE came, he would drive her; they would go off alone in the T-cart, and he would show her all the country round.

He was re-awakened by the words:

"Oh! I know he's going to shy!" At once there was a swerve. The roan was cantering.

They had passed a pig.

"Doesn't he look lovely now? Ought I to have whipped him when he shied?"

"Rather not."

"Why?"

"Because horses are horses, and pigs are pigs; it's natural for horses to shy at them."

"Oh!"

He looked up at her then, sidelong. The curve of her cheek and chin looked very soft, and rather jolly.

"I didn't know you, you know!" he said. "You've grown up so awfully."

"I knew you at once. Your voice is still furry."

There was another silence, till she said:

"He does pull, rather — doesn't he, going home?"

"Shall I drive?"

"Yes, please."

He stood up and took the reins, and she slipped past under them in front of him; her hair smelt exactly like hay, as she was softly bumped against him.

She kept regarding him steadily with very blue eyes, now that she was relieved of driving.

"Cicely was afraid you weren't coming," she said suddenly. "What sort of people are those old Stormers?"

He felt himself grow very red, choked something down, and answered:

"It's only he that's old. She's not more than about thirty-five."

"That IS old."

He restrained the words: "Of course it's old to a kid like you!" And, instead, he looked at her. Was she exactly a kid? She seemed quite tall (for a girl) and not very thin, and there was something frank and soft about her face, and as if she wanted you to be nice to her.

"Is she very pretty?"

This time he did not go red, such was the disturbance that question made in him. If he said: "Yes," it was like letting the world know his adoration; but to say anything less would be horrible, disloyal. So he did say: "Yes," listening hard to the tone of his own voice.

"I thought she was. Do you like her very much?" Again he struggled with that thing in his throat, and again said: "Yes."

He wanted to hate this girl, yet somehow could not — she looked so soft and confiding. She was staring before her now, her lips still just parted, so evidently THAT had not been because of Bolero's pulling; they were pretty all the same, and so was her short, straight little nose, and her chin, and she was awfully fair. His thoughts flew back to that other face — so splendid, so full of life. Suddenly he found himself unable to picture it — for the first time since he had started on his journey it would not come before him.

"Oh! Look!"

Her hand was pulling at his arm. There in the field over the hedge a buzzard hawk was dropping like a stone.

"Oh, Mark! Oh! Oh! It's got it!"

She was covering her face with both her hands, and the hawk, with a young rabbit in its claws, was sailing up again. It looked so beautiful that he did not somehow feel sorry for the rabbit; but he wanted to stroke and comfort her, and said:

"It's all right, Sylvia; it really is. The rabbit's dead already, you know. And it's quite natural."

She took her hands away from a face that looked just as if she were going to cry.

"Poor little rabbit! It was such a little one!"

XII

On the afternoon of the day following he sat in the smoking-room with a prayer book in his hand, and a frown on his forehead, reading the Marriage Service. The book had been effectively designed for not spoiling the figure when carried in a pocket. But this did not matter, for even if he could have read the words, he would not have known what they meant, seeing that he was thinking how he could make a certain petition to a certain person sitting just behind at a large bureau with a sliding top, examining artificial flies.

He fixed at last upon this form:

"Gordy!" (Why Gordy no one quite knew now — whether because his name was George, or by way of corruption from Guardian.) "When Cis is gone it'll be rather awful, won't it?"

"Not a bit."

Mr. Heatherley was a man of perhaps sixty-four, if indeed guardians have ages, and like a doctor rather than a squire; his face square and puffy, his eyes always half-closed, and his curly mouth using bluntly a voice of that refined coarseness peculiar to people of old family.

"But it will, you know!"

"Well, supposin' it is?"

"I only wondered if you'd mind asking Mr. and Mrs. Stormer to come here for a little — they were awfully kind to me out there."

"Strange man and woman! My dear fellow!"

"Mr. Stormer likes fishing."

"Does he? And what does she like?"

Very grateful that his back was turned, the boy said:

"I don't know — anything — she's awfully nice."

"Ah! Pretty?"

He answered faintly:

"I don't know what YOU call pretty, Gordy."

He felt, rather than saw, his guardian scrutinizing him with those half-closed eyes under their gouty lids.

"All right; do as you like. Have 'em here and have done with it, by all means."

Did his heart jump? Not quite; but it felt warm and happy, and he said:

"Thanks awfully, Gordy. It's most frightfully decent of you," and turned again to the Marriage Service. He could make out some of it. In places it seemed to him fine, and in other places queer. About obeying, for instance. If you loved anybody, it seemed rotten to expect them to obey you. If you loved them and they loved you, there couldn't ever be any question of obeying, because you would both do the things always of your own accord. And if they didn't love you, or you them, then — oh! then it would be simply too disgusting for anything, to go on living with a person you didn't love or who didn't love you. But of course SHE didn't love his tutor. Had she once? Those bright doubting eyes, that studiously satiric mouth came very clearly up before him. You could not love them; and yet — he was really very decent. A feeling as of pity, almost of affection, rose in him for his remote tutor. It was queer to feel so, since the last time they had talked together out there, on the terrace, he had not felt at all like that.

The noise of the bureau top sliding down aroused him; Mr. Heatherley was closing in the remains of the artificial flies. That meant he would be going out to fish. And the moment he heard the door shut, Mark sprang up, slid back the bureau top, and began to write his letter. It was hard work.

"DEAR MRS. STORMER,

"My guardian wishes me to beg you and Mr. Stormer to pay us

a visit as soon as you come back from the Tyrol. Please tell Mr. Stormer that only the very best fishermen — like him — can catch our trout; the rest catch our trees. This is me catching our trees (here followed a sketch). My sister is going to be married tomorrow, and it will be disgusting afterwards unless you come. So do come, please. And with my very best greetings,

"I am,

"Your humble servant,

"M. LENNAN."

When he had stamped this production and dropped it in the letterbox, he had the oddest feeling, as if he had been let out of school; a desire to rush about, to frolic. What should he do? Cis, of course, would be busy — they were all busy about the wedding. He would go and saddle Bolero, and jump him in the park; or should he go down along the river and watch the jays? Both seemed lonely occupations. And he stood in the window — dejected. At the age of five, walking with his nurse, he had been overheard remarking: "Nurse, I want to eat a biscuit — ALL THE WAY I want to eat a biscuit!" and it was still rather so with him perhaps — all the way he wanted to eat a biscuit. He bethought him then of his modelling, and went out to the little empty greenhouse where he kept his masterpieces. They seemed to him now quite horrible — and two of them, the sheep and the turkey, he marked out for summary destruction. The idea occurred to him that he might try and model that hawk escaping with the little rabbit; but when he tried, no nice feeling came, and flinging the things down he went out. He ran along the unweeded path to the tennis ground — lawn tennis was then just coming in. The grass looked very rough. But then, everything about that little manor house was left rather wild and anyhow; why, nobody quite knew, and nobody seemed to mind. He stood there scrutinizing the condition of the ground. A sound of humming came to his ears. He got up on the wall. There was Sylvia sitting in the field, making a wreath of honeysuckle. He stood very quiet and listened. She looked pretty — lost in her tune. Then he slid down off the wall, and said gently:

"Hallo!"

She looked round at him, her eyes very wide open.

"Your voice is jolly, Sylvia!"

"Oh, no!"

"It is. Come and climb a tree!"

"Where?"

"In the park, of course."

They were some time selecting the tree, many being too easy for him, and many too hard for her; but one was found at last, an oak of great age, and frequented by rooks. Then, insisting that she must be roped to him, he departed to the house for some blind-cord. The climb began at four o'clock — named by him the ascent of the Cimone della Pala. He led the momentous expedition, taking a hitch of the blind-cord round a branch before he permitted her to move. Two or three times he was obliged to make the cord fast and return to help her, for she was not an 'expert'; her arms seemed soft, and she was inclined to straddle instead of trusting to one foot. But at last they were settled, streaked indeed with moss, on the top branch but two. They rested there, silent, listening to the rooks soothing an outraged dignity. Save for this slowly subsiding demonstration it was marvellously peaceful and remote up there, half-way to a blue sky thinly veiled from them by the crinkled brown-green leaves. The peculiar dry mossy smell of an oak-tree was disturbed into the air by the least motion of their feet or hands against the bark. They could hardly see the ground, and all around, other gnarled trees barred off any view.

He said:

"If we stay up here till it's dark we might see owls."

"Oh, no! Owls are horrible!"

"What! They're LOVELY—especially the white ones."

"I can't stand their eyes, and they squeak so when they're hunting."

"Oh! but that's so jolly, and their eyes are beautiful."

"They're always catching mice and little chickens; all sorts of little things."

"But they don't mean to; they only want them to eat. Don't you think things are jolliest at night?"

She slipped her arm in his.

"No; I don't like the dark."

"Why not? It's splendid — when things get mysterious." He dwelt lovingly on that word.

"I don't like mysterious things. They frighten you."

"Oh, Sylvia!"

"No, I like early morning — especially in spring, when it's beginning to get leafy."

"Well, of course."

She was leaning against him, for safety, just a little; and stretching out his arm, he took good hold of the branch to make a back for her. There was a silence. Then he said:

"If you could only have one tree, which would you have?"

"Not oaks. Limes — no — birches. Which would you?"

He pondered. There were so many trees that were perfect. Birches and limes, of course; but beeches and cypresses, and yews, and cedars, and holm-oaks — almost, and plane-trees; then he said suddenly:

"Pines; I mean the big ones with reddish stems and branches pretty high up."

"Why?"

Again he pondered. It was very important to explain exactly why; his feelings about everything were concerned in this. And while he mused she gazed at him, as if surprised to see anyone think so deeply. At last he said:

"Because they're independent and dignified and never quite cold, and their branches seem to brood, but chiefly because the ones I mean are generally out of the common where you find them. You know — just one or two, strong and dark, standing out against the sky."

"They're TOO dark."

It occurred to him suddenly that he had forgotten larches. They, of course, could be heavenly, when you lay under them and looked up at the sky, as he had that afternoon out there. Then he heard her say:

"If I could only have one flower, I should have lilies of the valley, the small ones that grow wild and smell so jolly."

He had a swift vision of another flower, dark — very different, and was silent.

"What would you have, Mark?" Her voice sounded a little hurt. "You ARE thinking of one, aren't you?"

He said honestly:

"Yes, I am."

"Which?"

"It's dark, too; you wouldn't care for it a bit."

"How d'you know?"

"A clove carnation."

"But I do like it — only — not very much."

He nodded solemnly.

"I knew you wouldn't."

Then a silence fell between them. She had ceased to lean against him, and he missed the cosy friendliness of it. Now that their voices and the cawings of the rooks had ceased, there was nothing heard but the dry rustle of the leaves, and the plaintive cry of a buzzard hawk hunting over the little tor across the river. There were nearly always two up there, quartering the sky. To the boy it was lovely, that silence — like Nature talking to you — Nature always talked in silences. The beasts, the birds, the insects, only really showed themselves when you were still; you had to be awfully quiet, too, for flowers and plants, otherwise you couldn't see the real jolly separate life there was in them. Even the boulders down there, that old Godden thought had been washed up by the Flood, never showed you what queer shapes they had, and let you feel close to them, unless you were thinking of nothing else. Sylvia, after all, was better in that way than he had expected. She could keep quiet (he had thought girls hopeless); she was gentle, and it was rather jolly to watch her. Through the leaves there came the faint far tinkle of the tea-bell.

She said: "We must get down."

It was much too jolly to go in, really. But if she wanted her tea — girls always wanted tea! And, twisting the cord carefully round the branch, he began to superintend her descent. About to follow, he heard her cry:

"Oh, Mark! I'm stuck — I'm stuck! I can't reach it with my foot! I'm swinging!" And he saw that she WAS swinging by her hands and the cord.

"Let go; drop on to the branch below — the cord'll hold you straight till you grab the trunk."

Her voice mounted piteously:

"I can't — I really can't — I should slip!"

He tied the cord, and slithered hastily to the branch below her; then, bracing himself against the trunk, he clutched her round the waist and knees; but the taut cord held her up, and she would not come to anchor. He could not hold her and untie the cord, which was fast round her waist. If he let her go with one hand, and got out his knife, he would never be able to cut and hold her at the same time. For a moment he thought he had better climb up again and slack off the cord, but he could see by her face that she was getting frightened; he could feel it by the quivering of her body.

"If I heave you up," he said, "can you get hold again above?" And, without waiting for an answer, he heaved. She caught hold frantically.

"Hold on just for a second."

She did not answer, but he saw that her face had gone very

white. He snatched out his knife and cut the cord. She clung just for that moment, then came loose into his arms, and he hauled her to him against the trunk. Safe there, she buried her face on his shoulder. He began to murmur to her and smooth her softly, with quite a feeling of its being his business to smooth her like this, to protect her. He knew she was crying, but she let no sound escape, and he was very careful not to show that he knew, for fear she should feel ashamed. He wondered if he ought to kiss her. At last he did, on the top of her head, very gently. Then she put up her face and said she was a beast. And he kissed her again on an eyebrow.

After that she seemed all right, and very gingerly they descended to the ground, where shadows were beginning to lengthen over the fern and the sun to slant into their eyes.

XIII

The night after the wedding the boy stood at the window of his pleasant attic bedroom, with one wall sloping, and a faint smell of mice. He was tired and excited, and his brain, full of pictures. This was his first wedding, and he was haunted by a vision of his sister's little white form, and her face with its starry eyes. She was gone — his no more! How fearful the Wedding March had sounded on that organ — that awful old wheezer; and the sermon! One didn't want to hear that sort of thing when one felt inclined to cry. Even Gordy had looked rather boiled when he was giving her away. With perfect distinctness he could still see the group before the altar rails, just as if he had not been a part of it himself. Cis in her white, Sylvia in fluffy grey; his impassive brother-in-law's tall figure; Gordy looking queer in a black coat, with a very yellow face, and eyes still half-closed. The rotten part of it all had been that you wanted to be just FEELING, and you had to be thinking of the ring, and your gloves, and whether the lowest button of your white waistcoat was properly undone. Girls could do both, it seemed — Cis seemed to be seeing something wonderful all the time, and Sylvia had looked quite holy. He himself had been too conscious of the rector's voice, and the sort of professional manner with which he did it all, as if he were making up a prescription, with directions how to take it. And yet it was all rather beautiful in a kind of fashion, every face turned one way, and a tremendous hush — except for poor old Godden's blowing of his nose with his enormous red handkerchief; and the soft darkness up in the roof, and down in the pews; and the sunlight brightening the South windows. All the same, it would have been much jollier just taking hands by themselves somewhere, and saying out before God what they really felt — because, after all, God was everything, everywhere, not only in stuffy churches. That was how HE would like to be married, out of doors on a starry night like this, when everything felt wonderful all round you. Surely God wasn't half as small as people seemed always making Him — a sort of superior man a little bigger than themselves! Even the very most beautiful and wonderful and awful things one could imagine or make, could only be just nothing to a God who had a temple like the night out there. But then you couldn't be married alone, and no girl would ever like to be married without rings and flowers and dresses, and words that made it all feel small and cosy! Cis might have, perhaps, only she wouldn't, because of not hurting other people's feelings; but Sylvia — never — she would be afraid. Only, of course, she was young! And the thread of his thoughts broke — and scattered like beads from a string.

Leaning out, and resting his chin on his hands, he drew the night air into his lungs. Honeysuckle, or was it the scent of lilies still? The stars all out, and lots of owls tonight — four at least. What would night be like without owls and stars? But that was it — you never could think what things would be like if they weren't just what and where they were. You never knew what was coming, either; and yet, when it came, it seemed as if nothing else ever could have come. That was queer — you could do anything you liked until you'd done it, but when you HAD done it, then you knew, of course, that you must always have had to . . . What was that light, below and to the left? Whose room? Old Tingle's — no, the little spare room — Sylvia's! She must be awake, then! He leaned far out, and whispered in the voice she had said was still furry:

"Sylvia!"

The light flickered, he could just see her head appear, with hair all loose, and her face turning up to him. He could only half see, half imagine it, mysterious, blurry; and he whispered:

"Isn't this jolly?"

The whisper travelled back:

"Awfully."

"Aren't you sleepy?"

"No; are you?"

"Not a bit. D'you hear the owls?"

"Rather."

"Doesn't it smell good?"

"Perfect. Can you see me?"

"Only just, not too much. Can you?"

"I can't see your nose. Shall I get the candle?"

"No — that'd spoil it. What are you sitting on?"

"The window sill."

"It doesn't twist your neck, does it?"

"No — o — only a little bit."

"Are you hungry?"

"Yes."

"Wait half a shake. I'll let down some chocolate in my big bath towel; it'll swing along to you — reach out."

A dim white arm reached out.

"Catch! I say, you won't get cold?"

"Rather not."

"It's too jolly to sleep, isn't it?"

"Mark!"

"Yes."

"Which star is yours? Mine is the white one over the top branch of the big sycamore, from here."

"Mine is that twinkling red one over the summer house. Sylvia!"

"Yes."

"Catch!"

"Oh! I couldn't — what was it?"

"Nothing."

"No, but what WAS it?"

"Only my star. It's caught in your hair."

"Oh!"

"Listen!"

Silence, then, until her awed whisper:

"What?"

And his floating down, dying away:

"CAVE!"

What had stirred — some window opened? Cautiously he spied along the face of the dim house. There was no light anywhere, nor any shifting blur of white at her window below. All was dark, remote — still sweet with the scent of something jolly. And then he saw what that something was. All over the wall below his window white jessamine was in flower — stars, not only in the sky. Perhaps the sky was really a field of white flowers; and God walked there, and plucked the stars. . . .

The next morning there was a letter on his plate when he came down to breakfast. He couldn't open it with Sylvia on one side of him, and old Tingle on the other. Then with a sort of anger he did open it. He need not have been afraid. It was written so that anyone might have read; it told of a climb, of bad weather, said they were coming home. Was he relieved, disturbed, pleased at their coming back, or only uneasily ashamed? She had not got his second letter yet. He could feel old Tingle looking round at him with those queer sharp twinkling eyes of hers, and Sylvia regarding him quite frankly. And conscious that he was growing red, he said to himself: 'I won't!' And did not. In three days they would be at Oxford. Would they come on here at once? Old Tingle was speaking. He heard Sylvia answer: "No, I don't like 'bopsies'. They're so hard!" It was their old name for high cheekbones. Sylvia certainly had none, her cheeks went softly up to her eyes.

"Do you, Mark?"

He said slowly:

"On some people."

"People who have them are strong-willed, aren't they?"

Was SHE — Anna — strong-willed? It came to him that he did not know at all what she was.

When breakfast was over and he had got away to his old greenhouse, he had a strange, unhappy time. He was a beast, he had not been thinking of her half enough! He took the letter out, and frowned at it horribly. Why could he not feel more? What was the matter with him? Why was he such a brute — not to be thinking of her day and night? For long he stood, disconsolate, in the little dark greenhouse among the images of his beasts, the letter in his hand.

He stole out presently, and got down to the river unobserved. Comforting — that crisp, gentle sound of water; ever so comforting to sit on a stone, very still, and wait for things to happen round you. You lost yourself that way, just became branches, and stones, and water, and birds, and sky. You did not feel such a beast. Gordy would never understand why he did not care for fishing — one thing trying to catch another — instead of watching and understanding what things were. You never got to the end of looking into water, or grass or fern; always something queer and new. It was like that, too, with yourself, if you sat down and looked properly — most awfully interesting to see things working in your mind.

A soft rain had begun to fall, hissing gently on the leaves, but he had still a boy's love of getting wet, and stayed where he was, on the stone. Some people saw fairies in woods and down in water, or said they did; that did not seem to him much fun. What was really interesting was noticing that each thing was different from every other thing, and what made it so; you must see that before you could draw or model decently. It was fascinating to see your creatures coming out with shapes of their very own; they did that without your understanding how. But this vacation he was no good — couldn't draw or model a bit!

A jay had settled about forty yards away, and remained in full view, attending to his many-coloured feathers. Of all things, birds were the most fascinating! He watched it a long time, and when it flew on, followed it over the high wall up into the park. He heard the lunch-bell ring in the far distance, but did not go in. So long as he was out there in the soft rain with the birds and trees and other creatures, he was free from that unhappy feeling of the morning. He did not go back till nearly seven, properly wet through, and very hungry.

All through dinner he noticed that Sylvia seemed to be watching him, as if wanting to ask him something. She looked very soft in her white frock, open at the neck; and her hair almost the colour of special moonlight, so goldy-pale; and he wanted her to understand that it wasn't a bit because of her that he had been out alone all day. After dinner, when they were getting the table ready to play 'red nines,' he did murmur:

"Did you sleep last night — after?"

She nodded fervently to that.

It was raining really hard now, swishing and dripping out in the darkness, and he whispered:

"Our stars would be drowned tonight."

"Do you really think we have stars?"

"We might. But mine's safe, of course; your hair IS jolly, Sylvia."

She gazed at him, very sweet and surprised.

XIV

Anna did not receive the boy's letter in the Tyrol. It followed her to Oxford. She was just going out when it came, and she took it up with the mingled beatitude and almost sickening tremor that a lover feels touching the loved one's letter. She would not open it in the street, but carried it all the way to the garden of a certain College, and sat down to read it under the cedar-tree. That little letter, so short, boyish, and dry, transported her halfway to heaven. She was to see him again at once, not to wait weeks, with the fear that he would quite forget her! Her husband had said at breakfast that Oxford without 'the dear young clowns' assuredly was charming, but Oxford 'full of tourists and other strange bodies' as certainly was not. Where should they go? Thank heaven, the letter could be shown him! For all that, a little stab of pain went through her that there was not one word which made it unsuitable to show. Still, she was happy. Never had her favourite College garden seemed so beautiful, with each tree and flower so cared for, and the very wind excluded; never had the birds seemed so tame and friendly. The sun shone softly, even the clouds were luminous and joyful. She sat a long time, musing, and went back forgetting all she had come out to do. Having both courage and decision, she did not leave the letter to burn a hole in her corsets, but gave it to her husband at lunch, looking him in the face, and saying carelessly:

"Providence, you see, answers your question."

He read it, raised his eyebrows, smiled, and, without looking up, murmured:

"You wish to prosecute this romantic episode?"

Did he mean anything — or was it simply his way of putting things?

"I naturally want to be anywhere but here."

"Perhaps you would like to go alone?"

He said that, of course, knowing she could not say: Yes. And she answered simply: "No."

"Then let us both go — on Monday. I will catch the young man's trout; thou shalt catch — h'm! — he shall catch — What is it he catches — trees? Good! That's settled."

And, three days later, without another word exchanged on the subject, they started.

Was she grateful to him? No. Afraid of him? No. Scornful of him? Not quite. But she was afraid of HERSELF, horribly. How would she ever be able to keep herself in hand, how disguise from these people that she loved their boy? It was her desperate mood that she feared. But since she so much wanted all the best for him that life could give, surely she would have the strength to do nothing that might harm him. Yet she was afraid.

He was there at the station to meet them, in riding things and a nice rough Norfolk jacket that she did not recognize, though she thought she knew his clothes by heart; and as the train came slowly to a standstill the memory of her last moment with him, up in his room amid the luggage that she had helped to pack, very nearly overcame her. It seemed so hard to have to meet him coldly, formally, to have to wait — who knew how long — for a minute with him alone! And he was so polite, so beautifully considerate, with all the manners of a host; hoping she wasn't tired, hoping Mr. Stormer had brought his fishing-rod, though they had lots, of course, they could lend him; hoping the weather would be fine; hoping that they wouldn't mind having to drive three miles, and busying himself about their luggage. All this when she just wanted to take him in her arms and push his hair back from his forehead, and look at him!

He did not drive with them — he had thought they would be too crowded — but followed, keeping quite close in the dust to point out the scenery, mounted on a 'palfrey', as her husband called the roan with the black swish tail.

This countryside, so rich and yet a little wild, the independent-looking cottages, the old dark cosy manor-house, all was very new to one used to Oxford, and to London, and to little else of England. And all was delightful. Even Mark's guardian seemed to her delightful. For Gordy, when absolutely forced to face an unknown woman, could bring to the encounter a certain bluff ingratiation: His sister, too, Mrs. Doone, with her faded gentleness, seemed soothing.

When Anna was alone in her room, reached by an unexpected little stairway, she stood looking at its carved four-poster bed and the wide lattice window with chintz curtains, and the flowers in a blue bowl. Yes, all was delightful. And yet! What was it? What had she missed? Ah, she was a fool to fret! It was only his anxiety that they should be comfortable, his fear that he might betray himself. Out there those last few days — his eyes! And now! She brooded earnestly over what dress she should put on. She, who tanned so quickly, had almost lost her sunburn in the week of travelling and Oxford. Today her eyes looked tired, and she was pale. She was not going to disdain anything that might help. She had reached thirty-six last month, and he would be nineteen tomorrow! She decided on black. In black she knew that her neck looked whiter, and the colour of her eyes and hair stranger. She put on no jewellery, did not even pin a rose at her breast, took white gloves. Since her husband did not come to her room, she went up the little stairway to his. She surprised him ready dressed, standing by the fireplace, smiling faintly. What was he thinking of, standing there with that smile? Was there blood in him at all?

He inclined his head slightly and said:

"Good! Chaste as the night! Black suits you. Shall we find our way down to these savage halls?"

And they went down.

Everyone was already there, waiting. A single neighbouring squire and magistrate, by name Trusham, had been bidden, to make numbers equal.

Dinner was announced; they went in. At the round table in a dining-room, all black oak, with many candles, and terrible portraits of departed ancestors, Anna sat between the magistrate and Gordy. Mark was opposite, between a quaint-looking old lady and a young girl who had not been introduced, a girl in white, with very fair hair and very white skin, blue eyes, and lips a little parted; a daughter evidently of the faded Mrs. Doone. A girl like a silvery moth, like a forget-me-not! Anna found it hard to take her eyes away from this girl's face; not that she admired her exactly; pretty she was — yes; but weak, with those parted lips and soft chin, and almost wistful look, as if her deep-blue half-eager eyes were in spite of her. But she was young — so young! That was why not to watch her seemed impossible. "Sylvia Doone?" Indeed! Yes. A soft name, a pretty name — and very like her! Every time her eyes could travel away from her duty to Squire Trusham, and to Gordy (on both of whom she was clearly making an impression), she gazed at this girl, sitting there by the boy, and whenever those two young things smiled and spoke together she felt her heart contract and hurt her. Was THIS why that something had gone out of his eyes? Ah, she was foolish! If every girl or woman the boy knew was to cause such a feeling in her, what would life be like? And her will hardened against her fears. She was looking brilliant herself; and she saw that the girl in her turn could not help gazing at her eagerly, wistfully, a little bewildered — hatefully young. And the boy? Slowly, surely, as a magnet draws, Anna could feel that she was drawing him, could see him stealing chances to look at her. Once she surprised him full. What troubled eyes! It was not the old adoring face; yet she knew from its expression that she could make him want her — make him jealous — easily fire him with her kisses, if she would.

And the dinner wore to an end. Then came the moment when the girl and she must meet under the eyes of the mother, and that sharp, quaint-looking old governess. It would be a hard moment, that! And it came — a hard moment and a long one, for Gordy sat full span over his wine. But Anna had not served her time beneath the gaze of upper Oxford for nothing; she managed to be charming, full of interest and questions in her still rather foreign accent. Miss Doone — soon she became Sylvia — must show her all the treasures and antiquities. Was it too dark to go out just to look at the old house by night? Oh, no. Not a bit. There were goloshes in the hall. And they went, the girl leading, and talking of Anna knew not what, so absorbed was she in thinking how for a moment, just a moment, she could contrive to be with the boy alone.

It was not remarkable, this old house, but it was his home — might some day perhaps be his. And houses at night were strangely alive with their window eyes.

"That is my room," the girl said, "where the jessamine is — you can just see it. Mark's is above — look, under where the eave hangs out, away to the left. The other night —"

"Yes; the other night?"

"Oh, I don't —! Listen. That's an owl. We have heaps of owls. Mark likes them. I don't, much."

Always Mark!

"He's awfully keen, you see, about all beasts and birds — he models them. Shall I show you his workshop? — it's an old greenhouse. Here, you can see in."

There through the glass Anna indeed could just see the boy's quaint creations huddling in the dark on a bare floor, a grotesque company of small monsters. She murmured:

"Yes, I see them, but I won't really look unless he brings me himself."

"Oh, he's sure to. They interest him more than anything in the world."

For all her cautious resolutions Anna could not for the life of her help saying:

"What, more than you?"

The girl gave her a wistful stare before she answered:

"Oh! I don't count much."

Anna laughed, and took her arm. How soft and young it felt! A pang went through her heart, half jealous, half remorseful.

"Do you know," she said, "that you are very sweet?"

The girl did not answer.

"Are you his cousin?"

"No. Gordy is only Mark's uncle by marriage; my mother is Gordy's sister — so I'm nothing."

Nothing!

"I see — just what you English call 'a connection.'"

They were silent, seeming to examine the night; then the girl said:

"I wanted to see you awfully. You're not like what I thought."

"Oh! And what DID you think?"

"I thought you would have dark eyes, and Venetian red hair, and not be quite so tall. Of course, I haven't any imagination."

They were at the door again when the girl said that, and the hall light was falling on her; her slip of a white figure showed clear. Young — how young she looked! Everything she said — so young!

And Anna murmured: "And you are — more than I thought, too."

Just then the men came out from the dining-room; her husband with the look on his face that denoted he had been well listened to; Squire Trusham laughing as a man does who has no sense of humour; Gordy having a curly, slightly asphyxiated air; and the boy his pale, brooding look, as though he had lost touch with his surroundings. He wavered towards her, seemed to lose himself, went and sat down by the old governess. Was it because he did not dare to come up to her, or only because he saw the old lady sitting alone? It might well be that.

And the evening, so different from what she had dreamed of, closed in. Squire Trusham was gone in his high dog-cart, with his famous mare whose exploits had entertained her all through dinner. Her candle had been given her; she had said goodnight to all but Mark. What should she do when she had his hand in hers? She would be alone with him in that grasp, whose strength no one could see. And she did not know whether to clasp it passionately, or to let it go coolly back to its owner; whether to claim him or to wait. But she was unable to help pressing it feverishly. At once in his face she saw again that troubled look; and her heart smote her. She let it go, and that she might not see him say goodnight to the girl, turned and mounted to her room.

Fully dressed, she flung herself on the bed, and there lay, her handkerchief across her mouth, gnawing at its edges.

XV

Mark's nineteenth birthday rose in grey mist, slowly dropped its veil to the grass, and shone clear and glistening. He woke early. From his window he could see nothing in the steep park but the soft blue-grey, balloon-shaped oaks suspended one above the other among the round-topped boulders. It was in early morning that he always got his strongest feeling of wanting to model things; then and after dark, when, for want of light, it was no use. This morning he had the craving badly, and the sense of not knowing how weighed down his spirit. His drawings, his models — they were all so bad, so fumbly. If only this had been his twenty-first birthday, and he had his money, and could do what he liked. He would not stay in England. He would be off to Athens, or Rome, or even to Paris, and work till he COULD do something. And in his holidays he would study animals and birds in wild countries where there were plenty of them, and you could watch them in their haunts. It was stupid having to stay in a place like Oxford; but at the thought of what Oxford meant, his roaming fancy, like a bird hypnotized by a hawk, fluttered, stayed suspended, and dived back to earth. And that feeling of wanting to make things suddenly left him. It was as though he had woken up, his real self; then — lost that self again. Very quietly he made his way downstairs. The garden door was not shuttered, not even locked — it must have been forgotten overnight. Last night! He had never thought he would feel like this when she came — so bewildered, and confused; drawn towards her, but by something held back. And he felt impatient, angry with himself, almost with her. Why could he not be just simply happy, as this morning was happy? He got his field-glasses and searched the meadow that led down to the river. Yes, there were several rabbits out. With the white marguerites and the dew cobwebs, it was all moon-flowery and white; and the rabbits being there made it perfect. He wanted one badly to model from, and for a moment was tempted to get his rook rifle — but what was the good of a dead rabbit — besides, they looked so happy! He put the glasses down and went towards his greenhouse to get a drawing block, thinking to sit on the wall and make a sort of Midsummer Night's Dream sketch of flowers and rabbits. Someone was there, bending down and doing something to his creatures. Who had the cheek? Why, it was Sylvia — in her dressing-gown! He grew hot, then cold, with anger. He could not bear anyone in that holy place! It was hateful to have his things even looked at; and she — she seemed to be fingering them. He pulled the door open with a jerk, and said: "What are you doing?" He was indeed so stirred by righteous wrath that he hardly noticed the gasp she gave, and the collapse of her figure against the wall. She ran past him, and vanished without a word. He went up to his creatures and saw that she had placed on the head of each one of them a little sprig of jessamine flower. Why! It was idiotic! He could see nothing at first but the ludicrousness of flowers on the heads of his beasts! Then the desperation of this attempt to imagine something graceful, something that would give him pleasure touched him; for he saw now that this was a birthday decoration. From that it was only a second before he was horrified with himself. Poor little Sylvia! What a brute he was! She had plucked all that jessamine, hung out of her window and risked falling to get hold of it; and she had woken up early and come down in her dressing-gown just to do something that she thought he would like! Horrible — what he had done! Now, when it was too late, he saw, only too clearly, her startled white face and quivering lips, and the way she had shrunk against the wall. How pretty she had looked in her dressing-gown, with her hair all about her, frightened like that! He would do anything now to make up to her for having been such a perfect beast! The feeling, always a little with him, that he must look after her — dating, no doubt, from days when he had protected her from the bulls that were not there; and the feeling of her being so sweet and decent to him always; and some other feeling too — all these suddenly reached poignant climax. He simply must make it up to her! He ran back into the house and stole upstairs. Outside her room he listened with all his might, but could hear nothing; then tapped softly with one nail, and, putting his mouth to the keyhole, whispered: "Sylvia!" Again and again he whispered her name. He even tried the handle, meaning to open the door an inch, but it was bolted. Once he thought he heard a noise like sobbing, and this made him still more wretched. At last he gave it up; she would not come, would not be consoled. He deserved it, he knew, but it was very hard. And dreadfully dispirited he went up to his room, took a bit of paper, and tried to write:

"DEAREST SYLVIA,

"It was most awfully sweet of you to put your stars on my beasts. It was just about the most sweet thing you could have done. I am an awful brute, but, of course, if I had only known what you were doing, I should have loved it. Do forgive me; I deserve it, I know — only it IS my birthday.

"Your sorrowful

"MARK."

He took this down, slipped it under her door, tapped so that she might notice it, and stole away. It relieved his mind a little, and he went downstairs again.

Back in the greenhouse, sitting on a stool, he ruefully contemplated those chapletted beasts. They consisted of a crow, a sheep, a turkey, two doves, a pony, and sundry fragments. She had fastened the jessamine sprigs to the tops of their heads by a tiny daub of wet clay, and had evidently been surprised trying to put a sprig into the mouth of one of the doves, for it hung by a little thread of clay from the beak. He detached it and put it in his buttonhole. Poor little Sylvia! she took things awfully to heart. He would be as nice as ever he could to her all day. And, balancing on his stool, he stared fixedly at the wall against which she had fallen back; the line of her soft chin and throat seemed now to be his only memory. It was very queer how he could see nothing but that, the way the throat moved, swallowed — so white, so soft. And HE had made it go like that! It seemed an unconscionable time till breakfast.

As the hour approached he haunted the hall, hoping she might be first down. At last he heard footsteps, and waited, hidden behind the door of the empty dining-room, lest at sight of him she should turn back. He had rehearsed what he was going to do — bend down and kiss her hand and say: "Dulcinea del Toboso is the most beautiful lady in the world, and I the most unfortunate knight upon the earth," from his favourite passage out of his favourite book, 'Don Quixote'. She would surely forgive him then, and his heart would no longer hurt him. Certainly she could never go on making him so miserable if she knew his feelings! She was too soft and gentle for that. Alas! it was not Sylvia who came; but Anna, fresh from sleep, with her ice-green eyes and bright hair; and in sudden strange antipathy to her, that strong, vivid figure, he stood dumb. And this first lonely moment, which he had so many times in fancy spent locked in her arms, passed without even a kiss; for quickly one by one the others came. But of Sylvia only news through Mrs. Doone that she had a headache, and was staying in bed. Her present was on the sideboard, a book called 'Sartor Resartus.' "Mark — from Sylvia, August 1st, 1880," together with Gordy's cheque, Mrs. Doone's pearl pin, old Tingle's 'Stones of Venice,' and one other little parcel wrapped in tissue-paper — four ties of varying shades of green, red, and blue, hand-knitted in silk — a present of how many hours made short by the thought that he would wear the produce of that clicking. He did not fail in outer gratitude, but did he realize what had been knitted into those ties? Not then.

Birthdays, like Christmas days, were made for disenchantment. Always the false gaiety of gaiety arranged — always that pistol to the head: 'Confound you! enjoy yourself!' How could he enjoy himself with the thought of Sylvia in her room, made ill by his brutality! The vision of her throat working, swallowing her grief, haunted him like a little white, soft spectre all through the long drive out on to the moor, and the picnic in the heather, and the long drive home — haunted him so that when Anna touched or looked at him he had no spirit to answer, no spirit even to try and be with her alone, but almost a dread of it instead.

And when at last they were at home again, and she whispered: "What is it? What have I done?" he could only mutter:

"Nothing! Oh, nothing! It's only that I've been a brute!"

At that enigmatic answer she might well search his face.

"Is it my husband?"

He could answer that, at all events.

"Oh, no!"

"What is it, then? Tell me."

They were standing in the inner porch, pretending to examine the ancestral chart — dotted and starred with dolphins and little full-rigged galleons sailing into harbours — which always hung just there.

"Tell me, Mark; I don't like to suffer!"

What could he say, since he did not know himself? He stammered, tried to speak, could not get anything out.

"Is it that girl?"

Startled, he looked away, and said:

"Of course not."

She shivered, and went into the house. But he stayed, staring at the chart with a dreadful stirred-up feeling — of shame and irritation, pity, impatience, fear, all mixed. What had he done, said, lost? It was that horrid feeling of when one has not been kind and not quite true, yet might have been kinder if one had been still less true. Ah! but it was all so mixed up. It felt all bleak, too, and wintry in him, as if he had suddenly lost everybody's love. Then he was conscious of his tutor.

"Ah! friend Lennan — looking deeply into the past from the less romantic present? Nice things, those old charts. The dolphins are extremely jolly."

It was difficult to remember not to be ill-mannered then. Why did Stormer jeer like that? He just managed to answer:

"Yes, sir; I wish we had some now."

"There are so many moons we wish for, Lennan, and they none of them come tumbling down."

The voice was almost earnest, and the boy's resentment fled. He felt sorry, but why he did not know.

"In the meantime," he heard his tutor say, "let us dress for dinner."

When he came down to the drawing-room, Anna in her moonlight-coloured frock was sitting on the sofa talking to — Sylvia. He kept away from them; they could neither of them want him. But it did seem odd to him, who knew not too much concerning women, that she could be talking so gaily, when only half an hour ago she had said: "Is it that girl?"

He sat next her at dinner. Again it was puzzling that she should be laughing so serenely at Gordy's stories. Did the whispering in the porch, then, mean nothing? And Sylvia would not look at him; he felt sure that she turned her eyes away simply because she knew he was going to look in her direction. And this roused in him a sore feeling — everything that night seemed to rouse that feeling — of injustice; he was cast out, and he could not tell why. He had not meant to hurt either of them! Why should they both want to hurt him so? And presently there came to him a feeling that he did not care: Let them treat him as they liked! There were other things besides love! If they did not want him — he did not want them! And he hugged this reckless, unhappy, don't-care feeling to him with all the abandonment of youth.

But even birthdays come to an end. And moods and feelings that seem so desperately real die in the unreality of sleep.

XVI

If to the boy that birthday was all bewildered disillusionment, to Anna it was verily slow torture; SHE found no relief in thinking that there were things in life other than love. But next morning brought readjustment, a sense of yesterday's extravagance, a renewal of hope. Impossible surely that in one short fortnight she had lost what she had made so sure of! She had only to be resolute. Only to grasp firmly what was hers. After all these empty years was she not to have her hour? To sit still meekly and see it snatched from her by a slip of a soft girl? A thousand times, no! And she watched her chance. She saw him about noon sally forth towards the river, with his rod. She had to wait a little, for Gordy and his bailiff were down there by the tennis lawn, but they soon moved on. She ran out then to the park gate. Once through that she felt safe; her husband, she knew, was working in his room; the girl somewhere invisible; the old governess still at her housekeeping; Mrs. Doone writing letters. She felt full of hope and courage. This old wild tangle of a park, that she had not yet seen, was beautiful — a true trysting-place for fauns and nymphs, with its mossy trees and boulders and the high bracken. She kept along under the wall in the direction of the river, but came to no gate, and began to be afraid that she was going wrong. She could hear the river on the other side, and looked for some place where she could climb and see exactly where she was. An old ash-tree tempted her. Scrambling up into its fork, she could just see over. There was the little river within twenty yards, its clear dark water running between thick foliage. On its bank lay a huge stone balanced on another stone still more huge. And with his back to this stone stood the boy, his rod leaning beside him. And there, on the ground, her arms resting on her knees, her chin on her hands, that girl sat looking up. How eager his eyes now — how different from the brooding eyes of yesterday!

"So, you see, that was all. You might forgive me, Sylvia!"

And to Anna it seemed verily as if those two young faces formed suddenly but one — the face of youth.

If she had stayed there looking for all time, she could not have had graven on her heart a vision more indelible. Vision of Spring, of all that was gone from her for ever! She shrank back out of the fork of the old ash-tree, and, like a stricken beast, went hurrying, stumbling away, amongst the stones and bracken. She ran thus perhaps a quarter of a mile, then threw up her arms, fell down amongst the fern, and lay there on her face. At first her heart hurt her so that she felt nothing but that physical pain. If she could have died! But she knew it was nothing but breathlessness. It left her, and that which took its place she tried to drive away by pressing her breast against the ground, by clutching the stalks of the bracken — an ache, an emptiness too dreadful! Youth to youth! He was gone from her — and she was alone again! She did not cry. What good in crying? But gusts of shame kept sweeping through her; shame and rage. So this was all she was worth! The sun struck hot on her back in that lair of tangled fern, where she had fallen; she felt faint and sick. She had not known till now quite what this passion for the boy had meant to her; how much of her very belief in herself was bound up with it; how much clinging to her own youth. What bitterness! One soft slip of a white girl — one YOUNG thing — and she had become as nothing! But was that true? Could she not even now wrench him back to her with the passion that this child knew nothing of! Surely! Oh, surely! Let him but once taste the rapture she could give him! And at that thought she ceased clutching at the bracken stalks, lying as still as the very stones around her. Could she not? Might she not, even now? And all feeling, except just a sort of quivering, deserted her — as if she had fallen into a trance. Why spare this girl? Why falter? She was first! He had been hers out there. And she still had the power to draw him. At dinner the first evening she had dragged his gaze to her, away from that girl — away from youth, as a magnet draws steel. She could still bind him with chains that for a little while at all events he would not want to break! Bind him? Hateful word! Take him, hankering after what she could not give him — youth, white innocence, Spring? It would be infamous, infamous! She sprang up from the fern, and ran along the hillside, not looking where she went, stumbling among the tangled growth, in and out of the boulders, till she once more sank breathless on to a stone. It was bare of trees just here, and she could see, across the river valley, the high larch-crowned tor on the far side. The sky was clear — the sun bright. A hawk was wheeling over that hill; far up, very near the blue! Infamous! She could not do that! Could not drug him, drag him to her by his senses, by all that was least high in him, when she wished for him all the finest things that life could give, as if she had been his mother. She could not. It would be wicked! In that moment of intense spiritual agony, those two down there in the sun, by the grey stone and the dark water, seemed guarded from her, protected. The girl's white flower-face trembling up, the boy's gaze leaping down! Strange that a heart which felt that, could hate at the same moment that flower-face, and burn to kill with kisses that eagerness in the boy's eyes. The storm in her slowly passed. And she prayed just to feel nothing. It was natural that she should lose her hour! Natural that her thirst should go unslaked, and her passion never bloom; natural that youth should go to youth, this boy to his own kind, by the law of — love. The breeze blowing down the valley fanned her cheeks, and brought her a faint sensation of relief. Nobility! Was it just a word? Or did those that gave up happiness feel noble?

She wandered for a long time in the park. Not till late afternoon did she again pass out by the gate, through which she had entered, full of hope. She met no one before she reached her room; and there, to be safe, took refuge in her bed. She dreaded only lest the feeling of utter weariness should leave her. She wanted no vigour of mind or body till she was away from here. She meant neither to eat nor drink; only to sleep, if she could. Tomorrow, if there were any early train, she could be gone before she need see anyone; her husband must arrange. As to what he would think, and she could say — time enough to decide that. And what did it matter? The one vital thing now was not to see the boy, for she could not again go through hours of struggle like those. She rang the bell, and sent the startled maid with a message to her husband. And while she waited for him to come, her pride began revolting. She must not let him see. That would be horrible. And slipping out of bed she got a handkerchief and the eau-de-Cologne flask, and bandaged her forehead. He came almost instantly, entering in his quick, noiseless way, and stood looking at her. He did not ask what was the matter, but simply waited. And never before had she realized so completely how he began, as it were, where she left off; began on a plane from which instinct and feeling were as carefully ruled out as though they had been blasphemous. She summoned all her courage, and said: "I went into the park; the sun must have been too hot. I should like to go home tomorrow, if you don't mind. I can't bear not feeling well in other people's houses."

She was conscious of a smile flickering over his face; then it grew grave.

"Ah!" he said; "yes. The sun, a touch of that will last some days. Will you be fit to travel, though?"

She had a sudden conviction that he knew all about it, but that — since to know all about it was to feel himself ridiculous — he had the power of making himself believe that he knew nothing. Was this fine of him, or was it hateful?

She closed her eyes and said:

"My head is bad, but I SHALL be able. Only I don't want a fuss made. Could we go by a train before they are down?"

She heard him say:

"Yes. That will have its advantages."

There was not the faintest sound now, but of course he was still there. In that dumb, motionless presence was all her future. Yes, that would be her future — a thing without feeling, and without motion. A fearful curiosity came on her to look at it. She opened her gaze. He was still standing just as he had been, his eyes fixed on her. But one hand, on the edge of his coat pocket — out of the picture, as it were — was nervously closing and unclosing. And suddenly she felt pity. Not for her future — which must be like that; but for him. How dreadful to have grown so that all emotion was exiled — how dreadful! And she said gently:

"I am sorry, Harold."

As if he had heard something strange and startling, his eyes dilated in a curious way, he buried that nervous hand in his pocket, turned, and went out.

XVII

When young Mark came on Sylvia by the logan-stone, it was less surprising to him than if he had not known she was there — having watched her go. She was sitting, all humped together, brooding over the water, her sunbonnet thrown back; and that hair, in which his star had caught, shining faint-gold under the sun. He came on her softly through the grass, and, when he was a little way off, thought it best to halt. If he startled her she might run away, and he would not have the heart to follow. How still she was, lost in her brooding! He wished he could see her face. He spoke at last, gently:

"Sylvia! . . . Would you mind?"

And, seeing that she did not move, he went up to her. Surely she could not still be angry with him!

"Thanks most awfully for that book you gave me — it looks splendid!"

She made no answer. And leaning his rod against the stone, he sighed. That silence of hers seemed to him unjust; what was it she wanted him to say or do? Life was not worth living, if it was to be all bottled up like this.

"I never meant to hurt you. I hate hurting people. It's only that my beasts are so bad — I can't bear people to see them — especially you — I want to please you — I do really. So, you see, that was all. You MIGHT forgive me, Sylvia!"

Something over the wall, a rustling, a scattering in the fern — deer, no doubt! And again he said eagerly, softly:

"You might be nice to me, Sylvia; you really might."

Very quickly, turning her head away, she said:

"It isn't that any more. It's — it's something else."

"What else?"

"Nothing — only, that I don't count — now —"

He knelt down beside her. What did she mean? But he knew well enough.

"Of course, you count! Most awfully! Oh, don't be unhappy! I hate people being unhappy. Don't be unhappy, Sylvia!" And he began gently to stroke her arm. It was all strange and troubled within him; one thing only plain — he must not admit anything! As if reading that thought, her blue eyes seemed suddenly to search right into him. Then she pulled some blades of grass, and began plaiting them.

"SHE counts."

Ah! He was not going to say: She doesn't! It would be caddish to say that. Even if she didn't count — Did she still? — it would be mean and low. And in his eyes just then there was the look that had made his tutor compare him to a lion cub in trouble.

Sylvia was touching his arm.

"Mark!"

"Yes."

"Don't!"

He got up and took his rod. What was the use? He could not stay there with her, since he could not — must not speak.

"Are you going?"

"Yes."

"Are you angry? PLEASE don't be angry with me."

He felt a choke in his throat, bent down to her hand, and kissed it; then shouldered his rod, and marched away. Looking back once, he saw her still sitting there, gazing after him, forlorn, by that great stone. It seemed to him, then, there was nowhere he could go; nowhere except among the birds and beasts and trees, who did not mind even if you were all mixed up and horrible inside. He lay down in the grass on the bank. He could see the tiny trout moving round and round the stones; swallows came all about him, flying very low; a hornet, too, bore him company for a little. But he could take interest in nothing; it was as if his spirit were in prison. It would have been nice, indeed, to be that water, never staying, passing, passing; or wind, touching everything, never caught. To be able to do nothing without hurting someone — that was what was so ghastly. If only one were like a flower, that just sprang up and lived its life all to itself, and died. But whatever he did, or said now, would be like telling lies, or else being cruel. The only thing was to keep away from people. And yet how keep away from his own guests?

He went back to the house for lunch, but both those guests were out, no one seemed quite to know where. Restless, unhappy, puzzled, he wandered round and about all the afternoon. Just before dinner he was told of Mrs. Stormer's not being well, and that they would be leaving tomorrow. Going — after three days! That plunged him deeper into his strange and sorrowful confusion. He was reduced now to a complete brooding silence. He knew he was attracting attention, but could not help it. Several times during dinner he caught Gordy's eyes fixed on him, from under those puffy half-closed lids, with asphyxiated speculation. But he simply COULD not talk — everything that came into his mind to say seemed false. Ah! it was a sad evening — with its glimmering vision into another's sore heart, its confused gnawing sense of things broken, faith betrayed; and yet always the perplexed wonder — "How could I have helped it?" And always Sylvia's wistful face that he tried not to look at.

He stole out, leaving Gordy and his tutor still over their wine, and roamed about the garden a long time, listening sadly to the owls. It was a blessing to get upstairs, though of course he would not sleep.

But he did sleep, all through a night of many dreams, in the last of which he was lying on a mountain side, Anna looking down into his eyes, and bending her face to his. He woke just as her lips touched him. Still under the spell of that troubling dream, he became conscious of the sound of wheels and horses' hoofs on the gravel, and sprang out of bed. There was the waggonette moving from the door, old Godden driving, luggage piled up beside him, and the Stormers sitting opposite each other in the carriage. Going away like that — having never even said goodbye! For a moment he felt as people must when they have unwittingly killed someone — utterly stunned and miserable. Then he dashed into his clothes. He would not let her go thus! He would — he must — see her again! What had he done that she should go like this? He rushed downstairs. The hall was empty; nineteen minutes to eight! The train left at eight o'clock. Had he time to saddle Bolero? He rushed round to the stables; but the cob was out, being shoed. He would — he must get there in time. It would show her anyway that he was not quite a cad. He walked till the drive curved, then began running hard. A quarter of a mile, and already he felt better, not so miserable and guilty; it was something to feel you had a tough job in hand, all your work cut out — something to have to think of economizing strength, picking out the best going, keeping out of the sun, saving your wind uphill, flying down any slope. It was cool still, and the dew had laid the dust; there was no traffic and scarcely anyone to look back and gape as he ran by. What he would do, if he got there in time — how explain this mad three-mile run — he did not think. He passed a farm that he knew was just half-way. He had left his watch. Indeed, he had put on only his trousers, shirt, and Norfolk jacket; no tie, no hat, not even socks under his tennis shoes, and he was as hot as fire, with his hair flying back — a strange young creature indeed for anyone to meet. But he had lost now all feeling, save the will to get there. A flock of sheep came out of a field into the lane. He pushed through them somehow, but they lost him several seconds. More than a mile still; and he was blown, and his legs beginning to give! Downhill indeed they went of their own accord, but there was the long run-in, quite level; and he could hear the train, now slowly puffing its way along the valley. Then, in spite of exhaustion, his spirit rose. He would not go in looking like a scarecrow, utterly done, and make a scene. He must pull himself together at the end, and stroll in — as if he had come for fun. But how — seeing that at any moment he felt he might fall flat in the dust, and stay there for ever! And, as he ran, he made little desperate efforts to mop his face, and brush his clothes. There were the gates, at last — two hundred yards away. The train, he could hear no longer. It must be standing in the station. And a sob came from his overdriven lungs. He heard the guard's whistle as he reached the gates. Instead of making for the booking-office, he ran along the paling, where an entrance to the goods'-shed was open, and dashing through he fell back against the honeysuckle. The engine was just abreast of him; he snatched at his sleeve and passed it over his face, to wipe the sweat away. Everything was blurred. He must see — surely he had not come in time just not to see! He pushed his hands over his forehead and hair, and spied up dizzily at the slowly passing train. She was there, at a window! Standing, looking out! He dared not step forward, for fear of falling, but he put out his hand — She saw him. Yes, she saw him! Wasn't she going to make a sign? Not one? And suddenly he saw her tear at her dress, pluck something out, and throw it. It fell close to his feet. He did not pick it up — he wanted to see her face till she was gone. It looked wonderful — very proud, and pale. She put her hand up to her lips. Then everything went blurred again and when he could see once more, the train had vanished. But at his feet was what she had thrown. He picked it up! All dry and dark, it was the flower she had given him in the Tyrol, and stolen back from his buttonhole.

Creeping out, past the goods'-shed, he made his way to a field, and lay down with his face pressed to that withered thing which still had its scent. . . .

The asphyxiated speculation in his guardian's eyes had not been without significance. Mark did not go back to Oxford. He went instead to Rome — to live in his sister's house, and attend a school of sculpture. That was the beginning of a time when nothing counted except his work.

To Anna he wrote twice, but received no answer. From his tutor he had one little note:

"MY DEAR LENNAN,

"So! You abandon us for Art? Ah! well — it was your moon, if I remember — one of them. A worthy moon — a little dusty in these days — a little in her decline — but to you no doubt a virgin goddess, whose hem, etc.

"We shall retain the friendliest memories of you in spite of your defection.

"Once your tutor and still your friend,

"HAROLD STORMER."

After that vacation it was long — very long before he saw Sylvia again.

PART II — SUMMER

I

Gleam of a thousand lights; clack and mutter of innumerable voices, laughter, footsteps; hiss and rumble of passing trains taking gamblers back to Nice or Mentone; fevered wailing from the violins of four fiddlers with dark-white skins outside the cafe; and above, around, beyond, the dark sky, and the dark mountains, and the dark sea, like some great dark flower to whose heart is clinging a jewelled beetle. So was Monte Carlo on that May night of 1887.

But Mark Lennan, at one of the little marble-topped tables, was in too great maze and exaltation of spirit and of senses to be conscious of its glare and babel, even of its beauty. He sat so very still that his neighbours, with the instinctive aversion of the human creature to what is too remote from its own mood, after one good stare, turned their eyes away, as from something ludicrous, almost offensive.

He was lost, indeed, in memory of the minutes just gone by. For it had come at last, after all these weeks of ferment, after all this strange time of perturbation.

Very stealthily it had been creeping on him, ever since that chance introduction nearly a year ago, soon after he settled down in London, following those six years of Rome and Paris. First the merest friendliness, because she was so nice about his work; then respectful admiration, because she was so beautiful; then pity, because she was so unhappy in her marriage. If she had been happy, he would have fled. The knowledge that she had been unhappy long before he knew her had kept his conscience still. And at last one afternoon she said: "Ah! if you come out there too!" Marvelously subtle, the way that one little outslipped saying had worked in him, as though it had a life of its own — like a strange bird that had flown into the garden of his heart, and established itself with its new song and flutterings, its new flight, its wistful and ever clearer call. That and one moment, a few days later in her London drawing-room, when he had told her that he WAS coming, and she did not, could not, he felt, look at him. Queer, that nothing momentous said, done — or even left undone — had altered all the future!

And so she had gone with her uncle and aunt, under whose wing one might be sure she would meet with no wayward or exotic happenings. And he had received from her this little letter:

"HOTEL COEUR D'OR,

"MONTE CARLO.

"MY DEAR MARK,

"We've arrived. It is so good to be in the sun. The flowers are wonderful. I am keeping Gorbio and Roquebrune till you come.

"Your friend,

"OLIVE CRAMIER."

That letter was the single clear memory he had of the time between her going and his following. He received it one afternoon, sitting on an old low garden wall with the spring sun shining on him through apple-trees in blossom, and a feeling as if all the desire of the world lay before him, and he had but to stretch out his arms to take it.

Then confused unrest, all things vague; till at the end of his journey he stepped out of the train at Beaulieu with a furiously beating heart. But why? Surely he had not expected her to come out from Monte Carlo to meet him!

A week had gone by since then in one long effort to be with her and appear to others as though he did not greatly wish to be; two concerts, two walks with her alone, when all that he had said seemed as nothing said, and all her sayings but ghosts of what he wished to hear; a week of confusion, day and night, until, a few minutes ago, her handkerchief had fallen from her glove on to the dusty road, and he had picked it up and put it to his lips. Nothing could take away the look she had given him then. Nothing could ever again separate her from him utterly. She had confessed in it to the same sweet, fearful trouble that he himself was feeling. She had not spoken, but he had seen her lips part, her breast rise and fall. And HE had not spoken. What was the use of words?

He felt in the pocket of his coat. There, against his fingers, was that wisp of lawn and lace, soft, yet somehow alive; and stealthily he took it out. The whole of her, with her fragrance, seemed pressed to his face in the touch of that lawn border, roughened by little white stars. More secretly than ever he put it back; and for the first time looked round. These people! They belonged to a world that he had left. They gave him the same feeling that her uncle and aunt had given him just now, when they said goodnight, following her into their hotel. That good Colonel, that good Mrs. Ercott! The very concretion of the world he had been brought up in, of the English point of view; symbolic figures of health, reason, and the straight path, on which at that moment, seemingly, he had turned his back. The Colonel's profile, ruddy through its tan, with grey moustache guiltless of any wax, his cheery, high-pitched: "Goodnight, young Lennan!" His wife's curly smile, her flat, cosy, confidential voice — how strange and remote they had suddenly become! And all these people here, chattering, drinking — how queer and far away! Or was it just that he was queer and remote to them?

And getting up from his table, he passed the fiddlers with the dark-white skins, out into the Place.

II

He went up the side streets to the back of her hotel, and stood by the railings of the garden — one of those hotel gardens which exist but to figure in advertisements, with its few arid palms, its paths staring white between them, and a fringe of dusty lilacs and mimosas.

And there came to him the oddest feeling — that he had been there before, peering through blossoms at those staring paths and shuttered windows. A scent of wood-smoke was abroad, and some dry plant rustled ever so faintly in what little wind was stirring. What was there of memory in this night, this garden? Some dark sweet thing, invisible, to feel whose presence was at once ecstasy, and the irritation of a thirst that will not be quenched.

And he walked on. Houses, houses! At last he was away from them, alone on the high road, beyond the limits of Monaco. And walking thus through the night he had thoughts that he imagined no one had ever had before him. The knowledge that she loved him had made everything seem very sacred and responsible. Whatever he did, he must not harm her. Women were so helpless!

For in spite of six years of art in Rome and Paris, he still had a fastidious reverence for women. If she had loved her husband she would have been safe enough from him; but to be bound to a companionship that she gave unwillingly — this had seemed to him atrocious, even before he loved her. How could any husband ask that? Have so little pride — so little pity? The unpardonable thing! What was there to respect in such a marriage? Only, he must not do her harm! But now that her eyes had said, I love you! — What then? It was simply miraculous to know THAT, under the stars of this warm Southern night, burning its incense of trees and flowers!

Climbing up above the road, he lay down. If only she were there beside him! The fragrance of the earth not yet chilled, crept to his face; and for just a moment it seemed to him that she did come. If he could keep her there for ever in that embrace that was no embrace — in that ghostly rapture, on this wild fragrant bed that no lovers before had ever pressed, save the creeping things, and the flowers; save sunlight and moonlight with their shadows; and the wind kissing the earth! . . .

Then she was gone; his hands touched nothing but the crumbled pine dust, and the flowers of the wild thyme fallen into sleep.

He stood on the edge of the little cliff, above the road between the dark mountains and the sea black with depth. Too late for any passer-by; as far from what men thought and said and did as the very night itself with its whispering warmth. And he conjured up her face, making certain of it — the eyes, clear and brown, and wide apart; the close, sweet mouth; the dark hair; the whole flying loveliness.

Then he leaped down into the road, and ran — one could not walk, feeling this miracle, that no one had ever felt before, the miracle of love.

III

In their most reputable hotel 'Le Coeur d'Or', long since remodelled and renamed, Mrs. Ercott lay in her brass-bound bed looking by starlight at the Colonel in his brass-bound bed. Her ears were carefully freed from the pressure of her pillow, for she thought she heard a mosquito. Companion for thirty years to one whose life had been feverishly punctuated by the attentions of those little beasts, she had no love for them. It was the one subject on which perhaps her imagination was stronger than her common sense. For in fact there was not, and could not be, a mosquito, since the first thing the Colonel did, on arriving at any place farther South than Parallel 46 of latitude, was to open the windows very wide, and nail with many tiny tacks a piece of mosquito netting across that refreshing space, while she held him firmly by the coat-tails. The fact that other people did not so secure their windows did not at all trouble the Colonel, a true Englishman, who loved to act in his own way, and to think in the ways of other people. After that they would wait till night came, then burn a peculiar little lamp with a peculiar little smell, and, in the full glare of the gaslight, stand about on chairs, with slippers, and their eyes fixed on true or imaginary beasts. Then would fall little slaps, making little messes, and little joyous or doleful cries would arise: "I've got that one!" "Oh, John, I missed him!" And in the middle of the room, the Colonel, in pyjamas, and spectacles (only worn in very solemn moments, low down on his nose), would revolve slowly, turning his eyes, with that look in them of out-facing death which he had so long acquired, on every inch of wall and ceiling, till at last he would say: "Well,

Dolly, that's the lot!" At which she would say: "Give me a kiss, dear!" and he would kiss her, and get into his bed.

There was, then, no mosquito, save that general ghost of him which lingered in the mind of one devoted to her husband. Spying out his profile, for he was lying on his back, she refrained from saying: "John, are you awake?" A whiffling sound was coming from a nose, to which — originally straight — attention to military duties had given a slight crook, half an inch below the level of grizzled eyebrows raised a little, as though surprised at the sounds beneath. She could hardly see him, but she thought: "How good he looks!" And, in fact, he did. It was the face of a man incapable of evil, having in its sleep the candour of one at heart a child — that simple candour of those who have never known how to seek adventures of the mind, and have always sought adventures of the body. Then somehow she did say:

"John! Are you asleep?"

The Colonel, instantly alive, as at some old-time attack, answered:

"Yes."

"That poor young man!"

"Which?"

"Mark Lennan. Haven't you seen?"

"What?"

"My dear, it was under your nose. But you never do see these things!"

The Colonel slowly turned his head. His wife was an imaginative woman! She had always been so. Dimly he perceived that something romantic was about to come from her. But with that almost professional gentleness of a man who has cut the heads and arms off people in his time, he answered:

"What things?"

"He picked up her handkerchief."

"Whose?"

"Olive's. He put it in his pocket. I distinctly saw him."

There was silence; then Mrs. Ercott's voice rose again, impersonal, far away.

"What always astonishes me about young people is the way they think they're not seen — poor dears!"

Still there was silence.

"John! Are you thinking?"

For a considerable sound of breathing, not mere whiffling now, was coming from the Colonel — to his wife a sure sign.

And indeed he WAS thinking. Dolly was an imaginative woman, but something told him that in this case she might not be riding past the hounds.

Mrs. Ercott raised herself. He looked more good than ever; a little perplexed frown had climbed up with his eyebrows and got caught in the wrinkles across his forehead.

"I'm very fond of Olive," he said.

Mrs. Ercott fell back on her pillows. In her heart there was just that little soreness natural to a woman over fifty, whose husband has a niece.

"No doubt," she murmured.

Something vague moved deep down in the Colonel; he stretched out his hand. In that strip of gloom between the beds it encountered another hand, which squeezed it rather hard.

He said: "Look here, old girl!" and there was silence.

Mrs. Ercott in her turn was thinking. Her thoughts were flat and rapid like her voice, but had that sort of sentiment which accompanies the mental exercise of women with good hearts. Poor young man! And poor Olive! But was a woman ever to be pitied, when she was so pretty as that! Besides, when all was said and done, she had a fine-looking man for husband; in Parliament, with a career, and fond of her — decidedly. And their little house in London, so close to Westminster, was a distinct dear; and nothing could be more charming than their cottage by the river. Was Olive, then, to be pitied? And yet — she was not happy. It was no good pretending that she was happy. All very well to say that such things were within one's control, but if you read novels at all, you knew they weren't. There was such a thing as incompatibility. Oh yes! And there was the matter of difference in their ages! Olive was twenty-six, Robert Cramier forty-two. And now this young Mark Lennan was in love with her. What if she were in love with him! John would realize then, perhaps, that the young flew to the young. For men — even the best, like John, were funny! She would never dream of feeling for any of her nephews as John clearly felt for Olive.

The Colonel's voice broke in on her thoughts.

"Nice young fellow — Lennan! Great pity! Better sheer off — if he's getting —"

And, rather suddenly, she answered:

"Suppose he can't!"

"Can't?"

"Did you never hear of a 'grande passion'?"

The Colonel rose on his elbow. This was another of those occasions that showed him how, during the later years of his service in Madras and Upper Burmah, when Dolly's health had not been equal to the heat, she had picked up in London a queer way of looking at things — as if they were not — not so right or wrong as — as he felt them to be. And he repeated those two French words in his own way, adding:

"Isn't that just what I'm saying? The sooner he stands clear, the better."

But Mrs. Ercott, too, sat up.

"Be human," she said.

The Colonel experienced the same sensation as when one suddenly knows that one is not digesting food. Because young Lennan was in danger of getting into a dishonourable fix, he was told to be human! Really, Dolly was —! The white blur of her new boudoir cap suddenly impinged on his consciousness. Surely she was not getting — un-English! At her time of life!

"I'm thinking of Olive," he said; "I don't want her worried with that sort of thing."

"Perhaps Olive can manage for herself. In these days it doesn't do to interfere with love."

"Love!" muttered the Colonel. "What? Phew!"

If one's own wife called this — this sort of — thing, love — then, why had he been faithful to her — in very hot climates — all these years? A sense of waste, and of injustice, tried to rear its head against all the side of him that attached certain meanings to certain words, and acted up to them. And this revolt gave him a feeling, strange and so unpleasant. Love! It was not a word to use thus loosely! Love led to marriage; this could not lead to marriage, except through — the Divorce Court. And suddenly the Colonel had a vision of his dead brother Lindsay, Olive's father, standing there in the dark, with his grave, clear-cut, ivory-pale face, under the black hair supposed to be derived from a French ancestress who had escaped from the massacre of St. Bartholomew. Upright fellow always, Lindsay — even before he was made bishop! Queer somehow that Olive should be his daughter. Not that she was not upright; not at all! But she was soft! Lindsay was not! Imagine him seeing that young fellow putting her handkerchief in his pocket. But had young Lennan really done such a thing? Dolly was imaginative! He had mistaken it probably for his own; if he had chanced to blow his nose, he would have realized. For, coupled with the almost child-like candour of his mind, the Colonel had real administrative vigour, a true sense of practical values; an ounce of illustration was always worth to him a pound of theory! Dolly was given to riding off on theories. Thank God! she never acted on 'em!

He said gently:

"My dear! Young Lennan may be an artist and all that, but he's a gentleman! I know old Heatherley, his guardian. Why I introduced him to Olive myself!"

"What has that to do with it? He's in love with her."

One of the countless legion that hold a creed taken at face value, into whose roots and reasons they have never dreamed of going, the Colonel was staggered. Like some native on an island surrounded by troubled seas, which he has stared at with a certain contemptuous awe all his life, but never entered, he was disconcerted by thus being asked to leave the shore. And by his own wife!

Indeed, Mrs. Ercott had not intended to go so far; but there was in her, as in all women whose minds are more active than their husbands', a something worrying her always to go a little farther than she meant. With real compunction she heard the Colonel say:

"I must get up and drink some water."

She was out of bed in a moment. "Not without boiling!"

She had seriously troubled him, then! Now he would not sleep — the blood went to his head so quickly. He would just lie awake, trying not to disturb her. She could not bear him not to disturb her. It seemed so selfish of her! She ought to have known that the whole subject was too dangerous to discuss at night.

She became conscious that he was standing just behind her; his figure in its thin covering looked very lean, his face strangely worn.

"I'm sorry you put that idea into my head!" he said. "I'm fond of Olive."

Again Mrs. Ercott felt that jealous twinge, soon lost this time in the motherliness of a childless woman for her husband. He must not be troubled! He should not be troubled. And she said:

"The water's boiling! Now sip a good glass slowly, and get into bed, or I'll take your temperature!"

Obediently the Colonel took from her the glass, and as he sipped, she put her hand up and stroked his head.

IV

In the room below them the subject of their discussion was lying very wide awake. She knew that she had betrayed herself, made plain to Mark Lennan what she had never until now admitted to herself. But the love-look, which for the life of her she could not keep back, had been followed by a feeling of having 'lost caste.' For, hitherto, the world of women had been strictly divided by her into those who did and those who did not do such things; and to be no longer quite sure to which half she belonged was frightening. But what was the good of thinking, of being frightened? — it could not lead to anything. Yesterday she had not known this would come; and now she could not guess at tomorrow! Tonight was enough! Tonight with its swimming loveliness! Just to feel! To love, and to be loved!

A new sensation for her — as different from those excited by the courtships of her girlhood, or by her marriage, as light from darkness. For she had never been in love, not even with her husband. She knew it now. The sun was shining in a world where she had thought there was none. Nothing could come of it. But the sun was shining; and in that sunshine she must warm herself a little.

Quite simply she began to plan what he and she would do. There were six days left. They had not yet been to Gorbio, nor to Castellar — none of those long walks or rides they had designed to do for the beauty of them. Would he come early tomorrow? What could they do together? No one should know what these six days would be to her — not even he. To be with him, watch his face, hear his voice, and now and then just touch him! She

could trust herself to show no one. And then, it would be —
over! Though, of course, she would see him again in London.

And, lying there in the dark, she thought of their first meeting,
one Sunday morning, in Hyde Park. The Colonel religiously
observed Church Parade, and would even come all the way down
to Westminster, from his flat near Knightsbridge, in order to
fetch his niece up to it. She remembered how, during their stroll,
he had stopped suddenly in front of an old gentleman with a
puffy yellow face and eyes half open.

"Ah! Mr. Heatherley — you up from Devonshire? How's your
nephew — the — er — sculptor?"

And the old gentleman, glaring a little, as it seemed to her,
from under his eyelids and his grey top hat, had answered:
"Colonel Ercott, I think? Here's the fellow himself — Mark!" And
a young man had taken off his hat. She had only noticed at first
that his dark hair grew — not long — but very thick; and that his
eyes were very deep-set. Then she saw him smile; it made his face
all eager, yet left it shy; and she decided that he was nice. Soon
after, she had gone with the Ercotts to see his 'things'; for it was,
of course, and especially in those days, quite an event to know a
sculptor — rather like having a zebra in your park. The Colonel
had been delighted and a little relieved to find that the 'things'
were nearly all of beasts and birds. "Very interestin'" to one full
of curious lore about such, having in his time killed many of
them, and finding himself at the end of it with a curious aversion
to killing any more — which he never put into words.

Acquaintanceship had ripened fast after that first visit to his
studio, and now it was her turn to be relieved that Mark Lennan
devoted himself almost entirely to beasts and birds instead of to
the human form, so-called divine. Ah! yes — she would have
suffered; now that she loved him, she saw that. At all events she
could watch his work and help it with sympathy. That could not
be wrong. . . .

She fell asleep at last, and dreamed that she was in a boat alone on the river near her country cottage, drifting along among spiky flowers like asphodels, with birds singing and flying round her. She could move neither face nor limbs, but that helpless feeling was not unpleasant, till she became conscious that she was drawing nearer and nearer to what was neither water nor land, light nor darkness, but simply some unutterable feeling. And then she saw, gazing at her out of the rushes on the banks, a great bull head. It moved as she moved — it was on both sides of her, yet all the time only one head. She tried to raise her hands and cover her eyes, but could not — and woke with a sob. . . . It was light.

Nearly six o'clock already! Her dream made her disinclined to trust again to sleep. Sleep was a robber now — of each minute of these few days! She got up, and looked out. The morning was fine, the air warm already, sweet with dew, and heliotrope nailed to the wall outside her window. She had but to open her shutters and walk into the sun. She dressed, took her sunshade, stealthily slipped the shutters back, and stole forth. Shunning the hotel garden, where the eccentricity of her early wandering might betray the condition of her spirit, she passed through into the road toward the Casino. Without perhaps knowing it, she was making for where she had sat with him yesterday afternoon, listening to the band. Hatless, but defended by her sunshade, she excited the admiration of the few connoisseurs as yet abroad, strolling in blue blouses to their labours; and this simple admiration gave her pleasure. For once she was really conscious of the grace in her own limbs, actually felt the gentle vividness of her own face, with its nearly black hair and eyes, and creamy skin — strange sensation, and very comforting!

In the Casino gardens she walked more slowly, savouring the aromatic trees, and stopping to bend and look at almost every flower; then, on the seat, where she had sat with him yesterday, she rested. A few paces away were the steps that led to the railway-station, trodden upwards eagerly by so many, day after day, night after night, and lightly or sorrowfully descended. Above her, two pines, a pepper-tree, and a palm mingled their shade — so fantastic the jumbling of trees and souls in this strange place! She furled her sunshade and leaned back. Her gaze, free and friendly, passed from bough to bough. Against the bright sky, unbesieged as yet by heat or dust, they had a spiritual look, lying sharp and flat along the air. She plucked a cluster of pinkish berries from the pepper-tree, crushing and rubbing them between her hands to get their fragrance. All these beautiful and sweet things seemed to be a part of her joy at being loved, part of this sudden summer in her heart. The sky, the flowers, that jewel of green-blue sea, the bright acacias, were nothing in the world but love.

And those few who passed, and saw her sitting there under the pepper-tree, wondered no doubt at the stillness of this dame bien mise, who had risen so early.

V

In the small hours, which so many wish were smaller, the Colonel had awakened, with the affair of the handkerchief swelling visibly. His niece's husband was not a man that he had much liking for — a taciturn fellow, with possibly a bit of the brute in him, a man who rather rode people down; but, since Dolly and he were in charge of Olive, the notion that young Lennan was falling in love with her under their very noses was alarming to one naturally punctilious. It was not until he fell asleep again, and woke in full morning light, that the remedy occurred to him. She must be taken out of herself! Dolly and he had been slack; too interested in this queer place, this queer lot of people! They had neglected her, left her to. . . Boys and girls! — One ought always to remember. But it was not too late. She was old Lindsay's daughter; would not forget herself. Poor old Lindsay — fine fellow; bit too much, perhaps, of the — Huguenot in him! Queer, those throw-backs! Had noticed in horses, time and again — white hairs about the tail, carriage of the head — skip generations and then pop out. And Olive had something of his look — the same ivory skin, same colour of eyes and hair! Only she was not severe, like her father, not exactly! And once more there shot through the Colonel a vague dread, as of a trusteeship neglected. It disappeared, however, in his bath.

He was out before eight o'clock, a thin upright figure in hard straw hat and grey flannel clothes, walking with the indescribable loose poise of the soldier Englishman, with that air, different from the French, German, what not, because of shoulders ever asserting, through their drill, the right to put on mufti; with that perfectly quiet and modest air of knowing that, whatever might be said, there was only one way of wearing clothes and moving legs. And, as he walked, he smoothed his drooping grey moustache, considering how best to take his niece out of herself. He passed along by the Terrace, and stood for a moment looking down at the sea beyond the pigeon-shooting ground. Then he moved on round under the Casino into the gardens at the back. A beautiful spot! Wonderful care they had taken with the plants! It made him think a little of Tushawore, where his old friend the Rajah — precious old rascal! — had gardens to his palace rather like these. He paced again to the front. It was nice and quiet in the early mornings, with the sea down there, and nobody trying to get the better of anybody else. There were fellows never happy unless they were doing someone in the eye. He had known men who would ride at the devil himself, make it a point of honour to swindle a friend out of a few pounds! Odd place this 'Monte' — sort of a Garden of Eden gone wrong. And all the real, but quite inarticulate love of Nature, which had supported the Colonel through deserts and jungles, on transports at sea, and in mountain camps, awoke in the sweetness of these gardens. His dear mother! He had never forgotten the words with which she had shown him the sunset through the coppice down at old Withes Norton, when he was nine years old: "That is beauty, Jack! Do you feel it, darling?" He had not felt it at the time — not he; a thick-headed, scampering youngster. Even when he first went to India he had had no eye for a sunset. The rising generation were different. That young couple, for instance, under the pepper-tree, sitting there without a word, just looking at the trees. How long, he wondered, had they been sitting like that? And suddenly something in the Colonel leaped; his steel-coloured eyes took on their look of out-facing death. Choking down a cough, he faced about, back to where he had stood above the pigeon-shooting ground. . . . Olive and that young fellow! An assignation! At this time in the morning! The earth reeled. His brother's child — his favourite niece! The woman whom he most admired — the woman for whom his heart was softest. Leaning over the stone parapet, no longer seeing either the smooth green of the pigeon-shooting ground, or the smooth blue of the sea beyond, he was moved, distressed, bewildered beyond words. Before breakfast! That was the devil of it! Confession, as it were, of everything. Moreover, he had seen their hands touching on the seat. The blood rushed up to his face; he had seen, spied out, what was not intended for his eyes. Nice position — that! Dolly, too, last night, had seen. But that was different. Women might see things — it was expected of them. But for a man — a — a gentleman! The fullness of his embarrassment gradually disclosed itself. His hands were tied. Could he even consult Dolly? He had a feeling of isolation, of utter solitude. Nobody — not anybody in the world — could understand his secret and intense discomfort. To take up a position — the position he was bound to take up, as Olive's nearest relative and protector, and — what was it — chaperon, by the aid of knowledge come at in such a way, however unintentionally! Never in all his days in the regiment — and many delicate matters affecting honour had come his way — had he had a thing like this to deal with. Poor child! But he had no business to think of her like that. No, indeed! She had not behaved — as — And there he paused, curiously unable to condemn her. Suppose they got up and came that way!

He took his hands off the stone parapet, and made for his hotel. His palms were white from the force of his grip. He said to himself as he went along: "I must consider the whole question calmly; I must think it out." This gave him relief. With young Lennan, at all events, he could be angry. But even there he found, to his dismay, no finality of judgment. And this absence of finality, so unwonted, distressed him horribly. There was something in the way the young man had been sitting there beside her — so quiet, so almost timid — that had touched him. This was bad, by Jove — very bad! The two of them, they made, somehow, a nice couple! Confound it! This would not do! The chaplain of the little English church, passing at this moment, called out, "Fine morning, Colonel Ercott." The Colonel saluted, and did not answer. The greeting at the moment seemed to him paltry. No morning could be fine that contained such a discovery. He entered the hotel, passed into the dining-room, and sat down. Nobody was there. They all had their breakfast upstairs, even Dolly. Olive alone was in the habit of supporting him while he ate an English breakfast. And suddenly he perceived that he was face to face already with this dreadful situation. To have breakfast without, as usual, waiting for her, seemed too pointed. She might be coming in at any minute now. To wait for her, and have it, without showing anything — how could he do that?

He was conscious of a faint rustling behind him. There she was, and nothing decided. In this moment of hopeless confusion the Colonel acted by pure instinct, rose, patted her cheek, and placed a chair.

"Well, my dear," he said; "hungry?"

She was looking very dainty, very soft. That creamy dress showed off her dark hair and eyes, which seemed somehow to be — flying off somewhere; yes — it was queer, but that was the only way to put it. He got no reassurance, no comfort, from the sight of her. And slowly he stripped the skin from the banana with which he always commenced breakfast. One might just as well be asked to shoot a tame dove or tear a pretty flower to pieces as be expected to take her to task, even if he could, in honour. And he sought refuge in the words:

"Been out?" Then could have bitten his tongue off. Suppose she answered: "No."

But she did not so answer. The colour came into her cheeks, indeed, but she nodded: "It's so lovely!"

How pretty she looked saying that! He had put himself out of court now — could never tell her what he had seen, after setting, as it were, that trap for her; and presently he asked:

"Got any plans today?"

She answered, without flinching in the least:

"Mark Lennan and I were going to take mules from Mentone up to Gorbio."

He was amazed at her steadiness — never, to his knowledge, having encountered a woman armoured at every point to preserve a love that flies against the world. How tell what was under her smile! And in confusion of feeling that amounted almost to pain he heard her say:

"Will you and Aunt Dolly come?"

Between sense of trusteeship and hatred of spoiling sport; between knowledge of the danger she was in and half-pitying admiration at the sight of her; between real disapproval of an illicit and underhand business (what else was it, after all?) and some dim perception that here was something he did not begin to be able to fathom — something that perhaps no one but those two themselves could deal with — between these various extremes he was lost indeed. And he stammered out:

"I must ask your aunt; she's — she's not very good on a mule."

Then, in an impulse of sheer affection, he said with startling suddenness: "My dear, I've often meant to ask, are you happy at home?"

"At home?"

There was something sinister about the way she repeated that, as if the word "home" were strange to her.

She drank her coffee and got up; and the Colonel felt afraid of her, standing there — afraid of what she was going to tell him. He grew very red. But, worse than all, she said absolutely nothing; only shrugged her shoulders with a little smile that went to his heart.

VI

On the wild thyme, under the olives below the rock village of Gorbio, with their mules cropping at a little distance, those two sat after their lunch, listening to the cuckoos. Since their uncanny chance meeting that morning in the gardens, when they sat with their hands just touching, amazed and elated by their own good fortune, there was not much need to say what they felt, to break with words this rapture of belonging to each other — so shyly, so wildly, so, as it were, without reality. They were like epicures with old wine in their glasses, not yet tired of its fragrance and the spell of anticipation.

And so their talk was not of love, but, in that pathetic way of star-crossed lovers, of the things they loved; leaving out — each other.

It was the telling of her dream that brought the words from him at last; but she drew away, and answered:

"It can't — it mustn't be!"

Then he just clung to her hand; and presently, seeing that her eyes were wet, took courage enough to kiss her cheek.

Trembling and fugitive indeed that first passage of their love. Not much of the conquering male in him, nor in her of the ordinary enchantress.

And then they went, outwardly sober enough, riding their mules down the stony slopes back to Mentone.

But in the grey, dusty railway-carriage when she had left him, he was like a man drugged, staring at where she had sat opposite.

Two hours later, at dinner in her hotel, between her and Mrs. Ercott, with the Colonel opposite, he knew for the first time what he was faced with. To watch every thought that passed within him, lest it should by the slightest sign betray him; to regulate and veil every look and every word he spoke to her; never for a second to forget that these other persons were actual and dangerous, not merely the insignificant and grotesque shadows that they seemed. It would be perhaps for ever a part of his love for her to seem not to love her. He did not dare dream of fulfilment. He was to be her friend, and try to bring her happiness — burn and long for her, and not think about reward. This was his first real overwhelming passion — so different to the loves of spring — and he brought to it all that naivete, that touching quality of young Englishmen, whose secret instinct it is to back away from the full nature of love, even from admitting that it has that nature. They two were to love, and — not to love! For the first time he understood a little of what that meant. A few stolen adoring minutes now and then, and, for the rest, the presence of a world that must be deceived. Already he had almost a hatred of that orderly, brown-faced Colonel, with his eyes that looked so steady and saw nothing; of that flat, kindly lady, who talked so pleasantly throughout dinner, saying things that he had to answer without knowing what they signified. He realized, with a sense of shock, that he was deprived of all interests in life but one; not even his work had any meaning apart from HER. It lit no fire within him to hear Mrs. Ercott praise certain execrable pictures in the Royal Academy, which she had religiously visited the day before leaving home. And as the interminable meal wore on, he began even to feel grief and wonder that Olive could be so smiling, so gay, and calm; so, as it seemed to him, indifferent to this intolerable impossibility of exchanging even one look of love. Did she really love him — could she love him, and show not one little sign of it? And suddenly he felt her foot touch his own. It was the faintest sidelong, supplicating pressure, withdrawn at once, but it said: I know what you are suffering; I, too, but I love you. Characteristically, he felt that it cost her dear to make use of that little primitive device of common loves; the touch awoke within him only chivalry. He would burn for ever sooner than cause her the pain of thinking that he was not happy.

After dinner, they sat out on a balcony. The stars glowed above the palms; a frog was croaking. He managed to draw his chair so that he could look at her unseen. How deep, and softly dark her eyes, when for a second they rested on his! A moth settled on her knee — a cunning little creature, with its hooded, horned owl's face, and tiny black slits of eyes! Would it have come so confidingly to anyone but her? The Colonel knew its name — he had collected it. Very common, he said. The interest in it passed; but Lennan stayed, bent forward, gazing at that silk-covered knee.

The voice of Mrs. Ercott, sharper than its wont, said: "What day does Robert say he wants you back, my dear?"

He managed to remain gazing at the moth, even to take it gently from her knee, while he listened to her calm answer.

"Tuesday, I believe."

Then he got up, and let the moth fly into the darkness; his hands and lips were trembling, and he was afraid of their being seen. He had never known, had not dreamed, of such a violent, sick feeling. That this man could thus hale her home at will! It was grotesque, fantastic, awful, but — it was true! Next Tuesday she would journey back away from him to be again at the mercy of her Fate! The pain of this thought made him grip the railing, and grit his teeth, to keep himself from crying out. And another thought came to him: I shall have to go about with this feeling, day and night, and keep it secret.

They were saying goodnight; and he had to smirk and smile, and pretend — to her above all — that he was happy, and he could see that she knew it was pretence.

Then he was alone, with the feeling that he had failed her at the first shot; torn, too, between horror of what he suddenly saw

before him, and longing to be back in her presence at any cost. .
. . And all this on the day of that first kiss which had seemed to
him to make her so utterly his own.

He sat down on a bench facing the Casino. Neither the lights,
nor the people passing in and out, not even the gipsy bandsmen's
music, distracted his thoughts for a second. Could it be less than
twenty-four hours since he had picked up her handkerchief, not
thirty yards away? In that twenty-four hours he seemed to have
known every emotion that man could feel. And in all the world
there was now not one soul to whom he could speak his real
thoughts — not even to her, because from her, beyond all, he must
keep at any cost all knowledge of his unhappiness. So this was illicit
love — as it was called! Loneliness, and torture! Not jealousy — for
her heart was his; but amazement, outrage, fear. Endless lonely
suffering! And nobody, if they knew, would care, or pity him one
jot!

Was there really, then, as the ancients thought, a Daemon that
liked to play with men, as men liked to stir an earwig and turn it
over and put a foot on it in the end?

He got up and made his way towards the railway-station. There
was the bench where she had been sitting when he came on her
that very morning. The stars in their courses had seemed to fight
for them then; but whether for joy he no longer knew. And there
on the seat were still the pepper berries she had crushed and
strewn. He broke off another bunch and bruised them. That
scent was the ghost of sacred minutes when her hand lay against
his own. The stars in their courses — for joy or sorrow!

VII

There was no peace now for Colonel and Mrs. Ercott. They felt themselves conspirators, and of conspiracy they had never had the habit. Yet how could they openly deal with anxieties which had arisen solely from what they had chanced secretly to see? What was not intended for one's eyes and ears did not exist; no canon of conduct could be quite so sacred. As well defend the opening of another person's letters as admit the possibility of making use of adventitious knowledge. So far tradition, and indeed character, made them feel at one, and conspire freely. But they diverged on a deeper plane. Mrs. Ercott had SAID, indeed, that here was something which could not be controlled; the Colonel had FELT it — a very different thing! Less tolerant in theory, he was touched at heart; Mrs. Ercott, in theory almost approving — she read that dangerous authoress, George Eliot — at heart felt cold towards her husband's niece. For these reasons they could not in fact conspire without, in the end, saying suddenly: "Well, it's no good talking about it!" and almost at once beginning to talk about it again.

In proposing to her that mule, the Colonel had not had time, or, rather, not quite conviction enough as to his line of action, to explain so immediately the new need for her to sit upon it. It was only when, to his somewhat strange relief, she had refused the expedition, and Olive had started without them, that he told her of the meeting in the Gardens, of which he had been witness. She then said at once that if she had known she would, of course, have put up with anything in order to go; not because she approved of interfering, but because they must think of Robert!

And the Colonel had said: "D — n the fellow!" And there the matter had rested for the moment, for both of them were, wondering a little which fellow it was that he had damned. That indeed was the trouble. If the Colonel had not cared so much about his niece, and had liked, instead of rather disliking Cramier; if Mrs. Ercott had not found Mark Lennan a 'nice boy,' and had not secretly felt her husband's niece rather dangerous to her peace of mind; if, in few words, those three had been puppets made of wood and worked by law, it would have been so much simpler for all concerned. It was the discovery that there was a personal equation in such matters, instead of just a simple rule of three, which disorganized the Colonel and made him almost angry; which depressed Mrs. Ercott and made her almost silent. . . . These two good souls had stumbled on a problem which has divided the world from birth. Shall cases be decided on their individual merits, or according to formal codes?

Beneath an appearance and a vocabulary more orthodox than ever, the Colonel's allegiance to Authority and the laws of Form was really shaken; he simply could not get out of his head the sight of those two young people sitting side by side, nor the tone of Olive's voice, when she had repeated his regrettable words about happiness at home.

If only the thing had not been so human! If only she had been someone else's niece, it would clearly have been her duty to remain unhappy. As it was, the more he thought, the less he knew what to think. A man who had never had any balance to speak of at his bank, and from the nomadic condition of his life had no exaggerated feeling for a settled social status — deeming Society in fact rather a bore — he did not unduly exaggerate the worldly dangers of this affair; neither did he honestly believe that she would burn in everlasting torment if she did not succeed in remaining true to 'that great black chap', as he secretly called Cramier. His feeling was simply that it was an awful pity; a sort of unhappy conviction that it was not like the women of his family to fall upon such ways; that his dead brother would turn in his grave; in two words that it was 'not done.' Yet he was by no means of those who, giving latitude to women in general, fall with whips on those of their own family who take it. On the contrary, believing that 'Woman in general' should be stainless to the world's eye, he was inclined to make allowance for any individual woman that he knew and loved. A suspicion he had always entertained, that Cramier was not by breeding 'quite the clean potato' may insensibly have influenced him just a little. He had heard indeed that he was not even entitled to the name of Cramier, but had been adopted by a childless man, who had brought him up and left him a lot of money. There was something in this that went against the grain of the childless Colonel. He had never adopted, nor been adopted by anyone himself. There was a certain lack about a man who had been adopted, of reasonable guarantee — he was like a non-vintage wine, or a horse without a pedigree; you could not quite rely on what he might do, having no tradition in his blood. His appearance, too, and manner somehow lent colour to this distrust. A touch of the tar-brush somewhere, and a stubborn, silent, pushing fellow. Why on earth had Olive ever married him! But then women were such kittle cattle, poor things! and old Lindsay, with his vestments and his views on obedience, must have been a Tartar as a father, poor old chap! Besides, Cramier, no doubt, was what most women would call good-looking; more taking to the eye than such a quiet fellow as young Lennan, whose features were rather anyhow, though pleasant enough, and with a nice smile — the sort of young man one could not help liking, and who certainly would never hurt a fly! And suddenly there came the thought: Why should he not go to young Lennan and put it to him straight? That he was in love with Olive? Not quite — but the way to do it would come to him. He brooded long over this idea, and spoke of it to Mrs. Ercott, while shaving, the next morning. Her answer: "My dear John, bosh!" removed his last doubt.

Without saying where he was going, he strolled out the

moment after breakfast — and took a train to Beaulieu. At the young man's hotel he sent in his card, and was told that this Monsieur had already gone out for the day. His mood of marching straight up to the guns thus checked, he was left pensive and distraught. Not having seen Beaulieu (they spoke of it then as a coming place), he made his way up an incline. That whole hillside was covered with rose-trees. Thousands of these flowers were starring the lower air, and the strewn petals of blown and fallen roses covered the light soil. The Colonel put his nose to blossoms here and there, but they had little scent, as if they knew that the season was already over. A few blue-bloused peasants were still busy among them. And suddenly he came on young Lennan himself, sitting on a stone and dabbing away with his fingers at a lump of putty stuff. The Colonel hesitated. Apart from obvious reasons for discomfiture, he had that feeling towards Art common to so many of his caste. It was not work, of course, but it was very clever — a mystery to him how anyone could do it! On seeing him, Lennan had risen, dropping his handkerchief over what he was modelling — but not before the Colonel had received a dim impression of something familiar. The young man was very red — the Colonel, too, was conscious suddenly of the heat. He held out his hand.

"Nice quiet place this," he stammered; "never seen it before. I called at your hotel."

Now that he had his chance, he was completely at a loss. The sight of the face emerging from that lump of 'putty stuff' had quite unnerved him. The notion of this young man working at it up here all by himself, just because he was away an hour or two from the original, touched him. How on earth to say what he had come to say? It was altogether different from what he had thought. And it suddenly flashed through him — Dolly was right! She's always right — hang it!

"You're busy," he said; "I mustn't interrupt you."

"Not at all, sir. It was awfully good of you to look me up."

The Colonel stared. There was something about young Lennan that he had not noticed before; a 'Don't take liberties with me!' look that made things difficult. But still he lingered, staring wistfully at the young man, who stood waiting with such politeness. Then a safe question shot into his mind:

"Ah! And when do you go back to England? We're off on Tuesday."

While he spoke, a puff of wind lifted the handkerchief from the modelled face. Would the young fellow put it back? He did not. And the Colonel thought:

"It would have been bad form. He knew I wouldn't take advantage. Yes! He's a gentleman!"

Lifting his hand to the salute, he said: "Well, I must be getting back. See you at dinner perhaps?" And turning on his heel he marched away.

The remembrance of that face in the 'putty stuff' up there by the side of the road accompanied him home. It was bad — it was serious! And the sense that he counted for nothing in all of it grew and grew in him. He told no one of where he had been. . . .

When the Colonel turned with ceremony and left him, Lennan sat down again on the flat stone, took up his 'putty stuff,' and presently effaced that image. He sat still a long time, to all appearance watching the little blue butterflies playing round the red and tawny roses. Then his fingers began to work, feverishly shaping a head; not of a man, not of a beast, but a sort of horned, heavy mingling of the two. There was something frenetic in the movement of those rather short, blunt-ended fingers, as though they were strangling the thing they were creating.

VIII

In those days, such as had served their country travelled, as befitted Spartans, in ordinary first-class carriages, and woke in the morning at La Roche or some strange-sounding place, for paler coffee and the pale brioche. So it was with Colonel and Mrs. Ercott and their niece, accompanied by books they did not read, viands they did not eat, and one somnolent Irishman returning from the East. In the disposition of legs there was the usual difficulty, no one quite liking to put them up, and all ultimately doing so, save Olive. More than once during that night the Colonel, lying on the seat opposite, awoke and saw her sitting, withdrawn into her corner, with eyes still open. Staring at that little head which he admired so much, upright and unmoving, in its dark straw toque against the cushion, he would become suddenly alert. Kicking the Irishman slightly in the effort, he would slip his legs down, bend across to her in the darkness, and, conscious of a faint fragrance as of violets, whisper huskily: "Anything I can do for you, my dear?" When she had smiled and shaken her head, he would retreat, and after holding his breath to see if Dolly were asleep, would restore his feet, slightly kicking the Irishman. After one such expedition, for full ten minutes he remained awake, wondering at her tireless immobility. For indeed she was spending this night entranced, with the feeling that Lennan was beside her, holding her hand in his. She seemed actually to feel the touch of his finger against the tiny patch of her bare palm where the glove opened. It was wonderful, this uncanny communion in the dark rushing night — she would not have slept for worlds! Never before had she felt so close to him, not even when he had kissed her that once under the olives; nor even when at the concert yesterday his arm pressed hers; and his voice whispered words she heard so thirstily. And that golden fortnight passed and passed through her on an endless band of reminiscence. Its memories were like flowers, such scent and warmth and colour in them; and of all, none perhaps quite so poignant as the memory of the moment, at the door of their carriage, when he said, so low that she just heard: "Goodbye, my darling!"

He had never before called her that. Not even his touch on her cheek under the olives equalled the simple treasure of that word. And above the roar and clatter of the train, and the snoring of the Irishman, it kept sounding in her ears, hour after dark hour. It was perhaps not wonderful, that through all that night she never once looked the future in the face — made no plans, took no stock of her position; just yielded to memory, and to the half-dreamed sensation of his presence close beside her. Whatever might come afterwards, she was his this night. Such was the trance that gave to her the strange, soft, tireless immobility which so moved her Uncle whenever he woke up.

In Paris they drove from station to station in a vehicle unfit for three — 'to stretch their legs' — as the Colonel said. Since he saw in his niece no signs of flagging, no regret, his spirits were rising, and he confided to Mrs. Ercott in the buffet at the Gare du Nord, when Olive had gone to wash, that he did not think there was much in it, after all, looking at the way she'd travelled.

But Mrs. Ercott answered:

"Haven't you ever noticed that Olive never shows what she does not want to? She has not got those eyes for nothing."

"What eyes?"

"Eyes that see everything, and seem to see nothing."

Conscious that something was hurting her, the Colonel tried to take her hand.

But Mrs. Ercott rose quickly, and went where he could not follow.

Thus suddenly deserted, the Colonel brooded, drumming on the little table. What now! Dolly was unjust! Poor Dolly! He was as fond of her as ever! Of course! How could he help Olive's being young — and pretty; how could he help looking after her, and wanting to save her from this mess! Thus he sat wondering, dismayed by the unreasonableness of women. It did not enter his head that Mrs. Ercott had been almost as sleepless as his niece, watching through closed eyes every one of those little expeditions of his, and saying to herself: "Ah! He doesn't care how I travel!"

She returned serene enough, concealing her 'grief,' and soon they were once more whirling towards England.

But the future had begun to lay its hand on Olive; the spell of the past was already losing power; the sense that it had all been a dream grew stronger every minute. In a few hours she would re-enter the little house close under the shadow of that old Wren church, which reminded her somehow of childhood, and her austere father with his chiselled face. The meeting with her husband! How go through that! And tonight! But she did not care to contemplate tonight. And all those tomorrows wherein there was nothing she had to do of which it was reasonable to complain, yet nothing she could do without feeling that all the friendliness and zest and colour was out of life, and she a prisoner. Into those tomorrows she felt she would slip back, out of her dream; lost, with hardly perhaps an effort. To get away to the house on the river, where her husband came only at weekends, had hitherto been a refuge; only she would not see Mark there — unless —! Then, with the thought that she would, must still see him sometimes, all again grew faintly glamorous. If only she did see him, what would the rest matter? Never again as it had before!

The Colonel was reaching down her handbag; his cheery: "Looks as if it would be rough!" aroused her. Glad to be alone, and tired enough now, she sought the ladies' cabin, and slept through the crossing, till the voice of the old stewardess awakened her: "You've had a nice sleep. We're alongside, miss." Ah! if she were but THAT now! She had been dreaming that she was sitting in a flowery field, and Lennan had drawn her up by the hands, with the words: "We're here, my darling!"

On deck, the Colonel, laden with bags, was looking back for her, and trying to keep a space between him and his wife. He signalled with his chin. Threading her way towards him, she happened to look up. By the rails of the pier above she saw her husband. He was leaning there, looking intently down; his tall broad figure made the people on each side of him seem insignificant. The clean-shaved, square-cut face, with those almost epileptic, forceful eyes, had a stillness and intensity beside which the neighbouring faces seemed to disappear. She saw him very clearly, even noting the touch of silver in his dark hair, on each side under his straw hat; noting that he seemed too massive for his neat blue suit. His face relaxed; he made a little movement of one hand. Suddenly it shot through her: Suppose Mark had travelled with them, as he had wished to do? For ever and ever now, that dark massive creature, smiling down at her, was her enemy; from whom she must guard and keep herself if she could; keep, at all events, each one of her real thoughts and hopes! She could have writhed, and cried out; instead, she tightened her grip on the handle of her bag, and smiled. Though so skilled in knowledge of his moods, she felt, in his greeting, his fierce grip of her shoulders, the smouldering of some feeling the nature of which she could not quite fathom. His voice had a grim sincerity: "Glad you're back — thought you were never coming!" Resigned to his charge, a feeling of sheer physical faintness so beset her that she could hardly reach the compartment he had reserved. It seemed to her that, for all her foreboding, she had not till this moment had the smallest inkling of what was now before her; and at his muttered: "Must we have the old fossils in?" she looked back to assure herself that her Uncle and Aunt were following. To avoid having to talk, she feigned to have travelled badly, leaning back with closed eyes, in her corner. If only she could open them and see, not this square-jawed face with its intent gaze of possession, but that other with its eager eyes humbly adoring her. The interminable journey ended all too soon. She clung quite desperately to the Colonel's hand on the platform at Charing Cross. When his kind face vanished she would be lost indeed! Then, in the closed cab, she heard her husband's: "Aren't you going to kiss me?" and submitted to his embrace.

She tried so hard to think: What does it matter? It's not I, not my soul, my spirit — only my miserable lips!

She heard him say: "You don't seem too glad to see me!" And then: "I hear you had young Lennan out there. What was HE doing?"

She felt the turmoil of sudden fear, wondered whether she was showing it, lost it in unnatural alertness — all in the second before she answered: "Oh! just a holiday."

Some seconds passed, and then he said:

"You didn't mention him in your letters."

She answered coolly: "Didn't I? We saw a good deal of him."

She knew that he was looking at her — an inquisitive, half-menacing regard. Why — oh, why! — could she not then and there cry out: "And I love him — do you hear? — I love him!" So awful did it seem to be denying her love with these half lies! But it was all so much more grim and hopeless than even she had thought. How inconceivable, now, that she had ever given herself up to this man for life! If only she could get away from him to her room, and scheme and think! For his eyes never left her, travelling over her with their pathetic greed, their menacing inquiry, till he said: "Well, it's not done you any harm. You look very fit." But his touch was too much even for her self-command, and she recoiled as if he had struck her.

"What's the matter? Did I hurt you?"

It seemed to her that he was jeering — then realized as vividly that he was not. And the full danger to her, perhaps to Mark himself, of shrinking from this man, striking her with all its pitiable force, she made a painful effort, slipped her hand under his arm, and said: "I'm very tired. You startled me."

But he put her hand away, and turning his face, stared out of the window. And so they reached their home.

When he had left her alone, she remained where she was standing, by her wardrobe, without sound or movement, thinking: What am I going to do? How am I going to live?

IX

When Mark Lennan, travelling through from Beaulieu, reached his rooms in Chelsea, he went at once to the little pile of his letters, twice hunted through them, then stood very still, with a stunned, sick feeling. Why had she not sent him that promised note? And now he realized — though not yet to the full — what it meant to be in love with a married woman. He must wait in this suspense for eighteen hours at least, till he could call, and find out what had happened to prevent her, till he could hear from her lips that she still loved him. The chilliest of legal lovers had access to his love, but he must possess a soul that was on fire, in this deadly patience, for fear of doing something that might jeopardize her. Telegraph? He dared not. Write? She would get it by the first post; but what could he say that was not dangerous, if Cramier chanced to see? Call? Still more impossible till three o'clock, at very earliest, tomorrow. His gaze wandered round the studio. Were these household gods, and all these works of his, indeed the same he had left twenty days ago? They seemed to exist now only in so far as she might come to see them — come and sit in such a chair, and drink out of such a cup, and let him put this cushion for her back, and that footstool for her feet. And so vividly could he see her lying back in that chair looking across at him, that he could hardly believe she had never yet sat there. It was odd how — without any resolution taken, without admission that their love could not remain platonic, without any change in their relations, save one humble kiss and a few whispered words — everything was changed. A month or so ago, if he had wanted, he would have gone at once calmly to her house. It would have seemed harmless, and quite natural. Now it was impossible to do openly the least thing that strict convention did not find desirable. Sooner or later they would find him stepping over convention, and take him for what he was not — a real lover! A real lover! He knelt down before the empty chair and stretched out his arms. No substance — no warmth — no fragrance — nothing! Longing that passed through air, as the wind through grass.

He went to the little round window, which overlooked the river. The last evening of May; gloaming above the water, dusk resting in the trees, and the air warm! Better to be out, and moving in the night, out in the ebb and flow of things, among others whose hearts were beating, than stay in this place that without her was so cold and meaningless.

Lamps — the passion-fruit of towns — were turning from pallor to full orange, and the stars were coming out. Half-past nine! At ten o'clock, and not before, he would walk past her house. To have this something to look forward to, however furtive and barren, helped. But on a Saturday night there would be no sitting at the House. Cramier would be at home; or they would both be out; or perhaps have gone down to their river cottage. Cramier! What cruel demon had presided over that marring of her life! Why had he never met her till after she had bound herself to this man! From a negative contempt for one who was either not sensitive enough to recognize that his marriage was a failure, or not chivalrous enough to make that failure bear as little hardly as possible on his wife, he had come already to jealous hatred as of a monster. To be face to face with Cramier in a mortal conflict could alone have satisfied his feeling. . . . Yet he was a young man by nature gentle!

His heart beat desperately as he approached that street — one of those little old streets, so beautiful, that belonged to a vanished London. It was very narrow, there was no shelter; and he thought confusedly of what he could say, if met in this remote backwater that led nowhere. He would tell some lie, no doubt. Lies would now be his daily business. Lies and hatred, those violent things of life, would come to seem quite natural, in the violence of his love.

He stood a moment, hesitating, by the rails of the old church. Black, white-veined, with shadowy summits, in that half darkness, it was like some gigantic vision. Mystery itself seemed modelled there. He turned and walked quickly down the street close to the houses on the further side. The windows of her house were lighted! So, she was not away! Dim light in the dining-room, lights in the room above — her bedroom, doubtless. Was there no way to bring her to the window, no way his spirit could climb up there and beckon hers out to him? Perhaps she was not there, perhaps it was but a servant taking up hot water. He was at the end of the street by now, but to leave without once more passing was impossible. And this time he went slowly, his head down, feigning abstraction, grudging every inch of pavement, and all the time furtively searching that window with the light behind the curtains. Nothing! Once more he was close to the railings of the church, and once more could not bring himself to go away. In the little, close, deserted street, not a soul was moving, not even a cat or dog; nothing alive but many discreet, lighted windows. Like veiled faces, showing no emotion, they seemed to watch his indecision. And he thought: "Ah, well! I dare say there are lots like me. Lots as near, and yet as far away! Lots who have to suffer!" But what would he not have given for the throwing open of those curtains. Then, suddenly scared by an approaching figure, he turned and walked away.

X

At three o'clock next day he called.

In the middle of her white drawing-room, whose latticed window ran the whole length of one wall, stood a little table on which was a silver jar full of early larkspurs, evidently from her garden by the river. And Lennan waited, his eyes fixed on those blossoms so like to little blue butterflies and strange-hued crickets, tethered to the pale green stems. In this room she passed her days, guarded from him. Once a week, at most, he would be able to come there — once a week for an hour or two of the hundred and sixty-eight hours that he longed to be with her.

And suddenly he was conscious of her. She had come in without sound, and was standing by the piano, so pale, in her cream-white dress, that her eyes looked jet black. He hardly knew that face, like a flower closed against cold.

What had he done? What had happened in these five days to make her like this to him? He took her hands and tried to kiss them; but she said quickly:

"He's in!"

At that he stood silent, looking into that face, frozen to a dreadful composure, on the breaking up of which his very life seemed to depend. At last he said:

"What is it? Am I nothing to you, after all?"

But as soon as he had spoken he saw that he need not have asked, and flung his arms round her. She clung to him with desperation; then freed herself, and said:

"No, no; let's sit down quietly!"

He obeyed, half-divining, half-refusing to admit all that lay behind that strange coldness, and this desperate embrace; all the self-pity, and self-loathing, shame, rage, and longing of a married woman for the first time face to face with her lover in her husband's house.

She seemed now to be trying to make him forget her strange behaviour; to be what she had been during that fortnight in the sunshine. But, suddenly, just moving her lips, she said:

"Quick! When can we see each other? I will come to you to tea — tomorrow," and, following her eyes, he saw the door opening, and Cramier coming in. Unsmiling, very big in the low room, he crossed over to them, and offered his hand to Lennan; then drawing a low chair forward between their two chairs, sat down.

"So you're back," he said. "Have a good time?"

"Thanks, yes; very."

"Luck for Olive you were there; those places are dull holes."

"It was luck for me."

"No doubt." And with those words he turned to his wife. His elbows rested along the arms of his chair, so that his clenched palms were upwards; it was as if he knew that he was holding those two, gripped one in each hand.

"I wonder," he said slowly, "that fellows like you, with nothing in the world to tie them, ever sit down in a place like London. I should have thought Rome or Paris were your happy hunting-grounds." In his voice, in those eyes of his, a little bloodshot, with their look of power, in his whole attitude, there was a sort of muffled menace, and contempt, as though he were thinking: "Step into my path, and I will crush you!"

And Lennan thought:

"How long must I sit here?" Then, past that figure planted solidly between them, he caught a look from her, swift, sure, marvellously timed — again and again — as if she were being urged by the very presence of this danger. One of those glances would surely — surely be seen by Cramier. Is there need for fear that a swallow should dash itself against the wall over which it skims? But he got up, unable to bear it longer.

"Going?" That one suave word had an inimitable insolence.

He could hardly see his hand touching Cramier's heavy fist. Then he realized that she was standing so that their faces when they must say goodbye could not be seen. Her eyes were smiling, yet imploring; her lips shaped the word: "Tomorrow!" And squeezing her hand desperately, he got away.

He had never dreamed that to see her in the presence of the man who owned her would be so terrible. For a moment he thought that he must give her up, give up a love that would drive him mad.

He climbed on to an omnibus travelling West. Another twenty-four hours of starvation had begun. It did not matter at all what he did with them. They were simply so much aching that had to be got through somehow — so much aching; and what relief at the end? An hour or two with her, desperately holding himself in.

Like most artists, and few Englishmen, he lived on feelings rather than on facts; so, found no refuge in decisive resolutions. But he made many — the resolution to give her up; to be true to the ideal of service for no reward; to beseech her to leave Cramier and come to him — and he made each many times.

At Hyde Park Corner he got down, and went into the Park, thinking that to walk would help him.

A great number of people were sitting there, taking mysterious anodyne, doing the right thing; to avoid them, he kept along the rails, and ran almost into the arms of Colonel and Mrs. Ercott, who were coming from the direction of Knightsbridge, slightly flushed, having lunched and talked of 'Monte' at the house of a certain General.

They greeted him with the surprise of those who had said to each other many times: "That young man will come rushing back!" It was very nice — they said — to run across him. When did he arrive? They had thought he was going on to Italy — he was looking rather tired. They did not ask if he had seen her — being too kind, and perhaps afraid that he would say 'Yes,' which would be embarrassing; or that he would say 'No,' which would be still more embarrassing when they found that he ought to have said 'Yes.' Would he not come and sit with them a little — they were going presently to see how Olive was? Lennan perceived that they were warning him. And, forcing himself to look at them very straight, he said: "I have just been there."

Mrs. Ercott phrased her impressions that same evening: "He looks quite hunted, poor young man! I'm afraid there's going to be fearful trouble there. Did you notice how quickly he ran away from us? He's thin, too; if it wasn't for his tan, he'd look really ill. The boy's eyes are so pathetic; and he used to have such a nice smile in them."

The Colonel, who was fastening her hooks, paused in an operation that required concentration.

"It's a thousand pities," he muttered, "that he hasn't any work to do. That puddling about with clay or whatever he does is no good at all." And slowly fastening one hook, he unhooked several others.

Mrs. Ercott went on:

"And I saw Olive, when she thought I wasn't looking; it was just as if she'd taken off a mask. But Robert Cramier will never put up with it. He's in love with her still; I watched him. It's tragic, John."

The Colonel let his hands fall from the hooks.

"If I thought that," he said, "I'd do something."

"If you could, it would not be tragic."

The Colonel stared. There was always SOMETHING to be done.

"You read too many novels," he said, but without spirit.

Mrs. Ercott smiled, and made no answer to an aspersion she had heard before.

XI

When Lennan reached his rooms again after that encounter with the Ercotts, he found in his letterbox a visiting card: "Mrs. Doone" "Miss Sylvia Doone," and on it pencilled the words: "Do come and see us before we go down to Hayle — Sylvia." He stared blankly at the round handwriting he knew so well.

Sylvia! Nothing perhaps could have made so plain to him how in this tornado of his passion the world was drowned. Sylvia! He had almost forgotten her existence; and yet, only last year, after he definitely settled down in London, he had once more seen a good deal of her; and even had soft thoughts of her again — with her pale-gold hair, her true look, her sweetness. Then they had gone for the winter to Algiers for her mother's health.

When they came back, he had already avoided seeing her, though that was before Olive went to Monte Carlo, before he had even admitted his own feeling. And since — he had not once thought of her. Not once! The world had indeed vanished. "Do come and see us — Sylvia." The very notion was an irritation. No rest from aching and impatience to be had that way.

And then the idea came to him: Why not kill these hours of waiting for tomorrow's meeting by going on the river passing by her cottage? There was still one train that he could catch.

He reached the village after dark, and spent the night at the inn; got up early next morning, took a boat, and pulled downstream. The bluffs of the opposite bank were wooded with high trees. The sun shone softly on their leaves, and the bright stream was ruffled by a breeze that bent all the reeds and slowly swayed the water-flowers. One thin white line of wind streaked the blue sky. He shipped his sculls and drifted, listening to the wood-pigeons, watching the swallows chasing. If only she were here! To spend one long day thus, drifting with the stream! To have but one such rest from longing! Her cottage, he knew, lay on the same side as the village, and just beyond an island. She had told him of a hedge of yew-trees, and a white dovecote almost at the water's edge. He came to the island, and let his boat slide into the backwater. It was all overgrown with willow-trees and alders, dark even in this early morning radiance, and marvellously still. There was no room to row; he took the boathook and tried to punt, but the green water was too deep and entangled with great roots, so that he had to make his way by clawing with the hook at branches. Birds seemed to shun this gloom, but a single magpie crossed the one little clear patch of sky, and flew low behind the willows. The air here had a sweetish, earthy odour of too rank foliage; all brightness seemed entombed. He was glad to pass out again under a huge poplar-tree into the fluttering gold and silver of the morning. And almost at once he saw the yew-hedge at the border of some bright green turf, and a pigeon-house, high on its pole, painted cream-white. About it a number of ring-doves and snow-white pigeons were perched or flying; and beyond the lawn he could see the dark veranda of a low house, covered by wistaria just going out of flower. A drift of scent from late lilacs, and new-mown grass, was borne out to him, together with the sound of a mowing-machine, and the humming of many bees. It was beautiful here, and seemed, for all its restfulness, to have something of that flying quality he so loved about her face, about the sweep of her hair, the quick, soft turn of her eyes — or was that but the darkness of the yew-trees, the whiteness of the dovecote, and the doves themselves, flying?

He lay there a long time quietly beneath the bank, careful not to attract the attention of the old gardener, who was methodically pushing his machine across and across the lawn.

How he wanted her with him then! Wonderful that there could be in life such beauty and wild softness as made the heart ache with the delight of it, and in that same life grey rules and rigid barriers — coffins of happiness! That doors should be closed on love and joy! There was not so much of it in the world! She, who was the very spirit of this flying, nymph-like summer, was untimely wintered-up in bleak sorrow. There was a hateful unwisdom in that thought; it seemed so grim and violent, so corpse-like, gruesome, narrow and extravagant! What possible end could it serve that she should be unhappy! Even if he had not loved her, he would have hated her fate just as much — all such stories of imprisoned lives had roused his anger even as a boy.

Soft white clouds — those bright angels of the river, never very long away — had begun now to spread their wings over the woods; and the wind had dropped so that the slumbrous warmth and murmuring of summer gathered full over the water. The old gardener had finished his job of mowing, and came with a little basket of grain to feed the doves. Lennan watched them going to him, the ring-doves, very dainty, and capricious, keeping to themselves. In place of that old fellow, he was really seeing HER, feeding from her hands those birds of Cypris. What a group he could have made of her with them perching and flying round her! If she were his, what could he not achieve — to make her immortal — like the old Greeks and Italians, who, in their work, had rescued their mistresses from Time! . . .

He was back in his rooms in London two hours before he dared begin expecting her. Living alone there but for a caretaker who came every morning for an hour or two, made dust, and departed, he had no need for caution. And when he had procured flowers, and the fruits and cakes which they certainly would not eat — when he had arranged the tea-table, and made the grand tour at least twenty times, he placed himself with a book at the little round window, to watch for her approach.

There, very still, he sat, not reading a word, continually moistening his dry lips and sighing, to relieve the tension of his heart. At last he saw her coming. She was walking close to the railings of the houses, looking neither to right nor left. She had on a lawn frock, and a hat of the palest coffee-coloured straw, with a narrow black velvet ribbon. She crossed the side street, stopped for a second, gave a swift look round, then came resolutely on. What was it made him love her so? What was the secret of her fascination? Certainly, no conscious enticements. Never did anyone try less to fascinate. He could not recall one single little thing that she had done to draw him to her. Was it, perhaps, her very passivity, her native pride that never offered or asked anything, a sort of soft stoicism in her fibre; that and some mysterious charm, as close and intimate as scent was to a flower?

He waited to open till he heard her footstep just outside. She came in without a word, not even looking at him. And he, too, said not a word till he had closed the door, and made sure of her. Then they turned to each other. Her breast was heaving a little, under her thin frock, but she was calmer than he, with that wonderful composure of pretty women in all the passages of love, as who should say: This is my native air!

They stood and looked at each other, as if they could never have enough, till he said at last:

"I thought I should die before this moment came. There isn't a minute that I don't long for you so terribly that I can hardly live."

"And do you think that I don't long for you?"

"Then come to me!"

She looked at him mournfully and shook her head.

Well, he had known that she would not. He had not earned her. What right had he to ask her to fly against the world, to brave everything, to have such faith in him — as yet? He had no heart to press his words, beginning then to understand the paralyzing truth that there was no longer any resolving this or that; with love like his he had ceased to be a separate being with a separate will. He was entwined with her, could act only if her will and his were one. He would never be able to say to her: 'You must!' He loved her too much. And she knew it. So there was nothing for it but to forget the ache, and make the hour happy. But how about that other truth — that in love there is no pause, no resting? . . . With any watering, however scant, the flower will grow till its time comes to be plucked. . . . This oasis in the desert — these few minutes with her alone, were swept through and through with a feverish wind. To be closer! How not try to be that? How not long for her lips when he had but her hand to kiss? And how not be poisoned with the thought that in a few minutes she would leave him and go back to the presence of that other, who, even though she loathed him, could see and touch her when he would? She was leaning back in the very chair where in fancy he had seen her, and he only dared sit at her feet and look up. And this, which a week ago would have been rapture, was now almost torture, so far did it fall short of his longing. It was torture, too, to keep his voice in tune with the sober sweetness of her voice. And bitterly he thought: How can she sit there, and not want me, as I want her? Then at a touch of her fingers on his hair, he lost control, and kissed her lips. Her surrender lasted only for a second.

"No, no — you must not!"

That mournful surprise sobered him at once.

He got up, stood away from her, begged to be forgiven.

And, when she was gone, he sat in the chair where she had sat. That clasp of her, the kiss he had begged her to forget — to forget! — nothing could take that from him. He had done wrong; had startled her, had fallen short of chivalry! And yet — a smile of utter happiness would cling about his lips. His fastidiousness, his imagination almost made him think that this was all he wanted. If he could close his eyes, now, and pass out, before he lost that moment of half-fulfilment!

And, the smile still on his lips, he lay back watching the flies wheeling and chasing round the hanging-lamp. Sixteen of them there were, wheeling and chasing — never still!

XII

When, walking from Lennan's studio, Olive reentered her dark little hall, she approached its alcove and glanced first at the hat-stand. They were all there — the silk hat, the bowler, the straw! So he was in! And within each hat, in turn, she seemed to see her husband's head — with the face turned away from her — so distinctly as to note the leathery look of the skin of his cheek and neck. And she thought: "I pray that he will die! It is wicked, but I pray that he will die!" Then, quietly, that he might not hear, she mounted to her bedroom. The door into his dressing-room was open, and she went to shut it. He was standing there at the window.

"Ah! You're in! Been anywhere?"

"To the National Gallery."

It was the first direct lie she had ever told him, and she was surprised to feel neither shame nor fear, but rather a sense of pleasure at defeating him. He was the enemy, all the more the enemy because she was still fighting against herself, and, so strangely, in his behalf.

"Alone?"

"Yes."

"Rather boring, wasn't it? I should have thought you'd have got young Lennan to take you there."

"Why?"

By instinct she had seized on the boldest answer; and there was nothing to be told from her face. If he were her superior in strength, he was her inferior in quickness.

He lowered his eyes, and said:

"His line, isn't it?"

With a shrug she turned away and shut the door. She sat down on the edge of her bed, very still. In that little passage of wits she had won, she could win in many such; but the full hideousness of things had come to her. Lies! lies! That was to be her life! That; or to say farewell to all she now cared for, to cause despair not only in herself, but in her lover, and — for what? In order that her body might remain at the disposal of that man in the next room — her spirit having flown from him for ever. Such were the alternatives, unless those words: "Then come to me," were to be more than words. Were they? Could they be? They would mean such happiness if — if his love for her were more than a summer love? And hers for him? Was it — were they — more than summer loves? How know? And, without knowing, how give such pain to everyone? How break a vow she had thought herself quite above breaking? How make such a desperate departure from all the traditions and beliefs in which she had been brought up! But in the very nature of passion is that which resents the intrusion of hard and fast decisions. . . . And suddenly she thought: If our love cannot stay what it is, and if I cannot yet go to him for always, is there not still another way?

She got up and began to dress for dinner. Standing before her glass she was surprised to see that her face showed no signs of the fears and doubts that were now her comrades. Was it because, whatever happened, she loved and was beloved! She wondered how she had looked when he kissed her so passionately; had she shown her joy before she checked him?

In her garden by the river were certain flowers that, for all her care, would grow rank and of the wrong colour — wanting a different soil. Was she, then, like those flowers of hers? Ah! Let her but have her true soil, and she would grow straight and true enough!

Then in the doorway she saw her husband. She had never, till today, quite hated him; but now she did, with a real blind horrible feeling. What did he want of her standing there with those eyes fixed on her — those forceful eyes, touched with blood, that seemed at once to threaten, covet, and beseech! She drew her wrapper close round her shoulders. At that he came up and said:

"Look at me, Olive!"

Against instinct and will she obeyed, and he went on:

"Be careful! I say, be careful!"

Then he took her by the shoulders, and raised her up to him. And, quite unnerved, she stood without resisting.

"I want you," he said; "I mean to keep you."

Then, suddenly letting her go, he covered his eyes with his hands. That frightened her most — it was so unlike him. Not till now had she understood between what terrifying forces she was balancing. She did not speak, but her face grew white. From behind those hands he uttered a sound, not quite like a human noise, turned sharply, and went out. She dropped back into the chair before her mirror, overcome by the most singular feeling she had ever known; as if she had lost everything, even her love for Lennan, and her longing for his love. What was it all worth, what was anything worth in a world like this? All was loathsome, herself loathsome! All was a void! Hateful, hateful, hateful! It was like having no heart at all! And that same evening, when her husband had gone down to the House, she wrote to Lennan:

"Our love must never turn to earthiness as it might have this afternoon. Everything is black and hopeless. HE suspects. For you to come here is impossible, and too dreadful for us both. And I have no right to ask you to be furtive, I can't bear to think of you like that, and I can't bear it myself. I don't know what to do or say. Don't try to see me yet. I must have time, I must think."

XIII

Colonel Ercott was not a racing man, but he had in common with others of his countrymen a religious feeling in the matter of the Derby. His remembrances of it went back to early youth, for he had been born and brought up almost within sound of the coaching-road to Epsom. Every Derby and Oaks day he had gone out on his pony to watch the passing of the tall hats and feathers of the great, and the pot-hats and feathers of the lowly; and afterwards, in the fields at home, had ridden races with old Lindsay, finishing between a cow that judged and a clump of bulrushes representing the Grand Stand.

But for one reason or another he had never seen the great race, and the notion that it was his duty to see it had now come to him. He proposed this to Mrs. Ercott with some diffidence. She read so many books — he did not quite know whether she would approve. Finding that she did, he added casually:

"And we might take Olive."

Mrs. Ercott answered dryly:

"You know the House of Commons has a holiday?"

The Colonel murmured:

"Oh! I don't want that chap!"

"Perhaps," said Mrs. Ercott, "you would like Mark Lennan."

The Colonel looked at her most dubiously. Dolly could talk of it as a tragedy, and a — a grand passion, and yet make a suggestion like that! Then his wrinkles began slowly to come alive, and he gave her waist a squeeze.

Mrs. Ercott did not resist that treatment.

"Take Olive alone," she said. "I don't really care to go."

When the Colonel went to fetch his niece he found her ready, and very half-heartedly he asked for Cramier. It appeared she had not told him.

Relieved, yet somewhat disconcerted, he murmured:

"He won't mind not going, I suppose?"

"If he went, I should not."

At this quiet answer the Colonel was beset again by all his fears. He put his white 'topper' down, and took her hand.

"My dear," he said, "I don't want to intrude upon your feelings; but — but is there anything I can do? It's dreadful to see things going unhappily with you!" He felt his hand being lifted, her face pressed against it; and, suffering acutely, with his other hand, cased in a bright new glove, he smoothed her arm. "We'll have a jolly good day, sweetheart," he said, "and forget all about it."

She gave the hand a kiss and turned away. And the Colonel vowed to himself that she should not be unhappy — lovely creature that she was, so delicate, and straight, and fine in her pearly frock. And he pulled himself together, brushing his white 'topper' vigorously with his sleeve, forgetting that this kind of hat has no nap.

And so he was tenderness itself on the journey down, satisfying all her wants before she had them, telling her stories of Indian life, and consulting her carefully as to which horse they should back. There was the Duke's, of course, but there was another animal that appealed to him greatly. His friend Tabor had given him the tip — Tabor, who had the best Arabs in all India — and at a nice price. A man who practically never gambled, the Colonel liked to feel that his fancy would bring him in something really substantial — if it won; the idea that it could lose not really troubling him. However, they would see it in the paddock, and judge for themselves. The paddock was the place, away from all the dust and racket — Olive would enjoy the paddock! Once on the course, they neglected the first race; it was more important, the Colonel thought, that they should lunch. He wanted to see more colour in her cheeks, wanted to see her laugh. He had an invitation to his old regiment's drag, where the champagne was sure to be good. And he was so proud of her — would not have missed those young fellows' admiration of her for the world; though to take a lady amongst them was, in fact, against the rules. It was not, then, till the second race was due to start that they made their way into the paddock. Here the Derby horses were being led solemnly, attended each by a little posse of persons, looking up their legs and down their ribs to see whether they were worthy of support, together with a few who liked to see a whole horse at a time. Presently they found the animal which had been recommended to the Colonel. It was a chestnut, with a starred forehead, parading in a far corner. The Colonel, who really loved a horse, was deep in admiration. He liked its head and he liked its hocks; above all, he liked its eye. A fine creature, all sense and fire — perhaps just a little straight in the shoulder for coming down the hill! And in the midst of his examination he found himself staring at his niece. What breeding the child showed, with her delicate arched brows, little ears, and fine, close nostrils; and the way she moved — so sure and springy. She was too pretty to suffer! A shame! If she hadn't been so pretty that young fellow wouldn't have fallen in love with her. If she weren't so pretty — that husband of hers wouldn't —! And the Colonel dropped his gaze, startled by the discovery he had stumbled on. If she hadn't been so pretty! Was that the meaning of it all? The cynicism of his own reflection struck him between wind and water. And yet something in himself seemed to confirm it somehow. What then? Was he to let them tear her in two between them, destroying her, because she was so pretty? And somehow this discovery of his — that passion springs from worship of beauty and warmth, of form and colour — disturbed him horribly, for he had no habit of philosophy. The thought seemed to him strangely crude, even immoral. That she should be thus between two ravening desires — a bird between two hawks, a fruit between two mouths! It was a way of looking at things that had never before occurred to him. The idea of a husband clutching at his wife, the idea of that young man who looked so gentle, swooping down on her; and the idea that if she faded, lost her looks, went off, their greed, indeed, any man's, would die away — all these horrible ideas hurt him the more for the remarkable suddenness with which they had come to him. A tragic business! Dolly had said so. Queer and quick — were women! But his resolution that the day was to be jolly soon recurred to him, and he hastily resumed inspection of his fancy. Perhaps they ought to have a ten-pound note on it, and they had better get back to the Stand! And as they went the Colonel saw, standing beneath a tree at a little distance, a young man that he could have sworn was Lennan. Not likely for an artist chap to be down here! But it WAS undoubtedly young Lennan, brushed-up, in a top-hat. Fortunately, however, his face was not turned in their direction. He said nothing to Olive, not wishing — especially after those unpleasant thoughts — to take responsibility, and he kept her moving towards the gate, congratulating himself that his eyes had been so sharp. In the crush there he was separated from her a little, but she was soon beside him again; and more than ever he congratulated himself that nothing had occurred to upset her and spoil the day. Her cheeks were warm enough now, her dark eyes glowing. She was excited no doubt by thoughts of the race, and of the 'tenner' he was going to put on for her.

He recounted the matter afterwards to Mrs. Ercott. "That chestnut Tabor put me on to finished nowhere — couldn't get down the hill — knew it wouldn't the moment I set eyes on it. But the child enjoyed herself. Wish you'd been there, my dear!" Of his deeper thoughts and of that glimpse of young Lennan he did not speak, for on the way home an ugly suspicion had attacked him. Had the young fellow, after all, seen and managed to get close to her in the crush at the paddock gateway?

XIV

That letter of hers fanned the flame in Lennan as nothing had yet fanned it. Earthiness! Was it earthiness to love as he did? If so, then not for all the world would he be otherwise than earthy. In the shock of reading it, he crossed his Rubicon, and burned his boats behind him. No more did the pale ghost, chivalrous devotion, haunt him. He knew now that he could not stop short. Since she asked him, he must not, of course, try to see her just yet. But when he did, then he would fight for his life; the thought that she might be meaning to slip away from him was too utterly unbearable. But she could not be meaning that! She would never be so cruel! Ah! she would — she must come to him in the end! The world, life itself, would be well lost for love of her!

Thus resolved, he was even able to work again; and all that Tuesday he modelled at a big version of the fantastic, bull-like figure he had conceived after the Colonel left him up on the hillside at Beaulieu. He worked at it with a sort of evil joy. Into this creature he would put the spirit of possession that held her from him. And while his fingers forced the clay, he felt as if he had Cramier's neck within his grip. Yet, now that he had resolved to take her if he could, he had not quite the same hatred. After all, this man loved her too, could not help it that she loathed him; could not help it that he had the disposition of her, body and soul!

June had come in with skies of a blue that not even London glare and dust could pale. In every square and park and patch of green the air simmered with life and with the music of birds swaying on little boughs. Piano organs in the streets were no longer wistful for the South; lovers already sat in the shade of trees.

To remain indoors, when he was not working, was sheer torture; for he could not read, and had lost all interest in the little excitements, amusements, occupations that go to make up the normal life of man. Every outer thing seemed to have dropped off, shrivelled, leaving him just a condition of the spirit, a state of mind.

Lying awake he would think of things in the past, and they would mean nothing — all dissolved and dispersed by the heat of this feeling in him. Indeed, his sense of isolation was so strong that he could not even believe that he had lived through the facts which his memory apprehended. He had become one burning mood — that and nothing more.

To be out, especially amongst trees, was the only solace.

And he sat for a long time that evening under a large lime-tree on a knoll above the Serpentine. There was very little breeze, just enough to keep alive a kind of whispering. What if men and women, when they had lived their gusty lives, became trees! What if someone who had burned and ached were now spreading over him this leafy peace — this blue-black shadow against the stars? Or were the stars, perhaps, the souls of men and women escaped for ever from love and longing? He broke off a branch of the lime and drew it across his face. It was not yet in flower, but it smelled lemony and fresh even here in London. If only for a moment he could desert his own heart, and rest with the trees and stars!

No further letter came from her next morning, and he soon lost his power to work. It was Derby Day. He determined to go down. Perhaps she would be there. Even if she were not, he might find some little distraction in the crowd and the horses. He had seen her in the paddock long before the Colonel's sharp eyes detected him; and, following in the crush, managed to touch her hand in the crowded gateway, and whisper: "Tomorrow, the National Gallery, at four o'clock — by the Bacchus and Ariadne. For God's sake!" Her gloved hand pressed his hard; and she was gone. He stayed in the paddock, too happy almost to breathe. . . .

Next day, while waiting before that picture, he looked at it with wonder. For there seemed his own passion transfigured in the darkening star-crowned sky, and the eyes of the leaping god. In spirit, was he not always rushing to her like that? Minutes passed, and she did not come. What should he do if she failed him? Surely die of disappointment and despair. . . . He had little enough experience as yet of the toughness of the human heart; how life bruises and crushes, yet leaves it beating. . . . Then, from an unlikely quarter, he saw her coming.

They walked in silence down to the quiet rooms where the Turner watercolours hung. No one, save two Frenchmen and an old official, watched them passing slowly before those little pictures, till they came to the end wall, and, unseen, unheard by any but her, he could begin!

The arguments he had so carefully rehearsed were all forgotten; nothing left but an incoherent pleading. Life without her was not life; and they had only one life for love — one summer. It was all dark where she was not — the very sun itself was dark. Better to die than to live such false, broken lives, apart from each other. Better to die at once than to live wanting each other, longing and longing, and watching each other's sorrow. And all for the sake of what? It maddened, killed him, to think of that man touching her when he knew she did but hate him. It shamed all manhood; it could not be good to help such things to be. A vow when the spirit of it was gone was only superstition; it was wicked to waste one's life for the sake of that. Society — she knew, she must know — only cared for the forms, the outsides of things. And what did it matter what Society thought? It had no soul, no feeling, nothing. And if it were said they ought to sacrifice themselves for the sake of others, to make things happier in the world, she must know that was only true when love was light and selfish; but not when people loved as they did, with all their hearts and souls, so that they would die for each other any minute, so that without each other there was no meaning in anything. It would not help a single soul, for them to murder their love and all the happiness of their lives; to go on in a sort of living death. Even if it were wrong, he would rather do that wrong, and take the consequences! But it was not, it COULD not be wrong, when they felt like that!

And all the time that he was pouring forth those supplications, his eyes searched and searched her face. But there only came from her: "I don't know — I can't tell — if only I knew!" And then he was silent, stricken to the heart; till, at a look or a touch from her, he would break out again: "You do love me — you do; then what does anything else matter?"

And so it went on and on that summer afternoon, in the deserted room meant for such other things, where the two Frenchmen were too sympathetic, and the old official too drowsy, to come. Then it all narrowed to one fierce, insistent question:

"What is it — WHAT is it you're afraid of?"

But to that, too, he got only the one mournful answer, paralyzing in its fateful monotony.

"I don't know — I can't tell!"

It was awful to go on thus beating against this uncanny, dark, shadowy resistance; these unreal doubts and dreads, that by their very dumbness were becoming real to him, too. If only she could tell him what she feared! It could not be poverty — that was not like her — besides, he had enough for both. It could not be loss of a social position, which was but irksome to her! Surely it was not fear that he would cease to love her! What was it? In God's name — what?

Tomorrow — she had told him — she was to go down, alone, to the river-house; would she not come now, this very minute, to him instead? And they would start off — that night, back to the South where their love had flowered. But again it was: "I can't! I don't know — I must have time!" And yet her eyes had that brooding love-light. How COULD she hold back and waver? But, utterly exhausted, he did not plead again; did not even resist when she said: "You must go, now; and leave me to get back! I will write. Perhaps — soon — I shall know." He begged for, and took one kiss; then, passing the old official, went quickly up and out.

XV

He reached his rooms overcome by a lassitude that was not, however, quite despair. He had made his effort, failed — but there was still within him the unconquerable hope of the passionate lover. . . . As well try to extinguish in full June the beating of the heart of summer; deny to the flowers their deepening hues, or to winged life its slumbrous buzzing, as stifle in such a lover his conviction of fulfilment. . . .

He lay down on a couch, and there stayed a long time quite still, his forehead pressed against the wall. His will was already beginning to recover for a fresh attempt. It was merciful that she was going away from Cramier, going to where he had in fancy watched her feed her doves. No laws, no fears, not even her commands could stop his fancy from conjuring her up by day and night. He had but to close his eyes, and she was there.

A ring at the bell, repeated several times, roused him at last to go to the door. His caller was Robert Cramier. And at sight of him, all Lennan's lethargy gave place to a steely feeling. What had brought him here? Had he been spying on his wife? The old longing for physical combat came over him. Cramier was perhaps fifteen years his senior, but taller, heavier, thicker. Chances, then, were pretty equal!

"Won't you come in?" he said.

"Thanks."

The voice had in it the same mockery as on Sunday; and it shot through him that Cramier had thought to find his wife here. If so, he did not betray it by any crude look round. He came in with his deliberate step, light and well-poised for so big a man.

"So this," he said, "is where you produce your masterpieces! Anything great since you came back?"

Lennan lifted the cloths from the half-modelled figure of his bull-man. He felt malicious pleasure in doing that. Would Cramier recognize himself in this creature with the horn-like ears, and great bossed forehead? If this man who had her happiness beneath his heel had come here to mock, he should at all events get what he had come to give. And he waited.

"I see. You are giving the poor brute horns!"

If Cramier had seen, he had dared to add a touch of cynical humour, which the sculptor himself had never thought of. And this even evoked in the young man a kind of admiring compunction.

"Those are not horns," he said gently; "only ears."

Cramier lifted a hand and touched the edge of his own ear.

"Not quite like that, are they — human ears? But I suppose you would call this symbolic. What, if I may ask, does it represent?"

All the softness in Lennan vanished.

"If you can't gather that from looking, it must be a failure."

"Not at all. If I am right, you want something for it to tread on, don't you, to get your full effect?"

Lennan touched the base of the clay.

"The broken curve here" — then, with sudden disgust at this fencing, was silent. What had the man come for? He must want something. And, as if answering, Cramier said:

"To pass to another subject — you see a good deal of my wife. I just wanted to tell you that I don't very much care that you should. It is as well to be quite frank, I think."

Lennan bowed.

"Is that not," he said, "perhaps rather a matter for HER decision?"

That heavy figure — those threatening eyes! The whole thing was like a dream come true!

"I do not feel it so. I am not one of those who let things drift. Please understand me. You come between us at your peril."

Lennan kept silence for a moment, then he said quietly:

"Can one come between two people who have ceased to have anything in common?"

The veins in Cramier's forehead were swollen, his face and neck had grown crimson. And Lennan thought with strange elation: Now he's going to hit me! He could hardly keep his hands from shooting out and seizing in advance that great strong neck. If he could strangle, and have done with him!

But, quite suddenly, Cramier turned on his heel. "I have warned you," he said, and went.

Lennan took a long breath. So! That was over, and he knew where he was. If Cramier had struck out, he would surely have seized his neck and held on till life was gone. Nothing should have shaken him off. In fancy he could see himself swaying, writhing, reeling, battered about by those heavy fists, but always with his hands on the thick neck, squeezing out its life. He could feel, absolutely feel, the last reel and stagger of that great bulk crashing down, dragging him with it, till it lay upturned, still. He covered his eyes with his hands. . . . Thank God! The fellow had not hit out!

He went to the door, opened it, and stood leaning against the door-post. All was still and drowsy out there in that quiet backwater of a street. Not a soul in sight! How still, for London! Only the birds. In a neighbouring studio someone was playing Chopin. Queer! He had almost forgotten there was such a thing as Chopin. A mazurka! Spinning like some top thing, round and round — weird little tune! . . . Well, and what now? Only one thing certain. Sooner give up life than give her up! Far sooner! Love her, achieve her — or give up everything, and drown to that tune going on and on, that little dancing dirge of summer!

XVI

A t her cottage Olive stood often by the river.

What lay beneath all that bright water — what strange, deep, swaying, life so far below the ruffling of wind, and the shadows of the willow trees? Was love down there, too? Love between sentient things, where it was almost dark; or had all passion climbed up to rustle with the reeds, and float with the water-flowers in the sunlight? Was there colour? Or had colour been drowned? No scent and no music; but movement there would be, for all the dim groping things bending one way to the current — movement, no less than in the aspen-leaves, never quite still, and the winged droves of the clouds. And if it were dark down there, it was dark, too, above the water; and hearts ached, and eyes just as much searched for that which did not come.

To watch it always flowing by to the sea; never looking back, never swaying this way or that; drifting along, quiet as Fate — dark, or glamorous with the gold and moonlight of these beautiful days and nights, when every flower in her garden, in the fields, and along the river banks, was full of sweet life; when dog-roses starred the lanes, and in the wood the bracken was nearly a foot high.

She was not alone there, though she would much rather have been; two days after she left London her Uncle and Aunt had joined her. It was from Cramier they had received their invitation. He himself had not yet been down.

Every night, having parted from Mrs. Ercott and gone up the wide shallow stairs to her room, she would sit down at the window to write to Lennan, one candle beside her — one pale flame for comrade, as it might be his spirit. Every evening she poured out to him her thoughts, and ended always: "Have patience!" She was still waiting for courage to pass that dark hedge of impalpable doubts and fears and scruples, of a dread that she could not make articulate even to herself. Having finished, she would lean out into the night. The Colonel, his black figure cloaked against the dew, would be pacing up and down the lawn, with his goodnight cigar, whose fiery spark she could just discern; and, beyond, her ghostly dovehouse; and, beyond, the river — flowing. Then she would clasp herself close — afraid to stretch out her arms, lest she should be seen.

Each morning she rose early, dressed, and slipped away to the village to post her letter. From the woods across the river wild pigeons would be calling — as though Love itself pleaded with her afresh each day. She was back well before breakfast, to go up to her room and come down again as if for the first time. The Colonel, meeting her on the stairs, or in the hall, would say: "Ah, my dear! just beaten you! Slept well?" And, while her lips touched his cheek, slanted at the proper angle for uncles, he never dreamed that she had been three miles already through the dew.

Now that she was in the throes of an indecision, whose ending, one way or the other, must be so tremendous, now that she was in the very swirl, she let no sign at all escape her; the Colonel and even his wife were deceived into thinking that after all no great harm had been done. It was grateful to them to think so, because of that stewardship at Monte Carlo, of which they could not render too good account. The warm sleepy days, with a little croquet and a little paddling on the river, and much sitting out of doors, when the Colonel would read aloud from Tennyson, were very pleasant. To him — if not to Mrs. Ercott — it was especially jolly to be out of Town 'this confounded crowded time of year.' And so the days of early June went by, each finer than the last.

And then Cramier came down, without warning on a Friday evening. It was hot in London . . . the session dull. . . . The Jubilee turning everything upside down. . . . They were lucky to be out of Town!

A silent dinner — that!

Mrs. Ercott noticed that he drank wine like water, and for minutes at a time fixed his eyes, that looked heavy as if he had not been sleeping, not on his wife's face but on her neck. If Olive really disliked and feared him — as John would have it — she disguised her feelings very well! For so pale a woman she was looking brilliant that night. The sun had caught her cheeks, perhaps. That black low-cut frock suited her, with old Milanese-point lace matching her skin so well, and one carnation, of darkest red, at her breast. Her eyes were really sometimes like black velvet. It suited pale women to have those eyes, that looked so black at night! She was talking, too, and laughing more than usual. One would have said: A wife delighted to welcome her husband! And yet there was something — something in the air, in the feel of things — the lowering fixity of that man's eyes, or — thunder coming, after all this heat! Surely the night was unnaturally still and dark, hardly a breath of air, and so many moths out there, passing the beam of light, like little pale spirits crossing a river! Mrs. Ercott smiled, pleased at that image. Moths! Men were like moths; there were women from whom they could not keep away. Yes, there was something about Olive that drew men to her. Not meretricious — to do her justice, not that at all; but something soft, and-fatal; like one of these candle-flames to the poor moths. John's eyes were never quite as she knew them when he was looking at Olive; and Robert Cramier's — what a queer, drugged look they had! As for that other poor young fellow — she had never forgotten his face when they came on him in the Park!

And when after dinner they sat on the veranda, they were all more silent still, just watching, it seemed, the smoke of their cigarettes, rising quite straight, as though wind had been withdrawn from the world. The Colonel twice endeavoured to speak about the moon: It ought to be up by now! It was going to be full.

And then Cramier said: "Put on that scarf thing, Olive, and come round the garden with me."

Mrs. Ercott admitted to herself now that what John said was true. Just one gleam of eyes, turned quickly this way and that, as a bird looks for escape; and then Olive had got up and quietly gone with him down the path, till their silent figures were lost to sight.

Disturbed to the heart, Mrs. Ercott rose and went over to her husband's chair. He was frowning, and staring at his evening shoe balanced on a single toe. He looked up at her and put out his hand. Mrs. Ercott gave it a squeeze; she wanted comfort.

The Colonel spoke:

"It's heavy tonight, Dolly. I don't like the feel of it."

XVII

They had passed without a single word spoken, down through the laurels and guelder roses to the river bank; then he had turned to the right, and gone along it under the dove-house, to the yew-trees. There he had stopped, in the pitch darkness of that foliage. It seemed to her dreadfully still; if only there had been the faintest breeze, the faintest lisping of reeds on the water, one bird to make a sound; but nothing, nothing save his breathing, deep, irregular, with a quiver in it. What had he brought her here for? To show her how utterly she was his? Was he never going to speak, never going to say whatever it was he had in mind to say? If only he would not touch her!

Then he moved, and a stone dislodged fell with a splash into the water. She could not help a little gasp. How black the river looked! But slowly, beyond the dim shape of the giant poplar, a shiver of light stole outwards across the blackness from the far bank — the moon, whose rim she could now see rising, of a thick gold like a coin, above the woods. Her heart went out to that warm light. At all events there was one friendly inhabitant of this darkness.

Suddenly she felt his hands on her waist. She did not move, her heart beat too furiously; but a sort of prayer fluttered up from it against her lips. In the grip of those heavy hands was such quivering force!

His voice sounded very husky and strange: "Olive, this can't go on. I suffer. My God! I suffer!"

A pang went through her, a sort of surprise. Suffer! She might wish him dead, but she did not want him to suffer — God knew!

And yet, gripped by those hands, she could not say: I am sorry!

He made a sound that was almost a groan, and dropped on his knees. Feeling herself held fast, she tried to push his forehead back from her waist. It was fiery hot; and she heard him mutter: "Have mercy! Love me a little!" But the clutch of his hands, never still on the thin silk of her dress, turned her faint. She tried to writhe away, but could not; stood still again, and at last found her voice.

"Mercy? Can I MAKE myself love? No one ever could since the world began. Please, please get up. Let me go!"

But he was pulling her down to him so that she was forced on to her knees on the grass, with her face close to his. A low moaning was coming from him. It was horrible — so horrible! And he went on pleading, the words all confused, not looking in her face. It seemed to her that it would never end, that she would never get free of that grip, away from that stammering, whispering voice. She stayed by instinct utterly still, closing her eyes. Then she felt his gaze for the first time that evening on her face, and realized that he had not dared to look until her eyes were closed, for fear of reading what was in them. She said very gently:

"Please let me go. I think I'm going to faint."

He relaxed the grip of his arms; she sank down and stayed unmoving on the grass. After such utter stillness that she hardly knew whether he were there or not, she felt his hot hand on her bare shoulder. Was it all to begin again? She shrank down lower still, and a little moan escaped her. He let her go suddenly, and, when at last she looked up, was gone.

She got to her feet trembling, and moved quickly from under the yew-trees. She tried to think — tried to understand exactly what this portended for her, for him, for her lover. But she could not. There was around her thoughts the same breathless darkness that brooded over this night. Ah! but to the night had been given that pale-gold moon-ray, to herself nothing, no faintest gleam; as well try to pierce below the dark surface of that water!

She passed her hands over her face, and hair, and dress. How long had it lasted? How long had they been out here? And she began slowly moving back towards the house. Thank God! She had not yielded to fear or pity, not uttered falsities, not pretended she could love him, and betrayed her heart. That would have been the one unbearable thing to have been left remembering! She stood long looking down, as if trying to see the future in her dim flower-beds; then, bracing herself, hurried to the house. No one was on the veranda, no one in the drawing-room. She looked at the clock. Nearly eleven. Ringing for the servant to shut the windows, she stole up to her room. Had her husband gone away as he had come? Or would she presently again be face to face with that dread, the nerve of which never stopped aching now, dread of the night when he was near? She determined not to go to bed, and drawing a long chair to the window, wrapped herself in a gown, and lay back.

The flower from her dress, miraculously uncrushed in those dark minutes on the grass, she set in water beside her at the window — Mark's favourite flower, he had once told her; it was a comfort, with its scent, and hue, and memory of him.

Strange that in her life, with all the faces seen, and people known, she had not loved one till she had met Lennan! She had even been sure that love would never come to her; had not wanted it — very much; had thought to go on well enough, and pass out at the end, never having known, or much cared to know, full summer. Love had taken its revenge on her now for all slighted love offered her in the past; for the one hated love that had tonight been on its knees to her. They said it must always come once to every man and woman — this witchery, this dark sweet feeling, springing up, who knew how or why? She had not believed, but now she knew. And whatever might be coming, she would not have this different. Since all things changed, she must change and get old and be no longer pretty for him to look at, but this in her heart could not change. She felt sure of that. It was as if something said: This is for ever, beyond life, beyond death, this is for ever! He will be dust, and you dust, but your love will live! Somewhere — in the woods, among the flowers, or down in the dark water, it will haunt! For it only you have lived! ... Then she noticed that a slender silvery-winged thing, unlike any moth she had ever seen, had settled on her gown, close to her neck. It seemed to be sleeping, so delicate and drowsy, having come in from the breathless dark, thinking, perhaps, that her whiteness was a light. What dim memory did it rouse; something of HIM, something HE had done — in darkness, on a night like this. Ah, yes! that evening after Gorbio, the little owl-moth on her knee! He had touched her when he took that cosy wan velvet-eyed thing off her!

She leaned out for air. What a night! — whose stars were hiding in the sheer heavy warmth; whose small, round, golden moon had no transparency! A night like a black pansy with a little gold heart. And silent! For, of the trees, that whispered so much at night, not even the aspens had voice. The unstirring air had a dream-solidity against her cheeks. But in all the stillness, what sentiency, what passion — as in her heart! Could she not draw HIM to her from those woods, from that dark gleaming river, draw him from the flowers and trees and the passion-mood of the sky — draw him up to her waiting here, so that she was no more this craving creature, but one with him and the night! And she let her head droop down on her hands.

All night long she stayed there at the window. Sometimes dozing in the chair; once waking with a start, fancying that her husband was bending over her. Had he been — and stolen away? And the dawn came; dew-grey, filmy and wistful, woven round each black tree, and round the white dove-cot, and falling scarf-like along the river. And the chirrupings of birds stirred among leaves as yet invisible.

She slept then.

XVIII

When she awoke once more, in daylight, smiling, Cramier was standing beside her chair. His face, all dark and bitter, had the sodden look of a man very tired.

"So!" he said: "Sleeping this way doesn't spoil your dreams. Don't let me disturb them. I am just going back to Town."

Like a frightened bird, she stayed, not stirring, gazing at his back as he leaned in the window, till, turning round on her again, he said:

"But remember this: What I can't have, no one else shall! Do you understand? No one else!" And he bent down close, repeating: "Do you understand — you bad wife!"

Four years' submission to a touch she shrank from; one long effort not to shrink! Bad wife! Not if he killed her would she answer now!

"Do you hear?" he said once more: "Make up your mind to that. I mean it."

He had gripped the arms of her chair, till she could feel it quiver beneath her. Would he drive his fist into her face that she managed to keep still smiling? But there only passed into his eyes an expression which she could not read.

"Well," he said, "you know!" and walked heavily towards the door.

The moment he had gone she sprang up: Yes, she was a bad wife! A wife who had reached the end of her tether. A wife who hated instead of loving. A wife in prison! Bad wife! Martyrdom, then, for the sake of a faith in her that was lost already, could be but folly. If she seemed bad and false to him, there was no longer reason to pretend to be otherwise. No longer would she, in the words of the old song: — 'sit and sigh — pulling bracken, pulling bracken.' No more would she starve for want of love, and watch the nights throb and ache, as last night had throbbed and ached, with the passion that she might not satisfy.

And while she was dressing she wondered why she did not look tired. To get out quickly! To send her lover word at once to hasten to her while it was safe — that she might tell him she was coming to him out of prison! She would telegraph for him to come that evening with a boat, opposite the tall poplar. She and her Aunt and Uncle were to go to dinner at the Rectory, but she would plead headache at the last minute. When the Ercotts had gone she would slip out, and he and she would row over to the wood, and be together for two hours of happiness. And they must make a clear plan, too — for tomorrow they would begin their life together. But it would not be safe to send that message from the village; she must go down and over the bridge to the post-office on the other side, where they did not know her. It was too late now before breakfast. Better after, when she could slip away, knowing for certain that her husband had gone. It would still not be too late for her telegram — Lennan never left his rooms till the midday post which brought her letters.

She finished dressing, and knowing that she must show no trace of her excitement, sat quite still for several minutes, forcing herself into languor. Then she went down. Her husband had breakfasted and gone. At everything she did, and every word she spoke, she was now smiling with a sort of wonder, as if she were watching a self, that she had abandoned like an old garment, perform for her amusement. It even gave her no feeling of remorse to think she was going to do what would be so painful to the good Colonel. He was dear to her — but it did not matter. She was past all that. Nothing mattered — nothing in the world! It amused her to believe that her Uncle and Aunt misread her last night's walk in the dark garden, misread her languor and serenity. And at the first moment possible she flew out, and slipped away under cover of the yew-trees towards the river. Passing the spot where her husband had dragged her down to him on her knees in the grass, she felt a sort of surprise that she could ever have been so terrified. What was he? The past — nothing! And she flew on. She noted carefully the river bank opposite the tall poplar. It would be quite easy to get down from there into a boat. But they would not stay in that dark backwater. They would go over to the far side into those woods from which last night the moon had risen, those woods from which the pigeons mocked her every morning, those woods so full of summer. Coming back, no one would see her landing; for it would be pitch dark in the backwater. And, while she hurried, she looked back across her shoulder, marking where the water, entering, ceased to be bright. A dragon-fly brushed her cheek; she saw it vanish where the sunlight failed. How suddenly its happy flight was quenched in that dark shade, as a candle flame blown out. The tree growth there was too thick — the queer stumps and snags had uncanny shapes, as of monstrous creatures, whose eyes seemed to peer out at you. She shivered. She had seen those monsters with their peering eyes somewhere. Ah! In her dream at Monte Carlo of that bull-face staring from the banks, while she drifted by, unable to cry out. No! The backwater was not a happy place — they would not stay there a single minute. And more swiftly than ever she flew on along the path. Soon she had crossed the bridge, sent off her message, and returned. But there were ten hours to get through before eight o'clock, and she did not hurry now. She wanted this day of summer to herself alone, a day of dreaming till he came; this day for which all her life till now had been shaping her — the day of love. Fate was very wonderful! If she had ever loved before; if she had known joy in her marriage — she could never have been feeling what she was feeling now, what she well knew she would never feel again. She crossed a new-mown hayfield, and finding a bank, threw herself down on her back among its uncut grasses. Far away at the other end men were scything. It was all very beautiful — the soft clouds floating, the clover-stalks pushing themselves against her palms, and stems of the tall couch grass cool to her cheeks; little blue butterflies; a lark, invisible; the scent of the ripe hay; and the gold-fairy arrows of the sun on her face and limbs. To grow and reach the hour of summer; all must do that! That was the meaning of Life! She had no more doubts and fears. She had no more dread, no bitterness, and no remorse for what she was going to do. She was doing it because she must. . . . As well might grass stay its ripening because it shall be cut down! She had, instead, a sense of something blessed and uplifting. Whatever Power had made her heart, had placed within it this love. Whatever it was, whoever it was, could not be angry with her!

A wild bee settled on her arm, and she held it up between her and the sun, so that she might enjoy its dusky glamour. It would not sting her — not today! The little blue butterflies, too, kept alighting on her, who lay there so still. And the love-songs of the wood-pigeons never ceased, nor the faint swish of scything.

At last she rose to make her way home. A telegram had come saying simply: "Yes." She read it with an unmoved face, having resorted again to her mask of languor. Toward tea-time she confessed to headache, and said she would lie down. Up there in her room she spent those three hours writing — writing as best she could all she had passed through in thought and feeling, before making her decision. It seemed to her that she owed it to herself to tell her lover how she had come to what she had never thought to come to. She put what she had written in an envelope and sealed it. She would give it to him, that he might read and understand, when she had shown him with all of her how she loved him. It would pass the time for him, until tomorrow — until they set out on their new life together. For tonight they would make their plans, and tomorrow start.

At half-past seven she sent word that her headache was too bad to allow her to go out. This brought a visit from Mrs. Ercott: The Colonel and she were so distressed; but perhaps Olive was wise not to exert herself! And presently the Colonel himself spoke, lugubriously through the door: Not well enough to come? No fun without her! But she mustn't on any account strain herself! No, no!

Her heart smote her at that. He was always so good to her.

At last, watching from the corridor, she saw them sally forth down the drive — the Colonel a little in advance, carrying his wife's evening shoes. How nice he looked — with his brown face, and his grey moustache; so upright, and concerned with what he had in hand!

There was no languor in her now. She had dressed in white, and now she took a blue silk cloak with a hood, and caught up the flower that had so miraculously survived last night's wearing and pinned it at her breast. Then making sure no servant was about, she slipped downstairs and out. It was just eight, and the sun still glistened on the dovecote. She kept away from that lest the birds should come fluttering about her, and betray her by cooing. When she had nearly reached the tow-path, she stopped affrighted. Surely something had moved, something heavy, with a sound of broken branches. Was it the memory of last night come on her again; or, indeed, someone there? She walked back a few steps. Foolish alarm! In the meadow beyond a cow was brushing against the hedge. And, stealing along the grass, out on to the tow-path, she went swiftly towards the poplar.

XIX

A hundred times in these days of her absence Lennan had been on the point of going down, against her orders, just to pass the house, just to feel himself within reach, to catch a glimpse of her, perhaps, from afar. If his body haunted London, his spirit had passed down on to that river where he had drifted once already, reconnoitring. A hundred times — by day in fancy, and by night in dreams — pulling himself along by the boughs, he stole down that dim backwater, till the dark yews and the white dovecote came into view.

For he thought now only of fulfilment. She was wasting cruelly away! Why should he leave her where she was? Leave her to profane herself and all womanhood in the arms of a man she hated?

And on that day of mid-June, when he received her telegram, it was as if he had been handed the key of Paradise.

Would she — could she mean to come away with him that very night? He would prepare for that at all events. He had so often in mind faced this crisis in his affairs, that now it only meant translating into action what had been carefully thought out. He packed, supplied himself liberally with money, and wrote a long letter to his guardian. It would hurt the old man — Gordy was over seventy now — but that could not be helped. He would not post it till he knew for certain.

After telling how it had all come about, he went on thus: "I know that to many people, and perhaps to you, Gordy, it will seem very wrong, but it does not to me, and that is the simple truth. Everybody has his own views on such things, I suppose;

and as I would not — on my honour, Gordy — ever have held or wished to hold, or ever will hold in marriage or out of marriage, any woman who does not love me, so I do not think it is acting as I would resent others acting towards me, to take away from such unhappiness this lady for whom I would die at any minute. I do not mean to say that pity has anything to do with it — I thought so at first, but I know now that it is all swallowed up in the most mighty feeling I have ever had or ever shall have. I am not a bit afraid of conscience. If God is Universal Truth, He cannot look hardly upon us for being true to ourselves. And as to people, we shall just hold up our heads; I think that they generally take you at your own valuation. But, anyway, Society does not much matter. We shan't want those who don't want us — you may be sure. I hope he will divorce her quickly — there is nobody much to be hurt by that except you and Cis; but if he doesn't — it can't be helped. I don't think she has anything; but with my six hundred, and what I can make, even if we have to live abroad, we shall be all right for money. You have been awfully good to me always, Gordy, and I am very grieved to hurt you, and still more sorry if you think I am being ungrateful; but when one feels as I do — body and soul and spirit — there isn't any question; there wouldn't be if death itself stood in the way. If you receive this, we shall be gone together; I will write to you from wherever we pitch our tent, and, of course, I shall write to Cicely. But will you please tell Mrs. Doone and Sylvia, and give them my love if they still care to have it. Goodbye, dear Gordy. I believe you would have done the same, if you had been I. Always your affectionate — MARK."

In all those preparations he forgot nothing, employing every minute of the few hours in a sort of methodic exaltation. The last thing before setting out he took the damp cloths off his 'bull-man.' Into the face of the monster there had come of late a hungry, yearning look. The artist in him had done his work that unconscious justice; against his will had set down the truth. And, wondering whether he would ever work at it again, he redamped the cloths and wrapped it carefully.

He did not go to her village, but to one five or six miles down the river — it was safer, and the row would steady him. Hiring a skiff, he pulled up stream. He travelled very slowly to kill time, keeping under the far bank. And as he pulled, his very heart seemed parched with nervousness. Was it real that he was going to her, or only some fantastic trick of Fate, a dream from which he would wake to find himself alone again? He passed the dovecote at last, and kept on till he could round into the backwater and steal up under cover to the poplar. He arrived a few minutes before eight o'clock, turned the boat round, and waited close beneath the bank, holding to a branch, and standing so that he could see the path. If a man could die from longing and anxiety, surely Lennan must have died then!

All wind had failed, and the day was fallen into a wonderful still evening. Gnats were dancing in the sparse strips of sunlight that slanted across the dark water, now that the sun was low. From the fields, bereft of workers, came the scent of hay and the heavy scent of meadow-sweet; the musky odour of the backwater was confused with them into one brooding perfume. No one passed. And sounds were few and far to that wistful listener, for birds did not sing just there. How still and warm was the air, yet seemed to vibrate against his cheeks as though about to break into flame. That fancy came to him vividly while he stood waiting — a vision of heat simmering in little pale red flames. On the thick reeds some large, slow, dusky flies were still feeding, and now and then a moorhen a few yards away splashed a little, or uttered a sharp, shrill note. When she came — if she did come! — they would not stay here, in this dark earthy backwater; he would take her over to the other side, away to the woods! But the minutes passed, and his heart sank. Then it leaped up. Someone was coming — in white, with bare head, and something blue or black flung across her arm. It was she! No one else walked like that! She came very quickly. And he noticed that her hair looked like little wings on either side of her brow, as if her face were a white bird with dark wings, flying to love! Now she was close, so close that he could see her lips parted, and her eyes love-lighted — like nothing in the world but darkness wild with dew and starlight. He reached up and lifted her down into the boat, and the scent of some flower pressed against his face seemed to pierce into him and reach his very heart, awakening the memory of something past, forgotten. Then, seizing the branches, snapping them in his haste, he dragged the skiff along through the sluggish water, the gnats dancing in his face. She seemed to know where he was taking her, and neither of them spoke a single word, while he pulled out into the open, and over to the far bank.

There was but one field between them and the wood — a field of young wheat, with a hedge of thorn and alder. And close to that hedge they set out, their hands clasped. They had nothing to say yet — like children saving up. She had put on her cloak to hide her dress, and its silk swished against the silvery blades of the wheat. What had moved her to put on this blue cloak? Blue of the sky, and flowers, of birds' wings, and the black-burning blue of the night! The hue of all holy things! And how still it was in the late gleam of the sun! Not one little sound of beast or bird or tree; not one bee humming! And not much colour — only the starry white hemlocks and globe-campion flowers, and the low-flying glamour of the last warm light on the wheat.

XX

. . . Now over wood and river the evening drew in fast. And first the swallows, that had looked as if they would never stay their hunting, ceased; and the light, that had seemed fastened above the world, for all its last brightenings, slowly fell wingless and dusky.

The moon would not rise till ten! And all things waited. The creatures of night were slow to come forth after that long bright summer's day, watching for the shades of the trees to sink deeper and deeper into the now chalk-white water; watching for the chalk-white face of the sky to be masked with velvet. The very black-plumed trees themselves seemed to wait in suspense for the grape-bloom of night. All things stared, wan in that hour of passing day — all things had eyes wistful and unblessed. In those moments glamour was so dead that it was as if meaning had abandoned the earth. But not for long. Winged with darkness, it stole back; not the soul of meaning that had gone, but a witch-like and brooding spirit harbouring in the black trees, in the high dark spears of the rushes, and on the grim-snouted snags that lurked along the river bank. Then the owls came out, and night-flying things. And in the wood there began a cruel bird-tragedy — some dark pursuit in the twilight above the bracken; the piercing shrieks of a creature into whom talons have again and again gone home; and mingled with them, hoarse raging cries of triumph. Many minutes they lasted, those noises of the night, sound-emblems of all the cruelty in the heart of Nature; till at last death appeased that savagery. And any soul abroad, that pitied fugitives, might once more listen, and not weep. . . .

Then a nightingale began to give forth its long liquid gurgling; and a corn-crake churred in the young wheat. Again the night brooded, in the silent tops of the trees, in the more silent depths of the water. It sent out at long intervals a sigh or murmur, a tiny scuttling splash, an owl's hunting cry. And its breath was still hot and charged with heavy odour, for no dew was falling. . . .

XXI

It was past ten when they came out from the wood. She had wanted to wait for the moon to rise; not a gold coin of a moon as last night, but ivory pale, and with a gleaming radiance level over the fern, and covering the lower boughs, as it were, with a drift of white blossom.

Through the wicket gate they passed once more beside the moon-coloured wheat, which seemed of a different world from that world in which they had walked but an hour and a half ago.

And in Lennan's heart was a feeling such as a man's heart can only know once in all his life — such humble gratitude, and praise, and adoration of her who had given him her all. There should be nothing for her now but joy — like the joy of this last hour. She should never know less happiness! And kneeling down before her at the water's edge he kissed her dress, and hands, and feet, which tomorrow would be his forever.

Then they got into the boat.

The smile of the moonlight glided over each ripple, and reed, and closing water-lily; over her face, where the hood had fallen back from her loosened hair; over one hand trailing the water, and the other touching the flower at her breast; and, just above her breath, she said:

"Row, my dear love; it's late!"

Dipping his sculls, he shot the skiff into the darkness of the backwater. . . .

What happened then he never knew, never clearly — in all those after years. A vision of her white form risen to its feet, bending forward like a creature caught, that cannot tell which way to spring; a crashing shock, his head striking something hard! Nothingness! And then — an awful, awful struggle with roots and weeds and slime, a desperate agony of groping in that pitchy blackness, among tree-stumps, in dead water that seemed to have no bottom — he and that other, who had leaped at them in the dark with his boat, like a murdering beast; a nightmare search more horrible than words could tell, till in a patch of moonlight on the bank they laid her, who for all their efforts never stirred. . . . There she lay all white, and they two crouched at her head and feet — like dark creatures of the woods and waters over that which with their hunting they had slain.

How long they stayed there, not once looking at each other, not once speaking, not once ceasing to touch with their hands that dead thing — he never knew. How long in the summer night, with its moonlight and its shadows quivering round them, and the night wind talking in the reeds!

And then the most enduring of all sentient things had moved in him again; so that he once more felt. . . . Never again to see those eyes that had loved him with their light! Never again to kiss her lips! Frozen — like moonlight to the earth, with the flower still clinging at her breast. Thrown out on the bank like a plucked water-lily! Dead? No, no! Not dead! Alive in the night — alive to him — somewhere! Not on this dim bank, in this hideous backwater, with that dark dumb creature who had destroyed her! Out there on the river — in the wood of their happiness — somewhere alive! . . . And, staggering up past Cramier, who never moved, he got into his boat, and like one demented pulled out into the stream.

But once there in the tide, he fell huddled forward, motionless above his oars. . . .

And the moonlight flooded his dark skiff drifting down. And the moonlight effaced the ripples on the water that had stolen away her spirit. Her spirit mingled now with the white beauty and the shadows, for ever part of the stillness and the passion of a summer night; hovering, floating, listening to the rustle of the reeds, and the whispering of the woods; one with the endless dream — that spirit passing out, as all might wish to pass, in the hour of happiness.

PART III — AUTUMN

I

When on that November night Lennan stole to the open door of his dressing-room, and stood watching his wife asleep, Fate still waited for an answer.

A low fire was burning — one of those fires that throw faint shadows everywhere, and once and again glow so that some object shines for a moment, some shape is clearly seen. The curtains were not quite drawn, and a plane-tree branch with leaves still hanging, which had kept them company all the fifteen years they had lived there, was moving darkly in the wind, now touching the glass with a frail tap, as though asking of him, who had been roaming in that wind so many hours, to let it in. Unfailing comrades — London plane-trees!

He had not dared hope that Sylvia would be asleep. It was merciful that she was, whichever way the issue went — that issue so cruel. Her face was turned towards the fire, and one hand rested beneath her cheek. So she often slept. Even when life seemed all at sea, its landmarks lost, one still did what was customary. Poor tenderhearted thing — she had not slept since he told her, forty-eight hours, that seemed such years, ago! With her flaxen hair, and her touching candour, even in sleep, she looked like a girl lying there, not so greatly changed from what she had been that summer of Cicely's marriage down at Hayle. Her face had not grown old in all those twenty-eight years. There had been till now no special reason why it should. Thought, strong feeling, suffering, those were what changed faces; Sylvia had never thought very deeply, never suffered much, till now. And was it for him, who had been careful of her — very careful on the whole, despite man's selfishness, despite her never having understood the depths of him — was it for him of all people to hurt her so, to stamp her face with sorrow, perhaps destroy her utterly?

He crept a little farther in and sat down in the arm-chair beyond the fire. What memories a fire gathered into it, with its flaky ashes, its little leaf-like flames, and that quiet glow and flicker! What tale of passions! How like to a fire was a man's heart! The first young fitful leapings, the sudden, fierce, mastering heat, the long, steady sober burning, and then — that last flaming-up, that clutch back at its own vanished youth, the final eager flight of flame, before the ashes wintered it to nothing! Visions and memories he saw down in the fire, as only can be seen when a man's heart, by the agony of long struggle, has been stripped of skin, and quivers at every touch. Love! A strange haphazard thing was love — so spun between ecstacy and torture! A thing insidious, irresponsible, desperate. A flying sweetness, more poignant than anything on earth, more dark in origin and destiny. A thing without reason or coherence. A man's love-life — what say had he in the ebb and flow of it? No more than in the flights of autumn birds, swooping down, alighting here and there, passing on. The loves one left behind — even in a life by no means vagabond in love, as men's lives went! The love that thought the Tyrol skies would fall if he were not first with a certain lady. The love whose star had caught in the hair of Sylvia, now lying there asleep. A so-called love — that half-glamorous, yet sordid little meal of pleasure, which youth, however sensitive, must eat, it seems, some time or other with some young light of love — a glimpse of life that beforehand had seemed much and had meant little, save to leave him disillusioned with himself and sorry for his partner. And then the love that he could not, even after twenty years, bear to remember; that all-devouring summer passion, which in one night had gained all and lost all terribly, leaving on his soul a scar that could never be quite healed, leaving his spirit always a little lonely, haunted by the sense of what might have been. Of his share in that night of tragedy — that 'terrible accident on the river' — no one had ever dreamed. And then the long despair which had seemed the last death of love had slowly passed, and yet another love had been born — or rather born again, pale, sober, but quite real; the fresh springing-up of a feeling long forgotten, of that protective devotion of his boyhood. He still remembered the expression on Sylvia's face when he passed her by chance in Oxford Street, soon after he came back from his four years of exile in the East and Rome — that look, eager, yet reproachful, then stoically ironic, as if saying: 'Oh, no! after forgetting me four years and more — you can't remember me now!' And when he spoke, the still more touching pleasure in her face. Then uncertain months, with a feeling of what the end would be; and then their marriage. Happy enough — gentle, not very vivid, nor spiritually very intimate — his work always secretly as remote from her as when she had thought to please him by putting jessamine stars on the heads of his beasts. A quiet successful union, not meaning, he had thought, so very much to him nor so very much to her — until forty-eight hours ago he told her; and she had shrunk, and wilted, and gone all to pieces. And what was it he had told her?

A long story — that!

Sitting there by the fire, with nothing yet decided, he could see it all from the start, with its devilish, delicate intricacy, its subtle slow enchantment spinning itself out of him, out of his own state of mind and body, rather than out of the spell cast over him, as though a sort of fatal force, long dormant, were working up again to burst into dark flower. . . .

II

Yes, it had begun within him over a year ago, with a queer unhappy restlessness, a feeling that life was slipping, ebbing away within reach of him, and his arms never stretched out to arrest it. It had begun with a sort of long craving, stilled only when he was working hard — a craving for he knew not what, an ache which was worst whenever the wind was soft.

They said that about forty-five was a perilous age for a man — especially for an artist. All the autumn of last year he had felt this vague misery rather badly. It had left him alone most of December and January, while he was working so hard at his group of lions; but the moment that was finished it had gripped him hard again. In those last days of January he well remembered wandering about in the parks day after day, trying to get away from it. Mild weather, with a scent in the wind! With what avidity he had watched children playing, the premature buds on the bushes, anything, everything young — with what an ache, too, he had been conscious of innumerable lives being lived round him, and loves loved, and he outside, unable to know, to grasp, to gather them; and all the time the sands of his hourglass running out! A most absurd and unreasonable feeling for a man with everything he wanted, with work that he loved, quite enough money, and a wife so good as Sylvia — a feeling that no Englishman of forty-six, in excellent health, ought for a moment to have been troubled with. A feeling such as, indeed, no Englishman ever admitted having — so that there was not even, as yet, a Society for its suppression. For what was this disquiet feeling, but the sense that he had had his day, would never again know the stir and fearful joy of falling in love, but only just hanker after what was past and gone! Could anything be more reprehensible in a married man?

It was — yes — the last day of January, when, returning from one of those restless rambles in Hyde Park, he met Dromore. Queer to recognize a man hardly seen since school-days. Yet unmistakably, Johnny Dromore, sauntering along the rails of Piccadilly on the Green Park side, with that slightly rolling gait of his thin, horseman's legs, his dandified hat a little to one side, those strange, chaffing, goggling eyes, that look, as if making a perpetual bet. Yes — the very same teasing, now moody, now reckless, always astute Johnny Dromore, with a good heart beneath an outside that seemed ashamed of it. Truly to have shared a room at school — to have been at College together, were links mysteriously indestructible.

"Mark Lennan! By gum! haven't seen you for ages. Not since you turned out a full-blown — what d'you call it? Awfully glad to meet you, old chap!" Here was the past indeed, long vanished in feeling and thought and all; and Lennan's head buzzed, trying to find some common interest with this hunting, racing man-about-town.

Johnny Dromore come to life again — he whom the Machine had stamped with astute simplicity by the time he was twenty-two, and for ever after left untouched in thought and feeling — Johnny Dromore, who would never pass beyond the philosophy that all was queer and freakish which had not to do with horses, women, wine, cigars, jokes, good-heartedness, and that perpetual bet; Johnny Dromore, who, somewhere in him, had a pocket of depth, a streak of hunger, that was not just Johnny Dromore.

How queer was the sound of that jerky talk!

"You ever see old Fookes now? Been racin' at all? You live in Town? Remember good old Blenker?" And then silence, and then another spurt: "Ever go down to 'Bambury's? 'Ever go racin'? . . . Come on up to my 'digs.' You've got nothin' to do."

No persuading Johnny Dromore that a 'what d'you call it' could have anything to do. "Come on, old chap. I've got the hump. It's this damned east wind."

Well he remembered it, when they shared a room at 'Bambury's' — that hump of Johnny Dromore's, after some reckless spree or bout of teasing.

And down that narrow bye-street of Piccadilly he had gone, and up into those 'digs' on the first floor, with their little dark hall, their Van Beers' drawing and Vanity Fair cartoons, and prints of racehorses, and of the old Nightgown Steeplechase; with the big chairs, and all the paraphernalia of Race Guides and race-glasses, fox-masks and stags'-horns, and hunting-whips. And yet, something that from the first moment struck him as not quite in keeping, foreign to the picture — a little jumble of books, a vase of flowers, a grey kitten.

"Sit down, old chap. What'll you drink?"

Sunk into the recesses of a marvellous chair, with huge arms of tawny leather, he listened and spoke drowsily. 'Bambury's,' 'Oxford, Gordy's clubs — dear old Gordy, gone now! — things long passed by; they seemed all round him once again. And yet, always that vague sense, threading this resurrection, threading the smoke of their cigars, and Johnny Dromore's clipped talk — of something that did not quite belong. Might it be, perhaps, that sepia drawing — above the 'Tantalus' on the oak sideboard at the far end — of a woman's face gazing out into the room? Mysteriously unlike everything else, except the flowers, and this kitten that was pushing its furry little head against his hand. Odd how a single thing sometimes took possession of a room, however remote in spirit! It seemed to reach like a shadow over Dromore's outstretched limbs, and weathered, long-nosed face, behind his huge cigar; over the queer, solemn, chaffing eyes, with something brooding in the depths of them.

"Ever get the hump? Bally awful, isn't it? It's getting old. We're bally old, you know, Lenny!" Ah! No one had called him 'Lenny' for twenty years. And it was true; they were unmentionably old.

"When a fellow begins to feel old, you know, it's time he went broke — or something; doesn't bear sittin' down and lookin' at. Come out to 'Monte' with me!"

'Monte! 'That old wound, never quite healed, started throbbing at the word, so that he could hardly speak his: "No, I don't care for 'Monte'."

And, at once, he saw Dromore's eyes probing, questioning: "You married?"

"Yes."

"Never thought of you as married!"

So Dromore did think of him. Queer! He never thought of Johnny Dromore.

"Winter's bally awful, when you're not huntin'. You've changed a lot; should hardly have known you. Last time I saw you, you'd just come back from Rome or somewhere. What's it like bein' a — a sculptor? Saw something of yours once. Ever do things of horses?"

Yes; he had done a 'relief' of ponies only last year.

"You do women, too, I s'pose?"

"Not often."

The eyes goggled slightly. Quaint, that unholy interest! Just like boys, the Johnny Dromores — would never grow up, no matter how life treated them. If Dromore spoke out his soul, as he used to speak it out at 'Bambury's,' he would say: 'You get a pull there; you have a bally good time, I expect.' That was the way it took them; just a converse manifestation of the very same feeling towards Art that the pious Philistines had, with their deploring eyebrows and their 'peril to the soul'. Babes all! Not a glimmering of what Art meant — of its effort, and its yearnings!

"You make money at it?"

"Oh, yes."

Again that appreciative goggle, as who should say: 'Ho! there's more in this than I thought!'

A long silence, then, in the dusk with the violet glimmer from outside the windows, the fire flickering in front of them, the grey kitten purring against his neck, the smoke of their cigars going up, and such a strange, dozing sense of rest, as he had not known for many days. And then — something, someone at the door, over by the sideboard! And Dromore speaking in a queer voice:

"Come in, Nell! D'you know my daughter?"

A hand took Lennan's, a hand that seemed to waver between the aplomb of a woman of the world, and a child's impulsive warmth. And a voice, young, clipped, clear, said:

"How d'you do? She's rather sweet, isn't she — my kitten?"

Then Dromore turned the light up. A figure fairly tall, in a grey riding-habit, stupendously well cut; a face not quite so round as a child's nor so shaped as a woman's, blushing slightly, very calm; crinkly light-brown hair tied back with a black ribbon under a neat hat; and eyes like those eyes of Gainsborough's 'Perdita' — slow, grey, mesmeric, with long lashes curling up, eyes that draw things to them, still innocent.

And just on the point of saying: "I thought you'd stepped out of that picture" — he saw Dromore's face, and mumbled instead:

"So it's YOUR kitten?"

"Yes; she goes to everybody. Do you like Persians? She's all fur really. Feel!"

Entering with his fingers the recesses of the kitten, he said:

"Cats without fur are queer."

"Have you seen one without fur?"

"Oh, yes! In my profession we have to go below fur — I'm a sculptor."

"That must be awfully interesting."

What a woman of the world! But what a child, too! And now he could see that the face in the sepia drawing was older altogether — lips not so full, look not so innocent, cheeks not so round, and something sad and desperate about it — a face that life had rudely touched. But the same eyes it had — and what charm, for all its disillusionment, its air of a history! Then he noticed, fastened to the frame, on a thin rod, a dust-coloured curtain, drawn to one side. The self-possessed young voice was saying:

"Would you mind if I showed you my drawings? It would be awfully good of you. You could tell me about them." And with dismay he saw her open a portfolio. While he scrutinized those schoolgirl drawings, he could feel her looking at him, as animals do when they are making up their minds whether or no to like you; then she came and stood so close that her arm pressed his. He redoubled his efforts to find something good about the drawings. But in truth there was nothing good. And if, in other matters, he could lie well enough to save people's feelings, where Art was concerned he never could; so he merely said:

"You haven't been taught, you see."

"Will you teach me?"

But before he could answer, she was already effacing that naive question in her most grown-up manner.

"Of course I oughtn't to ask. It would bore you awfully."

After that he vaguely remembered Dromore's asking if he ever rode in the Row; and those eyes of hers following him about; and her hand giving his another childish squeeze. Then he was on his way again down the dimly-lighted stairs, past an interminable array of Vanity Fair cartoons, out into the east wind.

III

Crossing the Green Park on his way home, was he more, or less, restless? Difficult to say. A little flattered, certainly, a little warmed; yet irritated, as always when he came into contact with people to whom the world of Art was such an amusing unreality. The notion of trying to show that child how to draw — that feather-pate, with her riding and her kitten; and her 'Perdita' eyes! Quaint, how she had at once made friends with him! He was a little different, perhaps, from what she was accustomed to. And how daintily she spoke! A strange, attractive, almost lovely child! Certainly not more than seventeen — and — Johnny Dromore's daughter!

The wind was bitter, the lamps bright among the naked trees. Beautiful always — London at night, even in January, even in an east wind, with a beauty he never tired of. Its great, dark, chiselled shapes, its gleaming lights, like droves of flying stars come to earth; and all warmed by the beat and stir of innumerable lives — those lives that he ached so to know and to be part of.

He told Sylvia of his encounter. Dromore! The name struck her. She had an old Irish song, 'The Castle of Dromore,' with a queer, haunting refrain.

It froze hard all the week, and he began a life-size group of their two sheep-dogs. Then a thaw set in with that first south-west wind, which brings each February a feeling of Spring such as is never again recaptured, and men's senses, like sleepy bees in the sun, go roving. It awakened in him more violently than ever the thirst to be living, knowing, loving — the craving for something new. Not this, of course, took him back to Dromore's rooms; oh, no! just friendliness, since he had not even told his old room-mate where he lived, or said that his wife would be glad to make his acquaintance, if he cared to come round. For Johnny Dromore had assuredly not seemed too happy, under all his hard-bitten air. Yes! it was but friendly to go again.

Dromore was seated in his long arm-chair, a cigar between his lips, a pencil in his hand, a Ruff's Guide on his knee; beside him was a large green book. There was a festive air about him, very different from his spasmodic gloom of the other day; and he murmured without rising:

"Halo, old man! — glad to see you. Take a pew. Look here! Agapemone — which d'you think I ought to put her to — San Diavolo or Ponte Canet? — not more than four crosses of St. Paul. Goin' to get a real good one from her this time!"

He, who had never heard these sainted names, answered:

"Oh! Ponte Canet, without doubt. But if you're working I'll come in another time."

"Lord! no! Have a smoke. I'll just finish lookin' out their blood — and take a pull."

And so Lennan sat down to watch those researches, wreathed in cigar smoke and punctuated by muttered expletives. They were as sacred and absorbing, no doubt, as his own efforts to create in clay; for before Dromore's inner vision was the perfect racehorse — he, too, was creating. Here was no mere dodge for making money, but a process hallowed by the peculiar sensation felt when one rubbed the palms of the hands together, the sensation that accompanied all creative achievement. Once only Dromore paused to turn his head and say:

"Bally hard, gettin' a taproot right!"

Real Art! How well an artist knew that desperate search after the point of balance, the central rivet that must be found before a form would come to life. . . . And he noted that today there was no kitten, no flowers, no sense at all of an extraneous presence — even the picture was curtained. Had the girl been just a dream — a fancy conjured up by his craving after youth?

Then he saw that Dromore had dropped the large green book, and was standing before the fire.

"Nell took to you the other day. But you always were a lady's man. Remember the girl at Coaster's?"

Coaster's tea-shop, where he would go every afternoon that he had money, just for the pleasure of looking shyly at a face. Something beautiful to look at — nothing more! Johnny Dromore would no better understand that now than when they were at 'Bambury's.'

Not the smallest good even trying to explain! He looked up at the goggling eyes; he heard the bantering voice:

"I say — you ARE goin' grey. We're bally old, Lenny! A fellow gets old when he marries."

And he answered:

"By the way, I never knew that YOU had been."

From Dromore's face the chaffing look went, like a candle-flame blown out; and a coppery flush spread over it. For some seconds he did not speak, then, jerking his head towards the picture, he muttered gruffly:

"Never had the chance of marrying, there; Nell's 'outside.'"

A sort of anger leaped in Lennan; why should Dromore speak that word as if he were ashamed of his own daughter? Just like his sort — none so hidebound as men-about-town! Flotsam on the tide of other men's opinions; poor devils adrift, without the one true anchorage of their own real feelings! And doubtful whether Dromore would be pleased, or think him gushing, or even distrustful of his morality, he said:

"As for that, it would only make any decent man or woman nicer to her. When is she going to let me teach her drawing?"

Dromore crossed the room, drew back the curtain of the picture, and in a muffled voice, said:

"My God, Lenny! Life's unfair. Nell's coming killed her mother. I'd rather it had been me — bar chaff! Women have no luck."

Lennan got up from his comfortable chair. For, startled out of the past, the memory of that summer night, when yet another woman had no luck, was flooding his heart with its black, inextinguishable grief. He said quietly:

"The past IS past, old man."

Dromore drew the curtain again across the picture, and came back to the fire. And for a full minute he stared into it.

"What am I to do with Nell? She's growing up."

"What have you done with her so far?"

"She's been at school. In the summer she goes to Ireland — I've got a bit of an old place there. She'll be eighteen in July. I shall have to introduce her to women, and all that. It's the devil! How? Who?"

Lennan could only murmur: "My wife, for one."

He took his leave soon after. Johnny Dromore! Bizarre guardian for that child! Queer life she must have of it, in that bachelor's den, surrounded by Ruff's Guides! What would become of her? Caught up by some young spark about town; married to him, no doubt — her father would see to the thoroughness of that, his standard of respectability was evidently high! And after — go the way, maybe, of her mother — that poor thing in the picture with the alluring, desperate face. Well! It was no business of his!

IV

No business of his! The merest sense of comradeship, then, took him once more to Dromore's after that disclosure, to prove that the word 'outside' had no significance save in his friend's own fancy; to assure him again that Sylvia would be very glad to welcome the child at any time she liked to come.

When he had told her of that little matter of Nell's birth, she had been silent a long minute, looking in his face, and then had said: "Poor child! I wonder if SHE knows! People are so unkind, even nowadays!" He could not himself think of anyone who would pay attention to such a thing, except to be kinder to the girl; but in such matters Sylvia was the better judge, in closer touch with general thought. She met people that he did not — and of a more normal species.

It was rather late when he got to Dromore's diggings on that third visit.

"Mr. Dromore, sir," the man said — he had one of those strictly confidential faces bestowed by an all-wise Providence on servants in the neighbourhood of Piccadilly — "Mr. Dromore, sir, is not in. But he will be almost sure to be in to dress. Miss Nell is in, sir."

And there she was, sitting at the table, pasting photographs into an album — lonely young creature in that abode of male middle-age! Lennan stood, unheard, gazing at the back of her head, with its thick crinkly-brown hair tied back on her dark-red frock. And, to the confidential man's soft:

"Mr. Lennan, miss," he added a softer: "May I come in?"

She put her hand into his with intense composure.

"Oh, yes, do! if you don't mind the mess I'm making;" and, with a little squeeze of the tips of his fingers, added: "Would it bore you to see my photographs?"

And down they sat together before the photographs — snapshots of people with guns or fishing-rods, little groups of schoolgirls, kittens, Dromore and herself on horseback, and several of a young man with a broad, daring, rather good-looking face. "That's Oliver — Oliver Dromore — Dad's first cousin once removed. Rather nice, isn't he? Do you like his expression?"

Lennan did not know. Not her second cousin; her father's first cousin once removed! And again there leaped in him that unreasoning flame of indignant pity.

"And how about drawing? You haven't come to be taught yet."

She went almost as red as her frock.

"I thought you were only being polite. I oughtn't to have asked. Of course, I want to awfully — only I know it'll bore you."

"It won't at all."

She looked up at that. What peculiar languorous eyes they were!

"Shall I come tomorrow, then?"

"Any day you like, between half-past twelve and one."

"Where?"

He took out a card.

"Mark Lennan — yes — I like your name. I liked it the other day. It's awfully nice!"

What was in a name that she should like him because of it? His fame as a sculptor — such as it was — could have nothing to do with that, for she would certainly not know of it. Ah! but there was a lot in a name — for children. In his childhood what fascination there had been in the words macaroon, and Spaniard, and Carinola, and Aldebaran, and Mr. McCrae. For quite a week the whole world had been Mr. McCrae — a most ordinary friend of Gordy's.

By whatever fascination moved, she talked freely enough now —

of her school; of riding and motoring — she seemed to love going very fast; about Newmarket — which was 'perfect'; and theatres — plays of the type that Johnny Dromore might be expected to approve; these together with 'Hamlet' and 'King Lear' were all she had seen. Never was a girl so untouched by thought, or Art — yet not stupid, having, seemingly, a certain natural good taste; only, nothing, evidently, had come her way. How could it — 'Johnny Dromore duce, et auspice Johnny Dromore!' She had been taken, indeed, to the National Gallery while at school. And Lennan had a vision of eight or ten young maidens trailing round at the skirts of one old maiden, admiring Landseer's dogs, giggling faintly at Botticelli's angels, gaping, rustling, chattering like young birds in a shrubbery.

But with all her surroundings, this child of Johnny Dromoredom was as yet more innocent than cultured girls of the same age. If those grey, mesmeric eyes of hers followed him about, they did so frankly, unconsciously. There was no minx in her, so far.

An hour went by, and Dromore did not come. And the loneliness of this young creature in her incongruous abode began telling on Lennan's equanimity.

What did she do in the evenings?

"Sometimes I go to the theatre with Dad, generally I stay at home."

"And then?"

"Oh! I just read, or talk French."

"What? To yourself?"

"Yes, or to Oliver sometimes, when he comes in."

So Oliver came in!

"How long have you known Oliver?"

"Oh! ever since I was a child."

He wanted to say: And how long is that? But managed to refrain, and got up to go instead. She caught his sleeve and said:

"You're not to go!" Saying that she looked as a dog will, going to bite in fun, her upper lip shortened above her small white teeth set fast on her lower lip, and her chin thrust a little forward. A glimpse of a wilful spirit! But as soon as he had smiled, and murmured:

"Ah! but I must, you see!" she at once regained her manners, only saying rather mournfully: "You don't call me by my name. Don't you like it?"

"Nell?"

"Yes. It's really Eleanor, of course. DON'T you like it?"

If he had detested the name, he could only have answered: "Very much."

"I'm awfully glad! Goodbye."

When he got out into the street, he felt terribly like a man who, instead of having had his sleeve touched, has had his heart plucked at. And that warm, bewildered feeling lasted him all the way home.

Changing for dinner, he looked at himself with unwonted attention. Yes, his dark hair was still thick, but going distinctly grey; there were very many lines about his eyes, too, and those eyes, still eager when they smiled, were particularly deepset, as if life had forced them back. His cheekbones were almost 'bopsies' now, and his cheeks very thin and dark, and his jaw looked too set and bony below the almost black moustache. Altogether a face that life had worn a good deal, with nothing for a child to take a fancy to and make friends with, that he could see.

Sylvia came in while he was thus taking stock of himself, bringing a freshly-opened flask of eau-de-Cologne. She was always bringing him something — never was anyone so sweet in those ways. In that grey, low-cut frock, her white, still prettiness and pale-gold hair, so little touched by Time, only just fell short of real beauty for lack of a spice of depth and of incisiveness, just as her spirit lacked he knew not what of poignancy. He would not for the world have let her know that he ever felt that lack. If a man could not hide little rifts in the lute from one so good and humble and affectionate, he was not fit to live.

She sang 'The Castle of Dromore' again that night with its queer haunting lilt. And when she had gone up, and he was smoking over the fire, the girl in her dark-red frock seemed to come, and sit opposite with her eyes fixed on his, just as she had been sitting while they talked. Dark red had suited her! Suited the look on her face when she said:

"You're not to go!" Odd, indeed, if she had not some devil in her, with that parentage!

V

Next day they had summoned him from the studio to see a peculiar phenomenon — Johnny Dromore, very well groomed, talking to Sylvia with unnatural suavity, and carefully masking the goggle in his eyes! Mrs. Lennan ride? Ah! Too busy, of course. Helped Mark with his — er — No! Really! Read a lot, no doubt? Never had any time for readin' himself — awful bore not having time to read! And Sylvia listening and smiling, very still and soft.

What had Dromore come for? To spy out the land, discover why Lennan and his wife thought nothing of the word 'outside' — whether, in fact, their household was respectable. . . . A man must always look twice at 'what-d'you-call-ems,' even if they have shared his room at school! . . . To his credit, of course, to be so careful of his daughter, at the expense of time owed to the creation of the perfect racehorse! On the whole he seemed to be coming to the conclusion that they might be useful to Nell in the uncomfortable time at hand when she would have to go about; seemed even to be falling under the spell of Sylvia's transparent goodness — abandoning his habitual vigilance against being scored off in life's perpetual bet; parting with his armour of chaff. Almost a relief, indeed, once out of Sylvia's presence, to see that familiar, unholy curiosity creeping back into his eyes, as though they were hoping against parental hope to find something — er — amusing somewhere about that mysterious Mecca of good times — a 'what-d'you-call-it's' studio. Delicious to watch the conflict between relief and disappointment. Alas! no model — not even a statue without clothes; nothing but portrait heads, casts of animals, and such-like sobrieties — absolutely nothing that could bring a blush to the cheek of the young person, or a glow to the eyes of a Johnny Dromore.

With what curious silence he walked round and round the group of sheep-dogs, inquiring into them with that long crinkled nose of his! With what curious suddenness, he said: "Damned good! You wouldn't do me one of Nell on horseback?" With what dubious watchfulness he listened to the answer:

"I might, perhaps, do a statuette of her; if I did, you should have a cast."

Did he think that in some way he was being outmanoeuvered? For he remained some seconds in a sort of trance before muttering, as though clinching a bet:

"Done! And if you want to ride with her to get the hang of it, I can always mount you."

When he had gone, Lennan remained staring at his unfinished sheep-dogs in the gathering dusk. Again that sense of irritation at contact with something strange, hostile, uncomprehending! Why let these Dromores into his life like this? He shut the studio, and went back to the drawing-room. Sylvia was sitting on the fender, gazing at the fire, and she edged along so as to rest against his knees. The light from a candle on her writing-table was shining on her hair, her cheek, and chin, that years had so little altered. A pretty picture she made, with just that candle flame, swaying there, burning slowly, surely down the pale wax — candle flame, of all lifeless things most living, most like a spirit, so bland and vague, one would hardly have known it was fire at all. A drift of wind blew it this way and that: he got up to shut the window, and as he came back; Sylvia said:

"I like Mr. Dromore. I think he's nicer than he looks."

"He's asked me to make a statuette of his daughter on horseback."

"And will you?"

"I don't know."

"If she's really so pretty, you'd better."

"Pretty's hardly the word — but she's not ordinary."

She turned round, and looked up at him, and instinctively he felt that something difficult to answer was coming next.

"Mark."

"Yes."

"I wanted to ask you: Are you really happy nowadays?"

"Of course. Why not?"

What else to be said? To speak of those feelings of the last few months — those feelings so ridiculous to anyone who had them not — would only disturb her horribly.

And having received her answer, Sylvia turned back to the fire, resting silently against his knees. . . .

Three days later the sheep-dogs suddenly abandoned the pose into which he had lured them with such difficulty, and made for the studio door. There in the street was Nell Dromore, mounted on a narrow little black horse with a white star, a white hoof, and devilish little goat's ears, pricked, and very close together at the tips.

"Dad said I had better ride round and show you Magpie. He's not very good at standing still. Are those your dogs? What darlings!"

She had slipped her knee already from the pummel, and slid down; the sheep-dogs were instantly on their hind-feet, propping themselves against her waist. Lennan held the black horse — a bizarre little beast, all fire and whipcord, with a skin like satin, liquid eyes, very straight hocks, and a thin bang-tail reaching down to them. The little creature had none of those commonplace good looks so discouraging to artists.

He had forgotten its rider, till she looked up from the dogs, and said: "Do you like him? It IS nice of you to be going to do us."

When she had ridden away, looking back until she turned the corner, he tried to lure the two dogs once more to their pose. But they would sit no more, going continually to the door, listening and sniffing; and everything felt disturbed and out of gear.

That same afternoon at Sylvia's suggestion he went with her to call on the Dromores.

While they were being ushered in he heard a man's voice rather high-pitched speaking in some language not his own; then the girl:

"No, no, Oliver. 'Dans l'amour il y a toujours un qui aime, et l'autre qui se laisse aimer.'"

She was sitting in her father's chair, and on the window-sill they saw a young man lolling, who rose and stood stock-still, with an almost insolent expression on his broad, good-looking face. Lennan scrutinized him with interest — about twenty-four he might be, rather dandified, clean-shaved, with crisp dark hair and wide-set hazel eyes, and, as in his photograph, a curious look of daring. His voice, when he vouchsafed a greeting, was rather high and not unpleasant, with a touch of lazy drawl.

They stayed but a few minutes, and going down those dimly lighted stairs again, Sylvia remarked:

"How prettily she said goodbye — as if she were putting up her face to be kissed! I think she's lovely. So does that young man. They go well together."

Rather abruptly Lennan answered:

"Ah! I suppose they do."

VI

She came to them often after that, sometimes alone, twice with Johnny Dromore, sometimes with young Oliver, who, under Sylvia's spell, soon lost his stand-off air. And the statuette was begun. Then came Spring in earnest, and that real business of life — the racing of horses 'on the flat,' when Johnny Dromore's genius was no longer hampered by the illegitimate risks of 'jumpin'.' He came to dine with them the day before the first Newmarket meeting. He had a soft spot for Sylvia, always saying to Lennan as he went away: "Charmin' woman — your wife!" She, too, had a soft spot for him, having fathomed the utter helplessness of this worldling's wisdom, and thinking him pathetic.

After he was gone that evening, she said:

"Ought we to have Nell to stay with us while you're finishing her? She must be very lonely now her father's so much away."

It was like Sylvia to think of that; but would it be pleasure or vexation to have in the house this child with her quaint grown-upness, her confiding ways, and those 'Perdita' eyes? In truth he did not know.

She came to them with touching alacrity — very like a dog, who, left at home when the family goes for a holiday, takes at once to those who make much of it.

And she was no trouble, too well accustomed to amuse herself; and always quaint to watch, with her continual changes from child to woman of the world. A new sensation, this — of a young creature in the house. Both he and Sylvia had wanted children, without luck. Twice illness had stood in the way. Was it, perhaps, just that little lack in her — that lack of poignancy, which had prevented her from becoming a mother? An only child herself, she had no nieces or nephews; Cicely's boys had always been at school, and now were out in the world. Yes, a new sensation, and one in which Lennan's restless feelings seemed to merge and vanish.

Outside the hours when Nell sat to him, he purposely saw but little of her, leaving her to nestle under Sylvia's wing; and this she did, as if she never wanted to come out. Thus he preserved his amusement at her quaint warmths, and quainter calmness, his aesthetic pleasure in watching her, whose strange, half-hypnotized, half-hypnotic gaze, had a sort of dreamy and pathetic lovingness, as if she were brimful of affections that had no outlet.

Every morning after 'sitting' she would stay an hour bent over her own drawing, which made practically no progress; and he would often catch her following his movements with those great eyes of hers, while the sheep-dogs would lie perfectly still at her feet, blinking horribly — such was her attraction. His birds also, a jackdaw and an owl, who had the run of the studio, tolerated her as they tolerated no other female, save the housekeeper. The jackdaw would perch on her and peck her dress; but the owl merely engaged her in combats of mesmeric gazing, which never ended in victory for either.

Now that she was with them, Oliver Dromore began to haunt the house, coming at all hours, on very transparent excuses. She behaved to him with extreme capriciousness, sometimes hardly speaking, sometimes treating him like a brother; and in spite of all his nonchalance, the poor youth would just sit glowering, or gazing out his adoration, according to her mood.

One of these July evenings Lennan remembered beyond all others. He had come, after a hard day's work, out from his studio into the courtyard garden to smoke a cigarette and feel the sun on his cheek before it sank behind the wall. A piano-organ far away was grinding out a waltz; and on an hydrangea tub, under the drawing-room window, he sat down to listen. Nothing was visible from there, save just the square patch of a quite blue sky, and one soft plume of smoke from his own kitchen chimney; nothing audible save that tune, and the never-ending street murmur. Twice birds flew across — starlings. It was very peaceful, and his thoughts went floating like the smoke of his cigarette, to meet who-knew-what other thoughts — for thoughts, no doubt, had little swift lives of their own; desired, found their mates, and, lightly blending, sent forth offspring. Why not? All things were possible in this wonder-house of a world. Even that waltz tune, floating away, would find some melody to wed, and twine with, and produce a fresh chord that might float in turn to catch the hum of a gnat or fly, and breed again. Queer — how everything sought to entwine with something else! On one of the pinkish blooms of the hydrangea he noted a bee — of all things, in this hidden-away garden of tiles and gravel and plants in tubs! The little furry, lonely thing was drowsily clinging there, as if it had forgotten what it had come for — seduced, maybe, like himself, from labour by these last rays of the sun. Its wings, close-furled, were glistening; its eyes seemed closed. And the piano-organ played on, a tune of yearning, waiting, yearning. . . .

Then, through the window above his head, he heard Oliver Dromore — a voice one could always tell, pitched high, with its slight drawl — pleading, very softly at first, then insistent, imperious; and suddenly Nell's answering voice:

"I won't, Oliver! I won't! I won't!"

He rose to go out of earshot. Then a door slammed, and he saw her at the window above him, her waist on a level with his head; flushed, with her grey eyes ominously bright, her full lips parted. And he said:

"What is it, Nell?"

She leaned down and caught his hand; her touch was fiery hot.

"He kissed me! I won't let him — I won't kiss him!"

Through his head went a medley of sayings to soothe children that are hurt; but he felt unsteady, unlike himself. And suddenly she knelt, and put her hot forehead against his lips.

It was as if she had really been a little child, wanting the place kissed to make it well.

VII

After that strange outburst, Lennan considered long whether he should speak to Oliver. But what could he say, from what standpoint say it, and — with that feeling? Or should he speak to Dromore? Not very easy to speak on such a subject to one off whose turf all spiritual matters were so permanently warned. Nor somehow could he bring himself to tell Sylvia; it would be like violating a confidence to speak of the child's outburst and that quivering moment, when she had kneeled and put her hot forehead to his lips for comfort. Such a disclosure was for Nell herself to make, if she so wished.

And then young Oliver solved the difficulty by coming to the studio himself next day. He entered with 'Dromore' composure, very well groomed, in a silk hat, a cut-away black coat and charming lemon-coloured gloves; what, indeed, the youth did, besides belonging to the Yeomanry and hunting all the winter, seemed known only to himself. He made no excuse for interrupting Lennan, and for some time sat silently smoking his cigarette, and pulling the ears of the dogs. And Lennan worked on, waiting. There was always something attractive to him in this young man's broad, good-looking face, with its crisp dark hair, and half-insolent good humour, now so clouded.

At last Oliver got up, and went over to the unfinished 'Girl on the Magpie Horse'. Turning to it so that his face could not be seen, he said:

"You and Mrs. Lennan have been awfully kind to me; I behaved rather like a cad yesterday. I thought I'd better tell you. I want to marry Nell, you know."

Lennan was glad that the young man's face was so religiously averted. He let his hands come to anchor on what he was working at before he answered: "She's only a child, Oliver;" and then, watching his fingers making an inept movement with the clay, was astonished at himself.

"She'll be eighteen this month," he heard Oliver say. "If she once gets out — amongst people — I don't know what I shall do. Old Johnny's no good to look after her."

The young man's face was very red; he was forgetting to hide it now. Then it went white, and he said through clenched teeth: "She sends me mad! I don't know how not to — If I don't get her, I shall shoot myself. I shall, you know — I'm that sort. It's her eyes. They draw you right out of yourself — and leave you —" And from his gloved hand the smoked-out cigarette-end fell to the floor. "They say her mother was like that. Poor old Johnny! D'you think I've got a chance, Mr. Lennan? I don't mean now, this minute; I know she's too young."

Lennan forced himself to answer.

"I dare say, my dear fellow, I dare say. Have you talked with my wife?"

Oliver shook his head.

"She's so good — I don't think she'd quite understand my sort of feeling."

A queer little smile came up on Lennan's lips.

"Ah, well!" he said, "you must give the child time. Perhaps when she comes back from Ireland, after the summer."

The young man answered moodily:

"Yes. I've got the run of that, you know. And I shan't be able to keep away." He took up his hat. "I suppose I oughtn't to have come and bored you about this, but Nell thinks such a lot of you; and, you being different to most people — I thought you wouldn't mind." He turned again at the door. "It wasn't gas what I said just now — about not getting her. Fellows say that sort of thing, but I mean it."

He put on that shining hat and went.

And Lennan stood, staring at the statuette. So! Passion broke down even the defences of Dromoredom. Passion! Strange hearts it chose to bloom in!

'Being different to most people — I thought you wouldn't mind'! How had this youth known that Sylvia would not understand passion so out of hand as this? And what had made it clear that he (Lennan) would? Was there, then, something in his face? There must be! Even Johnny Dromore — most reticent of creatures — had confided to him that one hour of his astute existence, when the wind had swept him out to sea!

Yes! And that statuette would never be any good, try as he might. Oliver was right — it was her eyes! How they had smoked — in their childish anger — if eyes could be said to smoke, and how they had drawn and pleaded when she put her face to his in her still more childish entreaty! If they were like this now, what would they be when the woman in her woke? Just as well not to think of her too much! Just as well to work, and take heed that he would soon be forty-seven! Just as well that next week she would be gone to Ireland!

And the last evening before she went they took her to see "Carmen" at the Opera. He remembered that she wore a nearly high white frock, and a dark carnation in the ribbon tying her crinkly hair, that still hung loose. How wonderfully entranced she sat, drunk on that opera that he had seen a score of times; now touching his arm, now Sylvia's, whispering questions: "Who's that?" "What's coming now?" The Carmen roused her to adoration, but Don Jose was 'too fat in his funny little coat,' till, in the maddened jealousy of the last act, he rose superior. Then, quite lost in excitement, she clutched Lennan's arm; and her gasp, when Carmen at last fell dead, made all their neighbours jump. Her emotion was far more moving than that on the stage; he wanted badly to stroke, and comfort her and say: "There, there, my dear, it's only make-believe!" And, when it was over, and the excellent murdered lady and her poor fat little lover appeared before the curtain, finally forgetting that she was a woman of the world, she started forward in her seat and clapped, and clapped. Fortunate that Johnny Dromore was not there to see! But all things coming to an end, they had to get up and go. And, as they made their way out to the hall, Lennan felt a hot little finger crooked into his own, as if she simply must have something to squeeze. He really did not know what to do with it. She seemed to feel this half-heartedness, soon letting it go. All the way home in the cab she was silent. With that same abstraction she ate her sandwiches and drank her lemonade; took Sylvia's kiss, and, quite a woman of the world once more, begged that they would not get up to see her off — for she was to go at seven in the morning, to catch the Irish mail. Then, holding out her hand to Lennan, she very gravely said:

"Thanks most awfully for taking me tonight. Goodbye!"

He stayed full half an hour at the window, smoking. No street lamp shone just there, and the night was velvety black above the plane-trees. At last, with a sigh, he shut up, and went tiptoeing upstairs in darkness. Suddenly in the corridor the white wall seemed to move at him. A warmth, a fragrance, a sound like a tiny sigh, and something soft was squeezed into his hand. Then the wall moved back, and he stood listening — no sound, no anything! But in his dressing-room he looked at the soft thing in his hand. It was the carnation from her hair. What had possessed the child to give him that? Carmen! Ah! Carmen! And gazing at the flower, he held it away from him with a sort of terror; but its scent arose. And suddenly he thrust it, all fresh as it was, into a candle-flame, and held it, burning, writhing, till it blackened to velvet. Then his heart smote him for so cruel a deed. It was still beautiful, but its scent was gone. And turning to the window he flung it far out into the darkness.

VIII

Now that she was gone, it was curious how little they spoke of her, considering how long she had been with them. And they had from her but one letter written to Sylvia, very soon after she left, ending: "Dad sends his best respects, please; and with my love to you and Mr. Lennan, and all the beasts. — NELL.

"Oliver is coming here next week. We are going to some races."

It was difficult, of course, to speak of her, with that episode of the flower, too bizarre to be told — the sort of thing Sylvia would see out of all proportion — as, indeed, any woman might. Yet — what had it really been, but the uncontrolled impulse of an emotional child longing to express feelings kindled by the excitement of that opera? What but a child's feathery warmth, one of those flying peeps at the mystery of passion that young things take? He could not give away that pretty foolishness. And because he would not give it away, he was more than usually affectionate to Sylvia.

They had made no holiday plans, and he eagerly fell in with her suggestion that they should go down to Hayle. There, if anywhere, this curious restlessness would leave him. They had not been down to the old place for many years; indeed, since Gordy's death it was generally let.

They left London late in August. The day was closing in when they arrived. Honeysuckle had long been improved away from that station paling, against which he had stood twenty-nine years ago, watching the train carrying Anna Stormer away. In the hired fly Sylvia pressed close to him, and held his hand beneath the ancient dust-rug. Both felt the same

excitement at seeing again this old home. Not a single soul of
the past days would be there now — only the house and the
trees, the owls and the stars; the river, park, and logan stone!
It was dark when they arrived; just their bedroom and two
sitting-rooms had been made ready, with fires burning,
though it was still high summer. The same old execrable
Heatherleys looked down from the black oak panellings. The
same scent of apples and old mice clung here and there about
the dark corridors with their unexpected stairways. It was all
curiously unchanged, as old houses are when they are let
furnished.

Once in the night he woke. Through the wide-open,
uncurtained windows the night was simply alive with stars, such
swarms of them swinging and trembling up there; and, far away,
rose the melancholy, velvet-soft hooting of an owl.

Sylvia's voice, close to him, said:

"Mark, that night when your star caught in my hair? Do you
remember?"

Yes, he remembered. And in his drowsy mind just roused from
dreams, there turned and turned the queer nonsensical refrain:
"I never — never — will desert Mr. Micawber. . . ."

A pleasant month that — of reading, and walking with the
dogs the country round, of lying out long hours amongst the
boulders or along the river banks, watching beasts and birds.

The little old green-house temple of his early masterpieces was
still extant, used now to protect watering pots. But no vestige of
impulse towards work came to him down there. He was marking
time; not restless, not bored, just waiting — but for what, he had
no notion. And Sylvia, at any rate, was happy, blooming in these
old haunts, losing her fairness in the sun; even taking again to a
sunbonnet, which made her look extraordinarily young. The
trout that poor old Gordy had so harried were left undisturbed.
No gun was fired; rabbits, pigeons, even the few partridges
enjoyed those first days of autumn unmolested. The bracken and

leaves turned very early, so that the park in the hazy September sunlight had an almost golden hue. A gentle mellowness reigned over all that holiday. And from Ireland came no further news, save one picture postcard with the words: "This is our house. — NELL."

In the last week of September they went back to London. And at once there began in him again that restless, unreasonable aching — that sense of being drawn away out of himself; so that he once more took to walking the Park for hours, over grass already strewn with leaves, always looking — craving — and for what?

At Dromore's the confidential man did not know when his master would be back; he had gone to Scotland with Miss Nell after the St. Leger. Was Lennan disappointed? Not so — relieved, rather. But his ache was there all the time, feeding on its secrecy and loneliness, unmentionable feeling that it was. Why had he not realized long ago that youth was over, passion done with, autumn upon him? How never grasped the fact that 'Time steals away'? And, as before, the only refuge was in work. The sheep — dogs and 'The Girl on the Magpie Horse' were finished. He began a fantastic 'relief' — a nymph peering from behind a rock, and a wild-eyed man creeping, through reeds, towards her. If he could put into the nymph's face something of this lure of Youth and Life and Love that was dragging at him, into the man's face the state of his own heart, it might lay that feeling to rest. Anything to get it out of himself! And he worked furiously, laboriously, all October, making no great progress. . . . What could he expect when Life was all the time knocking with that muffled tapping at his door?

It was on the Tuesday, after the close of the last Newmarket meeting, and just getting dusk, when Life opened the door and walked in. She wore a dark-red dress, a new one, and surely her face — her figure — were very different from what he had remembered! They had quickened and become poignant. She was no longer a child — that was at once plain. Cheeks, mouth, neck, waist — all seemed fined, shaped; the crinkly, light-brown hair was coiled up now under a velvet cap; only the great grey eyes seemed quite the same. And at sight of her his heart gave a sort of dive and flight, as if all its vague and wistful sensations had found their goal.

Then, in sudden agitation, he realized that his last moment with this girl — now a child no longer — had been a secret moment of warmth and of emotion; a moment which to her might have meant, in her might have bred, feelings that he had no inkling of. He tried to ignore that fighting and diving of his heart, held out his hand, and murmured:

"Ah, Nell! Back at last! You've grown." Then, with a sensation of every limb gone weak, he felt her arms round his neck, and herself pressed against him. There was time for the thought to flash through him: This is terrible! He gave her a little convulsive squeeze — could a man do less? — then just managed to push her gently away, trying with all his might to think: She's a child! It's nothing more than after Carmen! She doesn't know what I am feeling! But he was conscious of a mad desire to clutch her to him. The touch of her had demolished all his vagueness, made things only too plain, set him on fire.

He said uncertainly:

"Come to the fire, my child, and tell me all about it."

If he did not keep to the notion that she was just a child, his head would go. Perdita — 'the lost one'! A good name for her, indeed, as she stood there, her eyes shining in the firelight — more mesmeric than ever they had been! And, to get away from the lure of those eyes, he bent down and raked the grate, saying:

"Have you seen Sylvia?" But he knew that she had not, even before she gave that impatient shrug. Then he pulled himself together, and said:

"What has happened to you, child?"

"I'm not a child."

"No, we've both grown older. I was forty-seven the other day."

She caught his hand — Heavens! how supple she was! — and murmured:

"You're not old a bit; you're quite young." At his wits' end, with his heart thumping, but still keeping his eyes away from her, he said:

"Where is Oliver?"

She dropped his hand at that.

"Oliver? I hate him!"

Afraid to trust himself near her, he had begun walking up and down. And she stood, following him with her gaze — the firelight playing on her red frock. What extraordinary stillness! What power she had developed in these few months! Had he let her see that he felt that power? And had all this come of one little moment in a dark corridor, of one flower pressed into his hand? Why had he not spoken to her roughly then — told her she was a romantic little fool? God knew what thoughts she had been feeding on! But who could have supposed — who dreamed — ? And again he fixed his mind resolutely on that thought: She's a child — only a child!

"Come!" he said: "tell me all about your time in Ireland?"

"Oh! it was just dull — it's all been dull away from you."

It came out without hesitancy or shame, and he could only murmur:

"Ah! you've missed your drawing!"

"Yes. Can I come tomorrow?"

That was the moment to have said: No! You are a foolish child, and I an elderly idiot! But he had neither courage nor clearness of mind enough; nor — the desire. And, without answering, he went towards the door to turn up the light.

"Oh, no! please don't! It's so nice like this!"

The shadowy room, the bluish dusk painted on all the windows, the fitful shining of the fire, the pallor and darkness of the dim casts and bronzes, and that one glowing figure there before the hearth! And her voice, a little piteous, went on:

"Aren't you glad I'm back? I can't see you properly out there."

He went back into the glow, and she gave a little sigh of satisfaction. Then her calm young voice said, ever so distinctly:

"Oliver wants me to marry him, and I won't, of course."

He dared not say: Why not? He dared not say anything. It was too dangerous. And then followed those amazing words: "You know why, don't you? Of course you do."

It was ridiculous, almost shameful to understand their meaning. And he stood, staring in front of him, without a word; humility, dismay, pride, and a sort of mad exultation, all mixed and seething within him in the queerest pudding of emotion. But all he said was:

"Come, my child; we're neither of us quite ourselves tonight. Let's go to the drawing-room."

IX

Back in the darkness and solitude of the studio, when she was gone, he sat down before the fire, his senses in a whirl. Why was he not just an ordinary animal of a man that could enjoy what the gods had sent? It was as if on a November day someone had pulled aside the sober curtains of the sky and there in a chink had been April standing — thick white blossom, a purple cloud, a rainbow, grass vivid green, light flaring from one knew not where, and such a tingling passion of life on it all as made the heart stand still! This, then, was the marvellous, enchanting, maddening end of all that year of restlessness and wanting! This bit of Spring suddenly given to him in the midst of Autumn. Her lips, her eyes, her hair; her touching confidence; above all — quite unbelievable — her love. Not really love perhaps, just childish fancy. But on the wings of fancy this child would fly far, too far — all wistfulness and warmth beneath that light veneer of absurd composure.

To live again — to plunge back into youth and beauty — to feel Spring once more — to lose the sense of all being over, save just the sober jogtrot of domestic bliss; to know, actually to know, ecstasy again, in the love of a girl; to rediscover all that youth yearns for, and feels, and hopes, and dreads, and loves. It was a prospect to turn the head even of a decent man. . . .

By just closing his eyes he could see her standing there with the firelight glow on her red frock; could feel again that marvellous thrill when she pressed herself against him in the half-innocent, seducing moment when she first came in; could feel again her eyes drawing — drawing him! She was a witch, a grey-eyed, brown-haired witch — even unto her love of red. She had the witch's power of lighting fever in the veins. And he simply wondered at himself, that he had not, as she stood there in the firelight, knelt, and put his arms round her and pressed his face against her waist. Why had he not? But he did not want to think; the moment thought began he knew he must be torn this way and that, tossed here and there between reason and desire, pity and passion. Every sense struggled to keep him wrapped in the warmth and intoxication of this discovery that he, in the full of Autumn, had awakened love in Spring. It was amazing that she could have this feeling; yet there was no mistake. Her manner to Sylvia just now had been almost dangerously changed; there had been a queer cold impatience in her look, frightening from one who but three months ago had been so affectionate. And, going away, she had whispered, with that old trembling-up at him, as if offering to be kissed: "I may come, mayn't I? And don't be angry with me, please; I can't help it." A monstrous thing at his age to let a young girl love him — compromise her future! A monstrous thing by all the canons of virtue and gentility! And yet — what future? — with that nature — those eyes — that origin — with that father, and that home? But he would not — simply must not think!

Nevertheless, he showed the signs of thought, and badly; for after dinner Sylvia, putting her hand on his forehead, said:

"You're working too hard, Mark. You don't go out enough."

He held those fingers fast. Sylvia! No, indeed he must not think! But he took advantage of her words, and said that he would go out and get some air.

He walked at a great pace — to keep thought away — till he reached the river close to Westminster, and, moved by sudden impulse, seeking perhaps an antidote, turned down into that little street under the big Wren church, where he had never been since the summer night when he lost what was then more to him than life. There SHE had lived; there was the house — those windows which he had stolen past and gazed at with such distress and longing. Who lived there now? Once more he seemed to see that face out of the past, the dark hair, and dark soft eyes, and sweet gravity; and it did not reproach him. For this new feeling was not a love like that had been. Only once could a man feel the love that passed all things, the love before which the world was but a spark in a draught of wind; the love that, whatever dishonour, grief, and unrest it might come through, alone had in it the heart of peace and joy and honour. Fate had torn that love from him, nipped it off as a sharp wind nips off a perfect flower. This new feeling was but a fever, a passionate fancy, a grasping once more at Youth and Warmth. Ah, well! but it was real enough! And, in one of those moments when a man stands outside himself, seems to be lifted away and see his own life twirling, Lennan had a vision of a shadow driven here and there; a straw going round and round; a midge in the grip of a mad wind. Where was the home of this mighty secret feeling that sprang so suddenly out of the dark, and caught you by the throat? Why did it come now and not then, for this one and not that other? What did man know of it, save that it made him spin and hover — like a moth intoxicated by a light, or a bee by some dark sweet flower; save that it made of him a distraught, humble, eager puppet of its fancy? Had it not once already driven him even to the edge of death; and must it now come on him again with its sweet madness, its drugging scent? What was it? Why was it? Why these passionate obsessions that could not decently be satisfied? Had civilization so outstripped man that his nature was cramped into shoes too small — like the feet of a Chinese woman? What was it? Why was it?

And faster than ever he walked away.

Pall Mall brought him back to that counterfeit presentment of the real — reality. There, in St. James's Street, was Johnny Dromore's Club; and, again moved by impulse, he pushed open its swing door. No need to ask; for there was Dromore in the hall, on his way from dinner to the card-room. The glossy tan of hard exercise and good living lay on his cheeks as thick as clouted cream. His eyes had the peculiar shine of superabundant vigour; a certain sub-festive air in face and voice and movements suggested that he was going to make a night of it. And the sardonic thought flashed through Lennan: Shall I tell him?

"Hallo, old chap! Awfully glad to see you! What you doin' with yourself? Workin' hard? How's your wife? You been away? Been doin' anything great?" And then the question that would have given him his chance, if he had liked to be so cruel:

"Seen Nell?"

"Yes, she came round this afternoon."

"What d'you think of her? Comin' on nicely, isn't she?"

That old query, half furtive and half proud, as much as to say: 'I know she's not in the stud-book, but, d — n it, I sired her!' And then the old sudden gloom, which lasted but a second, and gave way again to chaff.

Lennan stayed very few minutes. Never had he felt farther from his old school-chum.

No. Whatever happened, Johnny Dromore must be left out. It was a position he had earned with his goggling eyes, and his astute philosophy; from it he should not be disturbed.

He passed along the railings of the Green Park. On the cold air of this last October night a thin haze hung, and the acrid fragrance from little bonfires of fallen leaves. What was there about that scent of burned-leaf smoke that had always moved him so? Symbol of parting! — that most mournful thing in all the world. For what would even death be, but for parting? Sweet, long sleep, or new adventure. But, if a man loved others — to leave them, or be left! Ah! and it was not death only that brought partings!

He came to the opening of the street where Dromore lived. She would be there, sitting by the fire in the big chair, playing with her kitten, thinking, dreaming, and — alone! He passed on at such a pace that people stared; till, turning the last corner for home, he ran almost into the arms of Oliver Dromore.

The young man was walking with unaccustomed indecision, his fur coat open, his opera-hat pushed up on his crisp hair. Dark under the eyes, he had not the proper gloss of a Dromore at this season of the year.

"Mr. Lennan! I've just been round to you."

And Lennan answered dazedly:

"Will you come in, or shall I walk your way a bit?"

"I'd rather — out here, if you don't mind."

So in silence they went back into the Square. And Oliver said:

"Let's get over by the rails."

They crossed to the railings of the Square's dark garden, where nobody was passing. And with every step Lennan's humiliation grew. There was something false and undignified in walking with this young man who had once treated him as a father confessor to his love for Nell. And suddenly he perceived that they had made a complete circuit of the Square garden without speaking a single word.

"Yes?" he said.

Oliver turned his face away.

"You remember what I told you in the summer. Well, it's worse now. I've been going a mucker lately in all sorts of ways to try and get rid of it. But it's all no good. She's got me!"

And Lennan thought: You're not alone in that! But he kept silence. His chief dread was of saying something that he would remember afterwards as the words of Judas.

Then Oliver suddenly burst out:

"Why can't she care? I suppose I'm nothing much, but she's known me all her life, and she used to like me. There's something — I can't make out. Could you do anything for me with her?"

Lennan pointed across the street.

"In every other one of those houses, Oliver," he said, "there's probably some creature who can't make out why another creature doesn't care. Passion comes when it will, goes when it will; and we poor devils have no say in it."

"What do you advise me, then?"

Lennan had an almost overwhelming impulse to turn on his heel and leave the young man standing there. But he forced himself to look at his face, which even then had its attraction — perhaps more so than ever, so pallid and desperate it was. And he said slowly, staring mentally at every word:

"I'm not up to giving you advice. The only thing I might say is: One does not press oneself where one isn't wanted; all the same — who knows? So long as she feels you're there, waiting, she might turn to you at any moment. The more chivalrous you are, Oliver, the more patiently you wait, the better chance you have."

Oliver took those words of little comfort without flinching. "I see," he said. "Thanks! But, my God! it's hard. I never could wait." And with that epigram on himself, holding out his hand, he turned away.

Lennan went slowly home, trying to gauge exactly how anyone who knew all would judge him. It was a little difficult in this affair to keep a shred of dignity.

Sylvia had not gone up, and he saw her looking at him anxiously. The one strange comfort in all this was that his feeling for her, at any rate, had not changed. It seemed even to have deepened — to be more real to him.

How could he help staying awake that night? How could he help thinking, then? And long time he lay, staring at the dark.

As if thinking were any good for fever in the veins!

X

Passion never plays the game. It, at all events, is free from self-consciousness, and pride; from dignity, nerves, scruples, cant, moralities; from hypocrisies, and wisdom, and fears for pocket, and position in this world and the next. Well did the old painters limn it as an arrow or a wind! If it had not been as swift and darting, Earth must long ago have drifted through space untenanted — to let. . . .

After that fevered night Lennan went to his studio at the usual hour and naturally did not do a stroke of work. He was even obliged to send away his model. The fellow had been his hairdresser, but, getting ill, and falling on dark days, one morning had come to the studio, to ask with manifest shame if his head were any good. After having tested his capacity for standing still, and giving him some introductions, Lennan had noted him down: "Five feet nine, good hair, lean face, something tortured and pathetic. Give him a turn if possible." The turn had come, and the poor man was posing in a painful attitude, talking, whenever permitted, of the way things had treated him, and the delights of cutting hair. This morning he took his departure with the simple pleasure of one fully paid for services not rendered.

And so, walking up and down, up and down, the sculptor waited for Nell's knock. What would happen now? Thinking had made nothing clear. Here was offered what every warm-blooded man whose Spring is past desires — youth and beauty, and in that youth a renewal of his own; what all men save hypocrites and Englishmen would even admit that they desired. And it was offered to one who had neither religious nor moral scruples, as they are commonly understood. In theory he could accept. In practice he did not as yet know what he could do. One thing only he had discovered during the night's reflections: That those who scouted belief in the principle of Liberty made no greater mistake than to suppose that Liberty was dangerous because it made a man a libertine. To those with any decency, the creed of Freedom was — of all — the most enchaining. Easy enough to break chains imposed by others, fling his cap over the windmill, and cry for the moment at least: I am unfettered, free! Hard, indeed, to say the same to his own unfettered Self! Yes, his own Self was in the judgment-seat; by his own verdict and decision he must abide. And though he ached for the sight of her, and his will seemed paralyzed — many times already he had thought: It won't do! God help me!

Then twelve o'clock had come, and she had not. Would 'The Girl on the Magpie Horse' be all he would see of her today — that unsatisfying work, so cold, and devoid of witchery? Better have tried to paint her — with a red flower in her hair, a pout on her lips, and her eyes fey, or languorous. Goya could have painted her!

And then, just as he had given her up, she came.

After taking one look at his face, she slipped in ever so quietly, like a very good child. . . . Marvellous the instinct and finesse of the young when they are women! . . . Not a vestige in her of yesterday's seductive power; not a sign that there had been a yesterday at all — just confiding, like a daughter. Sitting there, telling him about Ireland, showing him the little batch of drawings she had done while she was away. Had she brought them because she knew they would make him feel sorry for her? What could have been less dangerous, more appealing to the protective and paternal side of him than she was that morning; as if she only wanted what her father and her home could not give her — only wanted to be a sort of daughter to him!

She went away demurely, as she had come, refusing to stay to lunch, manifestly avoiding Sylvia. Only then he realized that she must have taken alarm from the look of strain on his face, been afraid that he would send her away; only then perceived that, with her appeal to his protection, she had been binding him closer, making it harder for him to break away and hurt her. And the fevered aching began again — worse than ever — the moment he lost sight of her. And more than ever he felt in the grip of something beyond his power to fight against; something that, however he swerved, and backed, and broke away, would close in on him, find means to bind him again hand and foot.

In the afternoon Dromore's confidential man brought him a note. The fellow, with his cast-down eyes, and his well-parted hair, seemed to Lennan to be saying: "Yes, sir — it is quite natural that you should take the note out of eyeshot, sir — BUT I KNOW; fortunately, there is no necessity for alarm — I am strictly confidential."

And this was what the note contained:

"You promised to ride with me once — you DID promise, and you never have. Do please ride with me tomorrow; then you will get what you want for the statuette instead of being so cross with it. You can have Dad's horse — he has gone to Newmarket again, and I'm so lonely. Please — tomorrow, at half-past two — starting from here. — NELL."

To hesitate in view of those confidential eyes was not possible; it must be 'Yes' or 'No'; and if 'No', it would only mean that she would come in the morning instead. So he said:

"Just say 'All right!'"

"Very good, sir." Then from the door: "Mr. Dromore will be away till Saturday, sir."

Now, why had the fellow said that? Curious how this desperate secret feeling of his own made him see sinister meaning in this servant, in Oliver's visit of last night — in everything. It was vile — this suspiciousness! He could feel, almost see, himself deteriorating already, with this furtive feeling in his soul. It would soon be written on his face! But what was the use of troubling? What would come, would — one way or the other.

And suddenly he remembered with a shock that it was the first of November — Sylvia's birthday! He had never before forgotten it. In the disturbance of that discovery he was very near to going and pouring out to her the whole story of his feelings. A charming birthday present, that would make! Taking his hat, instead, he dashed round to the nearest flower shop. A Frenchwoman kept it.

What had she?

What did Monsieur desire? "Des oeillets rouges? J'en ai de bien beaux ce soir."

No — not those. White flowers!

"Une belle azalee?"

Yes, that would do — to be sent at once — at once!

Next door was a jeweller's. He had never really known if Sylvia cared for jewels, since one day he happened to remark that they were vulgar. And feeling that he had fallen low indeed, to be trying to atone with some miserable gewgaw for never having thought of her all day, because he had been thinking of another, he went in and bought the only ornament whose ingredients did not make his gorge rise, two small pear-shaped black pearls, one at each end of a fine platinum chain. Coming out with it, he noticed over the street, in a clear sky fast deepening to indigo, the thinnest slip of a new moon, like a bright swallow, with wings bent back, flying towards the ground. That meant — fine weather! If it could only be fine weather in his heart! And in order that the azalea might arrive first, he walked up and down the Square which he and Oliver had patrolled the night before.

When he went in, Sylvia was just placing the white azalea in the window of the drawing-room; and stealing up behind her he clasped the little necklet round her throat. She turned round and clung to him. He could feel that she was greatly moved. And remorse stirred and stirred in him that he was betraying her with his kiss.

But, even while he kissed her, he was hardening his heart.

XI

Next day, still following the lead of her words about fresh air and his tired look, he told her that he was going to ride, and did not say with whom. After applauding his resolution, she was silent for a little — then asked:

"Why don't you ride with Nell?"

He had already so lost his dignity, that he hardly felt disgraced in answering:

"It might bore her!"

"Oh, no; it wouldn't bore her."

Had she meant anything by that? And feeling as if he were fencing with his own soul, he said:

"Very well, I will."

He had perceived suddenly that he did not know his wife, having always till now believed that it was she who did not quite know him.

If she had not been out at lunch-time, he would have lunched out himself — afraid of his own face. For feverishness in sick persons mounts steadily with the approach of a certain hour. And surely his face, to anyone who could have seen him being conveyed to Piccadilly, would have suggested a fevered invalid rather than a healthy, middle-aged sculptor in a cab.

The horses were before the door — the little magpie horse, and a thoroughbred bay mare, weeded from Dromore's racing stable. Nell, too, was standing ready, her cheeks very pink, and her eyes very bright. She did not wait for him to mount her, but took the aid of the confidential man. What was it that made her look so perfect on that little horse — shape of limb, or something soft and fiery in her spirit that the little creature knew of?

They started in silence, but as soon as the sound of hoofs died on the tan of Rotten Row, she turned to him.

"It was lovely of you to come! I thought you'd be afraid — you ARE afraid of me."

And Lennan thought: You're right!

"But please don't look like yesterday. Today's too heavenly. Oh! I love beautiful days, and I love riding, and —" She broke off and looked at him. 'Why can't you just be nice to me' — she seemed to be saying — 'and love me as you ought!' That was her power — the conviction that he did, and ought to love her; that she ought to and did love him. How simple!

But riding, too, is a simple passion; and simple passions distract each other. It was a treat to be on that bay mare. Who so to be trusted to ride the best as Johnny Dromore?

At the far end of the Row she cried out: "Let's go on to Richmond now," and trotted off into the road, as if she knew she could do with him what she wished. And, following meekly, he asked himself: Why? What was there in her to make up to him for all that he was losing — his power of work, his dignity, his self-respect? What was there? Just those eyes, and lips, and hair?

And as if she knew what he was thinking, she looked round and smiled.

So they jogged on over the Bridge and across Barnes Common into Richmond Park.

But the moment they touched turf, with one look back at him, she was off. Had she all the time meant to give him this breakneck chase — or had the loveliness of that Autumn day gone to her head — blue sky and coppery flames of bracken in the sun, and the beech leaves and the oak leaves; pure Highland colouring come South for once.

When in the first burst he had tested the mare's wind, this chase of her, indeed, was sheer delight. Through glades, over fallen tree-trunks, in bracken up to the hocks, out across the open, past a herd of amazed and solemn deer, over rotten ground all rabbit-burrows, till just as he thought he was up to her, she slipped away by a quick turn round trees. Mischief incarnate, but something deeper than mischief, too! He came up with her at last, and leaned over to seize her rein. With a cut of her whip that missed his hand by a bare inch, and a wrench, she made him shoot past, wheeled in her tracks, and was off again like an arrow, back amongst the trees — lying right forward under the boughs, along the neck of her little horse. Then out from amongst the trees she shot downhill. Right down she went, full tilt, and after her went Lennan, lying back, and expecting the bay mare to come down at every stride. This was her idea of fun! She switched round at the bottom and went galloping along the foot of the hill; and he thought: Now I've got her! She could not break back up that hill, and there was no other cover for fully half a mile.

Then he saw, not thirty yards in front, an old sandpit; and Great God! she was going straight at it! And shouting frantically, he reined his mare outwards. But she only raised her whip, cut the magpie horse over the flank, and rode right on. He saw that little demon gather its feet and spring — down, down, saw him pitch, struggle, sink — and she, flung forward, roll over and lie on her back. He felt nothing at the moment, only had that fixed vision of a yellow patch of sand, the blue sky, a rook flying, and her face upturned. But when he came on her she was on her feet, holding the bridle of her dazed horse. No sooner did he touch her, than she sank down. Her eyes were closed, but he could feel that she had not fainted; and he just held her, and kept pressing his lips to her eyes and forehead. Suddenly she let her head fall back, and her lips met his. Then opening her eyes, she said: "I'm not hurt, only — funny. Has Magpie cut his knees?"

Not quite knowing what he did, he got up to look. The little horse was cropping at some grass, unharmed — the sand and fern had saved his knees. And the languid voice behind him said: "It's all right — you can leave the horses. They'll come when I call."

Now that he knew she was unhurt, he felt angry. Why had she behaved in this mad way — given him this fearful shock? But in that same languid voice she went on: "Don't be cross with me. I thought at first I'd pull up, but then I thought: 'If I jump he can't help being nice' — so I did — Don't leave off loving me because I'm not hurt, please."

Terribly moved, he sat down beside her, took her hands in his, and said:

"Nell! Nell! it's all wrong — it's madness!"

"Why? Don't think about it! I don't want you to think — only to love me."

"My child, you don't know what love is!"

For answer she only flung her arms round his neck; then, since he held back from kissing her, let them fall again, and jumped up.

"Very well. But I love you. You can think of THAT — you can't prevent me!" And without waiting for help, she mounted the magpie horse from the sand-heap where they had fallen.

Very sober that ride home! The horses, as if ashamed of their mad chase, were edging close to each other, so that now and then his arm would touch her shoulder. He asked her once what she had felt while she was jumping.

"Only to be sure my foot was free. It was rather horrid coming down, thinking of Magpie's knees;" and touching the little horse's goat-like ears, she added softly: "Poor dear! He'll be stiff tomorrow."

She was again only the confiding, rather drowsy, child. Or was it that the fierceness of those past moments had killed his power of feeling? An almost dreamy hour — with the sun going down, the lamps being lighted one by one — and a sort of sweet oblivion over everything!

At the door, where the groom was waiting, Lennan would have said goodbye, but she whispered: "Oh, no, please! I AM tired now — you might help me up a little."

And so, half carrying her, he mounted past the Vanity Fair

cartoons, and through the corridor with the red paper and the Van Beers' drawings, into the room where he had first seen her.

Once settled back in Dromore's great chair, with the purring kitten curled up on her neck, she murmured:

"Isn't it nice? You can make tea; and we'll have hot buttered toast."

And so Lennan stayed, while the confidential man brought tea and toast; and, never once looking at them, seemed to know all that had passed, all that might be to come.

Then they were alone again, and, gazing down at her stretched out in that great chair, Lennan thought:

"Thank God that I'm tired too — body and soul!"

But suddenly she looked up at him, and pointing to the picture that today had no curtain drawn, said:

"Do you think I'm like her? I made Oliver tell me about — myself this summer. That's why you needn't bother. It doesn't matter what happens to me, you see. And I don't care — because you can love me, without feeling bad about it. And you will, won't you?"

Then, with her eyes still on his face, she went on quickly:

"Only we won't talk about that now, will we? It's too cosy. I AM nice and tired. Do smoke!"

But Lennan's fingers trembled so that he could hardly light that cigarette. And, watching them, she said: "Please give me one. Dad doesn't like my smoking."

The virtue of Johnny Dromore! Yes! It would always be by proxy! And he muttered:

"How do you think he would like to know about this afternoon, Nell?"

"I don't care." Then peering up through the kitten's fur she murmured: "Oliver wants me to go to a dance on Saturday — it's for a charity. Shall I?"

"Of course; why not?"

"Will YOU come?"

"I?"

"Oh, do! You must! It's my very first, you know. I've got an extra ticket."

And against his will, his judgment — everything, Lennan answered: "Yes."

She clapped her hands, and the kitten crawled down to her knees.

When he got up to go, she did not move, but just looked up at him; and how he got away he did not know.

Stopping his cab a little short of home, he ran, for he felt cold and stiff, and letting himself in with his latch-key, went straight to the drawing-room. The door was ajar, and Sylvia standing at the window. He heard her sigh; and his heart smote him. Very still, and slender, and lonely she looked out there, with the light shining on her fair hair so that it seemed almost white. Then she turned and saw him. He noticed her throat working with the effort she made not to show him anything, and he said:

"Surely you haven't been anxious! Nell had a bit of a fall — jumping into a sandpit. She's quite mad sometimes. I stayed to tea with her — just to make sure she wasn't really hurt." But as he spoke he loathed himself; his voice sounded so false.

She only answered: "It's all right, dear," but he saw that she kept her eyes — those blue, too true eyes — averted, even when she kissed him.

And so began another evening and night and morning of fever, subterfuge, wariness, aching. A round of half-ecstatic torment, out of which he seemed no more able to break than a man can break through the walls of a cell. . . .

Though it live but a day in the sun, though it drown in tenebrous night, the dark flower of passion will have its hour. . . .

XII

To deceive undoubtedly requires a course of training. And, unversed in this art, Lennan was fast finding it intolerable to scheme and watch himself, and mislead one who had looked up to him ever since they were children. Yet, all the time, he had a feeling that, since he alone knew all the circumstances of his case, he alone was entitled to blame or to excuse himself. The glib judgments that moralists would pass upon his conduct could be nothing but the imbecilities of smug and pharisaic fools — of those not under this drugging spell — of such as had not blood enough, perhaps, ever to fall beneath it!

The day after the ride Nell had not come, and he had no word from her. Was she, then, hurt, after all? She had lain back very inertly in that chair! And Sylvia never asked if he knew how the girl was after her fall, nor offered to send round to inquire. Did she not wish to speak of her, or had she simply — not believed? When there was so much he could not talk of it seemed hard that just what happened to be true should be distrusted. She had not yet, indeed, by a single word suggested that she felt he was deceiving her, but at heart he knew that she was not deceived. . . . Those feelers of a woman who loves — can anything check their delicate apprehension? . . .

Towards evening, the longing to see the girl — a sensation as if she were calling him to come to her — became almost insupportable; yet, whatever excuse he gave, he felt that Sylvia would know where he was going. He sat on one side of the fire, she on the other, and they both read books; the only strange thing about their reading was, that neither of them ever turned a leaf. It was 'Don Quixote' he read, the page which had these words: "Let Altisidora weep or sing, still I am Dulcinea's and hers alone, dead or alive, dutiful and unchanged, in spite of all the necromantic powers in the world." And so the evening passed. When she went up to bed, he was very near to stealing out, driving up to the Dromores' door, and inquiring of the confidential man; but the thought of the confounded fellow's eyes was too much for him, and he held out. He took up Sylvia's book, De Maupassant's 'Fort comme la mort' — open at the page where the poor woman finds that her lover has passed away from her to her own daughter. And as he read, the tears rolled down his cheek. Sylvia! Sylvia! Were not his old favourite words from that old favourite book still true? "Dulcinea del Toboso is the most beautiful woman in the world, and I the most unfortunate knight upon the earth. It were unjust that such perfection should suffer through my weakness. No, pierce my body with your lance, knight, and let my life expire with my honour. . . ." Why could he not wrench this feeling from his heart, banish this girl from his eyes? Why could he not be wholly true to her who was and always had been wholly true to him? Horrible — this will-less, nerveless feeling, this paralysis, as if he were a puppet moved by a cruel hand. And, as once before, it seemed to him that the girl was sitting there in Sylvia's chair in her dark red frock, with her eyes fixed on him. Uncannily vivid — that impression! . . . A man could not go on long with his head in Chancery like this, without becoming crazed!

It was growing dusk on Saturday afternoon when he gave up that intolerable waiting and opened the studio door to go to Nell. It was now just two days since he had seen or heard of her. She had spoken of a dance for that very night — of his going to it. She MUST be ill!

But he had not taken six steps when he saw her coming. She had on a grey furry scarf, hiding her mouth, making her look much older. The moment the door was shut she threw it off, went to the hearth, drew up a little stool, and, holding her hands out to the fire, said:

"Have you thought about me? Have you thought enough now?"

And he answered: "Yes, I've thought, but I'm no nearer."

"Why? Nobody need ever know you love me. And if they did, I wouldn't care."

Simple! How simple! Glorious, egoistic youth!

He could not speak of Sylvia to this child — speak of his married life, hitherto so dignified, so almost sacred. It was impossible. Then he heard her say:

"It can't be wrong to love YOU! I don't care if it is wrong," and saw her lips quivering, and her eyes suddenly piteous and scared, as if for the first time she doubted of the issue. Here was fresh torment! To watch an unhappy child. And what was the use of even trying to make clear to her — on the very threshold of life — the hopeless maze that he was wandering in! What chance of making her understand the marsh of mud and tangled weeds he must drag through to reach her. "Nobody need know." So simple! What of his heart and his wife's heart? And, pointing to his new work — the first man bewitched by the first nymph — he said:

"Look at this, Nell! That nymph is you; and this man is me." She got up, and came to look. And while she was gazing he greedily drank her in. What a strange mixture of innocence and sorcery! What a wonderful young creature to bring to full knowledge of love within his arms! And he said: "You had better understand what you are to me — all that I shall never know again; there it is in that nymph's face. Oh, no! not YOUR face. And there am I struggling through slime to reach you — not MY face, of course."

She said: "Poor face!" then covered her own. Was she going to cry, and torture him still more? But, instead, she only murmured: "But you HAVE reached me!" swayed towards him, and put her lips to his.

He gave way then. From that too stormy kiss of his she drew back for a second, then, as if afraid of her own recoil, snuggled close again. But the instinctive shrinking of innocence had been enough for Lennan — he dropped his arms and said:

"You must go, child."

Without a word she picked up her fur, put it on, and stood waiting for him to speak. Then, as he did not, she held out something white. It was the card for the dance.

"You said you were coming?"

And he nodded. Her eyes and lips smiled at him; she opened the door, and, still with that slow, happy smile, went out. . . .

Yes, he would be coming; wherever she was, whenever she wanted him! . . .

His blood on fire, heedless of everything but to rush after happiness, Lennan spent those hours before the dance. He had told Sylvia that he would be dining at his Club — a set of rooms owned by a small coterie of artists in Chelsea. He had taken this precaution, feeling that he could not sit through dinner opposite her and then go out to that dance — and Nell! He had spoken of a guest at the Club, to account for evening dress — another lie, but what did it matter? He was lying all the time, if not in words, in action — must lie, indeed, to save her suffering!

He stopped at the Frenchwoman's flower shop.

"Que desirez-vous, monsieur? Des oeillets rouges — j'en ai de bien beaux, ce soir."

Des oeillets rouges? Yes, those tonight! To this address. No green with them; no card!

How strange the feeling — with the die once cast for love — of rushing, of watching his own self being left behind!

In the Brompton Road, outside a little restaurant, a thin musician was playing on a violin. Ah! and he knew this place; he would go in there, not to the Club — and the fiddler should have all he had to spare, for playing those tunes of love. He turned in. He had not been there since the day before that night on the river, twenty years ago. Never since; and yet it was not changed. The same tarnished gilt, and smell of cooking; the same macaroni in the same tomato sauce; the same Chianti flasks; the same staring, light-blue walls wreathed with pink flowers. Only the waiter different — hollow-cheeked, patient, dark of eye. He, too, should be well tipped! And that poor, over-hatted lady, eating her frugal meal — to her, at all events, a look of kindness. For all desperate creatures he must feel, this desperate night! And suddenly he thought of Oliver. Another desperate one! What should he say to Oliver at this dance — he, aged forty-seven, coming there without his wife! Some imbecility, such as: 'Watching the human form divine in motion,' 'Catching sidelights on Nell for the statuette' — some cant; it did not matter! The wine was drawn, and he must drink!

It was still early when he left the restaurant — a dry night, very calm, not cold. When had he danced last? With Olive Cramier, before he knew he loved her. Well, THAT memory could not be broken, for he would not dance tonight! Just watch, sit with the girl a few minutes, feel her hand cling to his, see her eyes turned back to him; and — come away! And then — the future! For the wine was drawn! The leaf of a plane-tree, fluttering down, caught on his sleeve. Autumn would soon be gone, and after Autumn — only Winter! She would have done with him long before he came to Winter. Nature would see to it that Youth called for her, and carried her away. Nature in her courses! But just to cheat Nature for a little while! To cheat Nature — what greater happiness!

Here was the place with red-striped awning, carriages driving away, loiterers watching. He turned in with a beating heart. Was he before her? How would she come to this first dance? With Oliver alone? Or had some chaperon been found? To have come because she — this child so lovely, born 'outside' — might have need of chaperonage, would have been some comfort to dignity, so wistful, so lost as his. But, alas! he knew he was only there because he could not keep away!

Already they were dancing in the hall upstairs; but not she, yet; and he stood leaning against the wall where she must pass. Lonely and out of place he felt; as if everyone must know why he was there. People stared, and he heard a girl ask: "Who's that against the wall with the hair and dark moustache?" — and her partner murmuring his answer, and her voice again: "Yes, he looks as if he were seeing sand and lions." For whom, then, did they take him? Thank heaven! They were all the usual sort. There would be no one that he knew. Suppose Johnny Dromore himself came with Nell! He was to be back on Saturday! What could he say, then? How meet those doubting, knowing eyes, goggling with the fixed philosophy that a man has but one use for woman? God! and it would be true! For a moment he was on the point of getting his coat and hat, and sneaking away. That would mean not seeing her till Monday; and he stood his ground. But after tonight there must be no more such risks — their meetings must be wisely planned, must sink underground. And then he saw her at the foot of the stairs in a dress of a shell-pink colour, with one of his flowers in her light-brown hair and the others tied to the handle of a tiny fan. How self-possessed she looked, as if this were indeed her native element — her neck and arms bare, her cheeks a deep soft pink, her eyes quickly turning here and there. She began mounting the stairs, and saw him. Was ever anything so lovely as she looked just then? Behind her he marked Oliver, and a tall girl with red hair, and another young man. He moved deliberately to the top of the stairs on the wall side, so that from behind they should not see her face when she greeted him. She put the little fan with the flowers to her lips; and, holding out her hand, said, quick and low:

"The fourth, it's a polka; we'll sit out, won't we?"

Then swaying a little, so that her hair and the flower in it almost touched his face, she passed, and there in her stead stood Oliver.

Lennan had expected one of his old insolent looks, but the young man's face was eager and quite friendly.

"It was awfully good of you to come, Mr. Lennan. Is Mrs. Lennan —"

And Lennan murmured:

"She wasn't able; she's not quite —" and could have sunk into the shining floor. Youth with its touching confidence, its eager trust! This was the way he was fulfilling his duty towards Youth!

When they had passed into the ballroom he went back to his position against the wall. They were dancing Number Three; his time of waiting, then, was drawing to a close. From where he stood he could not see the dancers — no use to watch her go round in someone else's arms.

Not a true waltz — some French or Spanish pavement song played in waltz time; bizarre, pathetic, whirling after its own happiness. That chase for happiness! Well, life, with all its prizes and its possibilities, had nothing that quite satisfied — save just the fleeting moments of passion! Nothing else quite poignant enough to be called pure joy! Or so it seemed to him.

The waltz was over. He could see her now, on a rout seat against the wall with the other young man, turning her eyes constantly as if to make sure that he was still standing there. What subtle fuel was always being added to the fire by that flattery of her inexplicable adoration — of those eyes that dragged him to her, yet humbly followed him, too! Five times while she sat there he saw the red-haired girl or Oliver bring men up; saw youths cast longing glances; saw girls watching her with cold appraisement, or with a touching, frank delight. From the moment that she came in, there had been, in her father's phrase, 'only one in it.' And she could pass all this by, and still want him. Incredible!

At the first notes of the polka he went to her. It was she who found their place of refuge — a little alcove behind two palm-plants. But sitting there, he realized, as never before, that there was no spiritual communion between him and this child. She could tell him her troubles or her joys; he could soothe or sympathize; but never would the gap between their natures and their ages be crossed. His happiness was only in the sight and touch of her. But that, God knew, was happiness enough — a feverish, craving joy, like an overtired man's thirst, growing with the drink on which it tries to slake itself. Sitting there, in the scent of those flowers and of some sweet essence in her hair, with her fingers touching his, and her eyes seeking his, he tried loyally not to think of himself, to grasp her sensations at this her first dance, and just help her to enjoyment. But he could not — paralyzed, made drunk by that insensate longing to take her in his arms and crush her to him as he had those few hours back. He could see her expanding like a flower, in all this light, and motion, and intoxicating admiration round her. What business had he in her life, with his dark hunger after secret hours; he — a coin worn thin already — a destroyer of the freshness and the glamour of her youth and beauty!

Then, holding up the flowers, she said:

"Did you give me these because of the one I gave you?"

"Yes."

"What did you do with that?"

"Burned it."

"Oh! but why?"

"Because you are a witch — and witches must be burned with all their flowers."

"Are you going to burn me?"

He put his hand on her cool arm.

"Feel! The flames are lighted."

"You may! I don't care!"

She took his hand and laid her cheek against it; yet, to the music, which had begun again, the tip of her shoe was already beating time. And he said:

"You ought to be dancing, child."

"Oh, no! Only it's a pity you don't want to."

"Yes! Do you understand that it must all be secret — underground?"

She covered his lips with the fan, and said: "You're not to think; you're not to think — never! When can I come?"

"I must find the best way. Not tomorrow. Nobody must know,

Nell — for your sake — for hers — nobody!"

She nodded, and repeated with a soft, mysterious wisdom: "Nobody." And then, aloud: "Here's Oliver! It was awfully good of you to come. Goodnight!"

And as, on Oliver's arm, she left their little refuge, she looked back.

He lingered — to watch her through this one dance. How they made all the other couples sink into insignificance, with that something in them both that was better than mere good looks — that something not outre or eccentric, but poignant, wayward. They went well together, those two Dromores — his dark head and her fair head; his clear, brown, daring eyes, and her grey, languorous, mesmeric eyes. Ah! Master Oliver was happy now, with her so close to him! It was not jealousy that Lennan felt. Not quite — one did not feel jealous of the young; something very deep — pride, sense of proportion, who knew what — prevented that. She, too, looked happy, as if her soul were dancing, vibrating with the music and the scent of the flowers. He waited for her to come round once more, to get for a last time that flying glance turned back; then found his coat and hat and went.

XIII

Outside, he walked a few steps, then stood looking back at the windows of the hall through some trees, the shadows of whose trunks, in the light of a street lamp, were spilled out along the ground like the splines of a fan. A church clock struck eleven. For hours yet she would be there, going round and round in the arms of Youth! Try as he might he could never recapture for himself the look that Oliver's face had worn — the look that was the symbol of so much more than he himself could give her. Why had she come into his life — to her undoing, and his own? And the bizarre thought came to him: If she were dead should I really care? Should I not be almost glad? If she were dead her witchery would be dead, and I could stand up straight again and look people in the face! What was this power that played with men, darted into them, twisted their hearts to rags; this power that had looked through her eyes when she put her fan, with his flowers, to her lips?

The thrumming of the music ceased; he walked away.

It must have been nearly twelve when he reached home. Now, once more, would begin the gruesome process of deception — flinching of soul, and brazening of visage. It would be better when the whole thievish business was irretrievably begun and ordered in its secret courses!

There was no light in the drawing-room, save just the glow of the fire. If only Sylvia might have gone to bed! Then he saw her, sitting motionless out there by the uncurtained window.

He went over to her, and began his hateful formula:

"I'm afraid you've been lonely. I had to stay rather late. A dull evening." And, since she did not move or answer, but just sat there very still and white, he forced himself to go close, bend down to her, touch her cheek; even to kneel beside her. She looked round then; her face was quiet enough, but her eyes were strangely eager. With a pitiful little smile she broke out:

"Oh, Mark! What is it — what is it? Anything is better than this!"

Perhaps it was the smile, perhaps her voice or eyes — but something gave way in Lennan. Secrecy, precaution went by the board. Bowing his head against her breast, he poured it all out, while they clung, clutched together in the half dark like two frightened children. Only when he had finished did he realize that if she had pushed him away, refused to let him touch her, it would have been far less piteous, far easier to bear, than her wan face and her hands clutching him, and her words: "I never thought — you and I — oh! Mark — you and I —" The trust in their life together, in himself, that those words revealed! Yet, not greater than he had had — still had! She could not understand — he had known that she could never understand; it was why he had fought so for secrecy, all through. She was taking it as if she had lost everything; and in his mind she had lost nothing. This passion, this craving for Youth and Life, this madness — call it what one would — was something quite apart, not touching his love and need of her. If she would only believe that! Over and over he repeated it; over and over again perceived that she could not take it in. The only thing she saw was that his love had gone from her to another — though that was not true! Suddenly she broke out of his arms, pushing him from her, and cried: "That girl — hateful, horrible, false!" Never had he seen her look like this, with flaming spots in her white cheeks, soft lips and chin distorted, blue eyes flaming, breast heaving, as if each breath were drawn from lungs that received no air. And then, as quickly, the fire went out of her; she sank down on the sofa; covering her face with her arms, rocking to and fro. She did not cry, but a little moan came from her now and then. And each one of those sounds was to Lennan like the cry of something he was murdering. At last he went and sat down on the sofa by her and said:

"Sylvia! Sylvia! Don't! oh! don't!" And she was silent, ceasing to rock herself; letting him smooth and stroke her. But her face she kept hidden, and only once she spoke, so low that he could hardly hear: "I can't — I won't keep you from her." And with the awful feeling that no words could reach or soothe the wound in that tender heart, he could only go on stroking and kissing her hands.

It was atrocious — horrible — this that he had done! God knew that he had not sought it — the thing had come on him. Surely even in her misery she could see that! Deep down beneath his grief and self-hatred, he knew, what neither she nor anyone else could know — that he could not have prevented this feeling, which went back to days before he ever saw the girl — that no man could have stopped that feeling in himself. This craving and roving was as much part of him as his eyes and hands, as overwhelming and natural a longing as his hunger for work, or his need of the peace that Sylvia gave, and alone could give him. That was the tragedy — it was all sunk and rooted in the very nature of a man. Since the girl had come into their lives he was no more unfaithful to his wife in thought than he had been before. If only she could look into him, see him exactly as he was, as, without part or lot in the process, he had been made — then she would understand, and even might not suffer; but she could not, and he could never make it plain. And solemnly, desperately, with a weary feeling of the futility of words, he went on trying: Could she not see? It was all a thing outside him — a craving, a chase after beauty and life, after his own youth! At that word she looked at him:

"And do you think I don't want my youth back?"

He stopped.

For a woman to feel that her beauty — the brightness of her

hair and eyes, the grace and suppleness of her limbs — were slipping from her and from the man she loved! Was there anything more bitter? — or any more sacred duty than not to add to that bitterness, not to push her with suffering into old age, but to help keep the star of her faith in her charm intact!

Man and woman — they both wanted youth again; she, that she might give it all to him; he, because it would help him towards something — new! Just that world of difference!

He got up, and said:

"Come, dear, let's try and sleep."

He had not once said that he could give it up. The words would not pass his lips, though he knew she must be conscious that he had not said them, must be longing to hear them. All he had been able to say was:

"So long as you want me, you shall never lose me . . . and, I will never keep anything from you again."

Up in their room she lay hour after hour in his arms, quite unresentful, but without life in her, and with eyes that, when his lips touched them, were always wet.

What a maze was a man's heart, wherein he must lose himself every minute! What involved and intricate turnings and turnings on itself; what fugitive replacement of emotion by emotion! What strife between pities and passions; what longing for peace! . . .

And in his feverish exhaustion, which was almost sleep, Lennan hardly knew whether it was the thrum of music or Sylvia's moaning that he heard; her body or Nell's within his arms. . . .

But life had to be lived, a face preserved against the world, engagements kept. And the nightmare went on for both of them, under the calm surface of an ordinary Sunday. They were like people walking at the edge of a high cliff, not knowing from step to step whether they would fall; or like swimmers struggling for issue out of a dark whirlpool.

In the afternoon they went together to a concert; it was just something to do — something that saved them for an hour or two from the possibility of speaking on the one subject left to them. The ship had gone down, and they were clutching at anything that for a moment would help to keep them above water.

In the evening some people came to supper; a writer and two painters, with their wives. A grim evening — never more so than when the conversation turned on that perennial theme — the freedom, spiritual, mental, physical, requisite for those who practise Art. All the stale arguments were brought forth, and had to be joined in with unmoved faces. And for all their talk of freedom, Lennan could see the volte-face his friends would be making, if they only knew. It was not 'the thing' to seduce young girls — as if, forsooth, there were freedom in doing only what people thought 'the thing'! Their cant about the free artist spirit experiencing everything, would wither the moment it came up against a canon of 'good form,' so that in truth it was no freer than the bourgeois spirit, with its conventions; or the priest spirit, with its cry of 'Sin!' No, no! To resist — if resistance were possible to this dragging power — maxims of 'good form,' dogmas of religion and morality, were no help — nothing was any help, but some feeling stronger than passion itself. Sylvia's face, forced to smile! — that, indeed was a reason why they should condemn him! None of their doctrines about freedom could explain that away — the harm, the death that came to a man's soul when he made a loving, faithful creature suffer.

But they were gone at last — with their "Thanks so much!" and their "Delightful evening!"

And those two were face to face for another night.

He knew that it must begin all over again — inevitable, after the stab of that wretched argument plunged into their hearts and turned and turned all the evening.

"I won't, I mustn't keep you starved, and spoil your work. Don't think of me, Mark! I can bear it!"

And then a breakdown worse than the night before. What genius, what sheer genius Nature had for torturing her creatures! If anyone had told him, even so little as a week ago, that he could have caused such suffering to Sylvia — Sylvia, whom as a child with wide blue eyes and a blue bow on her flaxen head he had guarded across fields full of imaginary bulls; Sylvia, in whose hair his star had caught; Sylvia, who day and night for fifteen years had been his devoted wife; whom he loved and still admired — he would have given him the lie direct. It would have seemed incredible, monstrous, silly. Had all married men and women such things to go through — was this but a very usual crossing of the desert? Or was it, once for all, shipwreck? death — unholy, violent death — in a storm of sand?

Another night of misery, and no answer to that question yet.

He had told her that he would not see Nell again without first letting her know. So, when morning came, he simply wrote the words: "Don't come today!" — showed them to Sylvia, and sent them by a servant to Dromore's.

Hard to describe the bitterness with which he entered his studio that morning. In all this chaos, what of his work? Could he ever have peace of mind for it again? Those people last night had talked of 'inspiration of passion, of experience.' In pleading with her he had used the words himself. She — poor soul! — had but repeated them, trying to endure them, to believe them true. And were they true? Again no answer, or certainly none that he could give. To have had the waters broken up; to be plunged into emotion; to feel desperately, instead of stagnating — some day he might be grateful — who knew? Some day there might be fair country again beyond this desert, where he could work even better than before. But just now, as well expect creative work from a condemned man. It seemed to him that he was equally destroyed whether he gave Nell up, and with her, once for all, that roving, seeking instinct, which ought, forsooth, to have been satisfied, and was not; or whether he took Nell, knowing that in doing so he was torturing a woman dear to him! That was as far as he could see today. What he would come to see in time God only knew! But: 'Freedom of the Spirit!' That was a phrase of bitter irony indeed! And, there, with his work all round him, like a man tied hand and foot, he was swept by such a feeling of exasperated rage as he had never known. Women! These women! Only let him be free of both, of all women, and the passions and pities they aroused, so that his brain and his hands might live and work again! They should not strangle, they should not destroy him!

Unfortunately, even in his rage, he knew that flight from them both could never help him. One way or the other the thing would have to be fought through. If it had been a straight fight even; a clear issue between passion and pity! But both he loved, and both he pitied. There was nothing straight and clear about it anywhere; it was all too deeply rooted in full human nature. And the appalling sense of rushing ceaselessly from barrier to barrier began really to affect his brain.

True, he had now and then a lucid interval of a few minutes, when the ingenious nature of his own torments struck him as supremely interesting and queer; but this was not precisely a relief, for it only meant, as in prolonged toothache, that his power of feeling had for a moment ceased. A very pretty little hell indeed!

All day he had the premonition, amounting to certainty, that Nell would take alarm at those three words he had sent her, and come in spite of them. And yet, what else could he have written? Nothing save what must have alarmed her more, or plunged him deeper. He had the feeling that she could follow his moods, that her eyes could see him everywhere, as a cat's eyes can see in darkness. That feeling had been with him, more or less, ever since the last evening of October, the evening she came back from her summer — grown-up. How long ago? Only six days — was it possible? Ah, yes! She knew when her spell was weakening, when the current wanted, as it were, renewing. And about six o'clock — dusk already — without the least surprise, with only a sort of empty quivering, he heard her knock. And just behind the closed door, as near as he could get to her, he stood, holding his breath. He had given his word to Sylvia — of his own accord had given it. Through the thin wood of the old door he could hear the faint shuffle of her feet on the pavement, moved a few inches this way and that, as though supplicating the inexorable silence. He seemed to see her head, bent a little forward listening. Three times she knocked, and each time Lennan writhed. It was so cruel! With that seeing-sense of hers she must know he was there; his very silence would be telling her — for his silence had its voice, its pitiful breathless sound. Then, quite distinctly, he heard her sigh, and her footsteps move away; and covering his face with his hands he rushed to and fro in the studio, like a madman.

No sound of her any more! Gone! It was unbearable; and, seizing his hat, he ran out. Which way? At random he ran towards the Square. There she was, over by the railings; languidly, irresolutely moving towards home.

XIV

But now that she was within reach, he wavered; he had given his word — was he going to break it? Then she turned, and saw him; and he could not go back. In the biting easterly wind her face looked small, and pinched, and cold, but her eyes only the larger, the more full of witchery, as if beseeching him not to be angry, not to send her away.

"I had to come; I got frightened. Why did you write such a tiny little note?"

He tried to make his voice sound quiet and ordinary.

"You must be brave, Nell. I have had to tell her."

She clutched at his arm; then drew herself up, and said in her clear, clipped voice:

"Oh! I suppose she hates me, then!"

"She is terribly unhappy."

They walked a minute, that might have been an hour, without a word; not round the Square, as he had walked with Oliver, but away from the house. At last she said in a half-choked voice: "I only want a little bit of you."

And he answered dully: "In love, there are no little bits — no standing still."

Then, suddenly, he felt her hand in his, the fingers lacing, twining restlessly amongst his own; and again the half-choked voice said:

"But you WILL let me see you sometimes! You must!"

Hardest of all to stand against was this pathetic, clinging, frightened child. And, not knowing very clearly what he said, he murmured:

"Yes — yes; it'll be all right. Be brave — you must be brave, Nell. It'll all come right."

But she only answered:

"No, no! I'm not brave. I shall do something."

Her face looked just as when she had ridden at that gravel pit. Loving, wild, undisciplined, without resource of any kind — what might she not do? Why could he not stir without bringing disaster upon one or other? And between these two, suffering so because of him, he felt as if he had lost his own existence. In quest of happiness, he had come to that!

Suddenly she said:

"Oliver asked me again at the dance on Saturday. He said you had told him to be patient. Did you?"

"Yes."

"Why?"

"I was sorry for him."

She let his hand go.

"Perhaps you would like me to marry him."

Very clearly he saw those two going round and round over the shining floor.

"It would be better, Nell."

She made a little sound — of anger or dismay.

"You don't REALLY want me, then?"

That was his chance. But with her arm touching his, her face so pale and desperate, and those maddening eyes turned to him, he could not tell that lie, and answered:

"Yes — I want you, God knows!"

At that a sigh of content escaped her, as if she were saying to herself: 'If he wants me he will not let me go.' Strange little tribute to her faith in love and her own youth!

They had come somehow to Pall Mall by now. And scared to find himself so deep in the hunting-ground of the Dromores, Lennan turned hastily towards St. James's Park, that they might cross it in the dark, round to Piccadilly. To be thus slinking out of the world's sight with the daughter of his old room-mate — of all men in the world the last perhaps that he should do this to! A nice treacherous business! But the thing men called honour — what was it, when her eyes were looking at him and her shoulder touching his?

Since he had spoken those words, "Yes, I want you," she had been silent — fearful perhaps to let other words destroy their comfort. But near the gate by Hyde Park Corner she put her hand again into his, and again her voice, so clear, said:

"I don't want to hurt anybody, but you WILL let me come sometimes — you will let me see you — you won't leave me all alone, thinking that I'll never see you again?"

And once more, without knowing what he answered, Lennan murmured:

"No, no! It'll be all right, dear — it'll all come right. It must — and shall."

Again her fingers twined amongst his, like a child's. She seemed to have a wonderful knowledge of the exact thing to say and do to keep him helpless. And she went on:

"I didn't try to love you — it isn't wrong to love — it wouldn't hurt her. I only want a little of your love."

A little — always a little! But he was solely bent on comforting her now. To think of her going home, and sitting lonely, frightened, and unhappy, all the evening, was dreadful. And holding her fingers tight, he kept on murmuring words of would-be comfort.

Then he saw that they were out in Piccadilly. How far dared he go with her along the railings before he said goodbye? A man was coming towards them, just where he had met Dromore that first fatal afternoon nine months ago; a man with a slight lurch in his walk and a tall, shining hat a little on one side. But thank Heaven! — it was not Dromore — only one somewhat like him, who in passing stared sphinx-like at Nell. And Lennan said:

"You must go home now, child; we mustn't be seen together."

For a moment he thought she was going to break down, refuse to leave him. Then she threw up her head, and for a second stood like that, quite motionless, looking in his face. Suddenly stripping off her glove, she thrust her warm, clinging hand into his. Her lips smiled faintly, tears stood in her eyes; then she drew her hand away and plunged into the traffic. He saw her turn the corner of her street and disappear. And with the warmth of that passionate little hand still stinging his palm, he almost ran towards Hyde Park.

Taking no heed of direction, he launched himself into its dark space, deserted in this cold, homeless wind, that had little sound and no scent, travelling its remorseless road under the grey-black sky.

The dark firmament and keen cold air suited one who had little need of aids to emotion — one who had, indeed, but the single wish to get rid, if he only could, of the terrible sensation in his head, that bruised, battered, imprisoned feeling of a man who paces his cell — never, never to get out at either end. Without thought or intention he drove his legs along; not running, because he knew that he would have to stop the sooner. Alas! what more comic spectacle for the eyes of a good citizen than this married man of middle age, striding for hours over those dry, dark, empty pastures — hunted by passion and by pity, so that he knew not even whether he had dined! But no good citizen was abroad of an autumn night in a bitter easterly wind. The trees were the sole witnesses of this grim exercise — the trees, resigning to the cold blast their crinkled leaves that fluttered past him, just a little lighter than the darkness. Here and there his feet rustled in the drifts, waiting their turn to serve the little bonfires, whose scent still clung in the air. A desperate walk, in this heart of London — round and round, up and down, hour after hour, keeping always in the dark; not a star in the sky, not a human being spoken to or even clearly seen, not a bird or beast; just the gleam of the lights far away, and the hoarse muttering of the traffic! A walk as lonely as the voyage of the human soul is lonely from birth to death with nothing to guide it but the flickering glow from its own frail spirit lighted it knows not where. . . .

And, so tired that he could hardly move his legs, but free at last of that awful feeling in his head — free for the first time for days and days — Lennan came out of the Park at the gate where he had gone in, and walked towards his home, certain that tonight, one way or the other, it would be decided. . . .

XV

This then — this long trouble of body and of spirit — was what he remembered, sitting in the armchair beyond his bedroom fire, watching the glow, and Sylvia sleeping there exhausted, while the dark plane-tree leaves tap-tapped at the window in the autumn wind; watching, with the uncanny certainty that he would not pass the limits of this night without having made at last a decision that would not alter. For even conflict wears itself out; even indecision has this measure set to its miserable powers of torture, that any issue in the end is better than the hell of indecision itself. Once or twice in those last days even death had seemed to him quite tolerable; but now that his head was clear and he had come to grips, death passed out of his mind like the shadow that it was. Nothing so simple, extravagant, and vain could serve him. Other issues had reality; death — none. To leave Sylvia, and take this young love away; there was reality in that, but it had always faded as soon as it shaped itself; and now once more it faded. To put such a public and terrible affront on a tender wife whom he loved, do her to death, as it were, before the world's eyes — and then, ever remorseful, grow old while the girl was still young? He could not. If Sylvia had not loved him, yes; or, even if he had not loved her; or if, again, though loving him she had stood upon her rights — in any of those events he might have done it. But to leave her whom he did love, and who had said to him so generously: "I will not hamper you — go to her" — would be a black atrocity. Every memory, from their boy-and-girl lovering to the desperate clinging of her arms these last two nights —

memory with its innumerable tentacles, the invincible strength of its countless threads, bound him to her too fast. What then? Must it come, after all, to giving up the girl? And sitting there, by that warm fire, he shivered. How desolate, sacrilegious, wasteful to throw love away; to turn from the most precious of all gifts; to drop and break that vase! There was not too much love in the world, nor too much warmth and beauty — not, anyway, for those whose sands were running out, whose blood would soon be cold.

Could Sylvia not let him keep both her love and the girl's? Could she not bear that? She had said she could; but her face, her eyes, her voice gave her the lie, so that every time he heard her his heart turned sick with pity. This, then, was the real issue. Could he accept from her such a sacrifice, exact a daily misery, see her droop and fade beneath it? Could he bear his own happiness at such a cost? Would it be happiness at all? He got up from the chair and crept towards her. She looked very fragile sleeping there! The darkness below her closed eyelids showed cruelly on that too fair skin; and in her flax-coloured hair he saw what he had never noticed — a few strands of white. Her softly opened lips, almost colourless, quivered with her uneven breathing; and now and again a little feverish shiver passed up as from her heart. All soft and fragile! Not much life, not much strength; youth and beauty slipping! To know that he who should be her champion against age and time would day by day be placing one more mark upon her face, one more sorrow in her heart! That he should do this — they both going down the years together!

As he stood there holding his breath, bending to look at her, that slurring swish of the plane-tree branch, flung against and against the window by the autumn wind, seemed filling the whole world. Then her lips moved in one of those little, soft hurrying whispers that unhappy dreamers utter, the words all blurred with their wistful rushing.

And he thought: I, who believe in bravery and kindness; I, who hate cruelty — if I do this cruel thing, what shall I have to live for; how shall I work; how bear myself? If I do it, I am lost — an outcast from my own faith — a renegade from all that I believe in.

And, kneeling there close to that face so sad and lonely, that heart so beaten even in its sleep, he knew that he could not do it — knew it with sudden certainty, and a curious sense of peace. Over! — the long struggle — over at last! Youth with youth, summer to summer, falling leaf with falling leaf! And behind him the fire flickered, and the plane-tree leaves tap-tapped.

He rose, and crept away stealthily downstairs into the drawing-room, and through the window at the far end out into the courtyard, where he had sat that day by the hydrangea, listening to the piano-organ. Very dark and cold and eerie it was there, and he hurried across to his studio. There, too, it was cold, and dark, and eerie, with its ghostly plaster presences, stale scent of cigarettes, and just one glowing ember of the fire he had left when he rushed out after Nell — those seven hours ago.

He went first to the bureau, turned up its lamp, and taking out some sheets of paper, marked on them directions for his various works; for the statuette of Nell, he noted that it should be taken with his compliments to Mr. Dromore. He wrote a letter to his banker directing money to be sent to Rome, and to his solicitor telling him to let the house. He wrote quickly. If Sylvia woke, and found him still away, what might she not think? He took a last sheet. Did it matter what he wrote, what deliberate lie, if it helped Nell over the first shock?

"DEAR NELL,

"I write this hastily in the early hours, to say that we are called out to Italy to my only sister, who is very ill. We leave by the first morning boat, and may be away some time. I will write again. Don't fret, and God bless you.

"M. L."

He could not see very well as he wrote. Poor, loving, desperate child! Well, she had youth and strength, and would soon have — Oliver! And he took yet another sheet.

"DEAR OLIVER,

"My wife and I are obliged to go post-haste to Italy. I watched you both at the dance the other night. Be very gentle with Nell; and — good luck to you! But don't say again that I told you to be patient; it is hardly the way to make her love you.

"M. LENNAN."

That, then, was all — yes, all! He turned out the little lamp, and groped towards the hearth. But one thing left. To say goodbye! To her, and Youth, and Passion! — to the only salve for the aching that Spring and Beauty bring — the aching for the wild, the passionate, the new, that never quite dies in a man's heart. Ah! well, sooner or later, all men had to say goodbye to that. All men — all men!

He crouched down before the hearth. There was no warmth in that fast-blackening ember, but it still glowed like a dark-red flower. And while it lived he crouched there, as though it were that to which he was saying goodbye. And on the door he heard the girl's ghostly knocking. And beside him — a ghost among the ghostly presences — she stood. Slowly the glow blackened, till the last spark had faded out.

Then by the glimmer of the night he found his way back, softly as he had come, to his bedroom.

Sylvia was still sleeping; and, to watch for her to wake, he sat down again by the fire, in silence only stirred by the frail tap-tapping of those autumn leaves, and the little catch in her breathing now and then. It was less troubled than when he had bent over her before, as though in her sleep she knew. He must not miss the moment of her waking, must be beside her before she came to full consciousness, to say: "There, there! It's all over; we are going away at once — at once." To be ready to offer that quick solace, before she had time to plunge back into her sorrow, was an island in this black sea of night, a single little refuge point for his bereaved and naked being. Something to do — something fixed, real, certain. And yet another long hour before her waking, he sat forward in the chair, with that wistful eagerness, his eyes fixed on her face, staring through it at some vision, some faint, glimmering light — far out there beyond — as a traveller watches a star. . . .

How I Became a Holy Mother and other stories
Ruth Prawer Jhabvala. Introduced by Francis King
'Every one of them is brilliant. They are richly, slyly comic and quite desperately sad… that sharp eye for the give-away gesture, that keen perception of human loneliness and the various guises it assumes. In her quiet, undemonstrative way, Ruth Prawer Jhabvala is a truly astonishing writer.' *Observer*

The Green Hat
Michael Arlen. Introduced by Kirsty Gunn
The Green Hat perfectly reflects the atmosphere of the 1920s – the post-war fashion for verbal smartness, youthful cynicism and the spirit of rebellion of the 'bright young things' of Mayfair.

Juan in America
Eric Linklater. Introduced by Alexander Linklater
Unwillingly on the brink of the Slump, America at the end of the '20s is brought to life by a series of implausible predicants as Juan stumbles from state to state, somehow evading consequences as he goes.

The Voyage
Charles Morgan. Introduced by Valentine Cunningham
'As one reads one forgets everything, enchanted by the beauty of the setting, fascinated by the subtlety of the spiritual reading, the provisional speculations, the ethereal love-story.' *Daily Telegraph*